Draco's
Child

Draco's
Child

SHARON PLUMB

thistledown press

Thistledown Press Ltd.
633 Main Street
Saskatoon, Saskatchewan, S7H 0J8
www.thistledownpress.com

Library and Archives Canada Cataloguing in Publication
Plumb, Sharon, 1962 –
Draco's child / Sharon Plumb.

ISBN 978-1-897235-70-6

I. Title.

PS8631.L84D73 2010   jC813'.6   C2010-900918-5

Cover art by Rebbecca K. Ivic
Author photograph: Howard Hamilton
Cover and book design by Jackie Forrie
Printed and bound in Canada

Thistledown Press gratefully acknowledges the financial assistance of the Canada Council for the Arts, the Saskatchewan Arts Board, and the Government of Canada through the Book Publishing Industry Development Program for its publishing program.

ACNOWLEDGEMENTS

This book feels like a small miracle to me, given that I have held it as a virtual book in my mind for sixteen years now! Many people have journeyed with it, from scattered ideas, through series of drafts, to the book you are holding in your hand.

My husband, Howard, read far too many drafts, took the boys to the farm on weekends so I could write, and generally made it possible for me to do this. My son, Richard, source and sounding board for ideas of all kinds, and whose logical mind catches inconsistencies and analyzes plots at lightning speed, is responsible for many things in the story that make sense. My parents, sister Linda, and sons Billy and Arthur made me feel like a writer long before I dared use the term.

Alison Lohans and Anne Patton, writing team extra-ordinaire, taught me to see the story through my characters' eyes, and thus made it live. Sandra Davis and Sheena Koops and the other members of the Saskatchewan Children's Writers' Round Robin gave me a community to write in.

Paul Woods told me in grade 7 that I should be a writer. Gillian Harding-Russell taught the course that inspired me to start writing this novel. Joanne Gerber believed in the story and gave me valuable suggestions. Sandra Davis, Heather Becker, Shirley Carbno, Christine Carbno, Chris Danyluk, Billy Hamilton, and Eli Koziel read various drafts, gave feedback, and encouraged me to keep at it. Sandi and Katie were willing to proofread on short notice.

The team at Thistledown Press took a chance on this story and did all the things necessary to turn it into a real, beautiful book. My editor, Rod McIntyre, liked it! His insightful comments made me think about what I was really trying to say, and his sharp eyes caught the silly/confusing/wrong things I actually wrote before they went to press. Any remaining errors are completely my fault.

To all of these people, thank you.

To Howard, the brightest star in my sky.

Prologue

THE STAR DRAGON IS FLYING TOO *fast to stop. Its twinkling rider bounces on its back, gripping the dragon's long neck with both hands. "Look out!" Varia calls, but the dragon doesn't hear. It should be more careful, riding a supernova's gale-force wind! Varia covers her eyes. Between her fingers, she sees the squat mushroom constellation, smack in the dragon's path. It pulls its cap stars in around its stalk, trying to make itself tiny. But mushrooms, even star mushrooms, can't move out of the way. The dragon's flat head slams into it — and slips right through, followed by its twinkling body, with the rider pressed flat along its back. Stars brushing stars.*

The mushroom's cap ripples and flares. Dusty star-spores burst from beneath it: magenta, cyan, dazzling white. They engulf the mushroom, the dragon, the rider, and Varia's field of vision in a hurricane of light. The dragon shoots out of the storm — but something is wrong. A star in the middle of its back is pulsating wildly. The dragon skids to a stop at the top of the sky and roars a shower of sparks.

Varia lowers her hands. She knows that dragon, recognizes both its angular head and its impetuous flight. Draco. She smiles. It's been a long time.

Draco's rider leaps off his back. It's a child, Varia sees, a star child. The child strokes the dragon's heaving side and bends close to examine the injured star.

For the first time, Varia sees the star child's face. Its translucent skin shimmers inside its outline of stars. The supernova glows faintly through its cheek. Its hair tosses wildly around its face like a sun's corona, and its mouth stars curve down like an overturned crescent moon. Its burning eyes stare, not twinkling, at Draco's injured star, and at the planet she can now see orbiting it. It's her own star, Sigma Draconis, also called Alsafi, and her own planet, ignobly named "The Kettle," where she is standing in the clearing between the kitchen and the sleeping hut. Varia shivers and hugs herself in the chilly air.

Radiant eyes stare into hers. She shivers — from excitement or dread? Holding her gaze, the star child raises both twinkling arms and flings itself into a somersault. She watches it shrink as it falls, spinning, through the clouds, over the signal tower, past the trees, and into her up-stretched hands.

Chapter 1

In all the nights Varia could remember, from her last one on Earth, through light-years on the spaceship, and now six seasons on The Kettle, she had never before woken from a dream to find that it was really happening. But when she pushed aside her grass blanket and tiptoed past the other sleeping mats and out the door to look at the sky, there was Sidran. He stood beside the signal tower, holding something. The tower's metal bars and Sidran's white face and red hair glowed like fire in its light.

It was a torch, Varia tried to tell herself, or a reed cage full of glow-bugs. But she had seen the fiery ball plummeting through the sky. She knew what was in Sidran's hands.

She watched the star child unfold itself and leap to the ground. She watched it stare up into Sidran's face, then lead him toward the poisonous woods. Varia raced toward them. "Sidran!" she screamed. "Don't go!" Sidran didn't turn his head. Mom would know what to do, but there was no time to get her. In the last second before the star glow vanished into the darkness of the forest, Varia plunged in after them.

Sidran was just out of reach ahead of her. Varia pushed aside a tree branch and opened her eyes wide to pull in more of the flickering light. If she could only see the next safe place to plant her bare foot, she might be able to grab Sidran's nightshirt and shake him out of his dream walk. He must be sleepwalking; awake, he would never go into the woods. She stepped into a lighter patch of shadow. Something mushy squeezed up between her toes, and a musty fungus scent invaded her nostrils. She shuddered and scraped it off her foot onto a tree root.

Sidran must be walking in the star child's footprints, if a constellation could make footprints. She would walk in Sidran's if she could see them. The star child was only half Sidran's height, so when the three of them lined up, Sidran's body blocked most of the glow on her path. All Varia could then see through the web of tree branches was the silhouette of his nightshirt under the ring of his wild, red hair — like the picture of a solar eclipse Dad had once shown her. In the dark woods, her legs tangled in bushes, or she sank through loose moss, or sharp roots jabbed her feet. Invisible branches scraped her face and neck, even though she held both hands in front of her.

Varia gave up calling Sidran's name. Neither he nor the star child paid her any attention, until she wasn't even sure if they knew she was following. It made her wonder if she too was still dreaming. But she couldn't be. If her feet were this cold in bed, she would wake up for sure. Sidran and the star child kept walking . . . and walking . . .

Darkness crowded her from the sides and from behind. Keeping up with the light was more than a matter of helping Sidran. If she got left behind she would never find her way home, even in morning's light, even if she survived the night. Like the other colonists, Varia didn't venture past the rim of the forest. After Reyk and Thora's mysterious deaths, no one had dared.

Something creaked above her. There couldn't be any animals tracking her, she reminded herself; there weren't any here, unless you counted insects and worms. And the plants, no matter how malevolent, couldn't travel. As long as she kept moving, she should be safe. She stumbled ahead, tripped over a root, dodged a cluster of grasping leaves, and bumped her head under a low branch. This was enough.

Varia lunged forward. If she could only get hold of Sidran's shoulders and turn him around, make him look straight into her eyes, he might wake up from his trance. True, they didn't like each other much, but they had grown up together on the ship, and now that the other lander was missing they were the only two people of their age in the settlement. He couldn't just leave her alone here.

Something grabbed her hair.

Varia screamed. Surely Sidran would hear her now! Or the star child. Even an alien wouldn't ignore a scream, would it? It would. She thrashed wildly — and found herself fighting a scraggly, low-hanging branch. The light bobbed away from her. Why had she ever followed them? Even if she could catch Sidran and wake him, how would she ever convince the star child to take them back to the settlement?

The light was still faintly visible when Varia freed herself and stumbled into a mat of low, prickly plants. She tiptoed through in giant steps, trying to ignore the thorns stabbing her unprotected toes. "Wait!" she called, knowing no one was listening. The light flickered. Varia leapt forward — and found herself smack on her hands and knees in the prickles.

It took her a moment to catch her breath. A sharp pain stabbed her forehead, and something trickled into her eye. She wiped it away. If she were home, Mom would tie a mouldy piece of bread to her head to stop the bleeding and prevent an infection. "Lots of antibiotics are derived from mould," she would snap. "Stop wrinkling your nose." Varia pressed one hand against the cut, and shielding her head with her elbows, stood up. The light had vanished.

Varia looked frantically in all directions — if you could call it "looking" when there was only darkness. There was no sound, not even wind. There was blood on her forehead, and thorns in her feet. The leaves must be on high alert. It was only a matter of time now until the venom took effect, and the hungry roots opened to drink her blood after she collapsed . . .

"Sidran! Star child!" The forest drank her words.

But something was glowing off to the side. The light stood still; they were finally waiting for her! She scrambled toward them, crying and laughing, arms in front, lifting her feet high to avoid tripping on a high root or a low branch. Her scraped knees slammed into a fallen log. Blinking away tears, she threaded herself between the spiky branches. From the other side, she could see the source of the light. It wasn't the star child. It was a clump of fat mushrooms, glowing green at the base of a large tree.

Varia crowded her body into the green glow. Suddenly she was angry. What was Sidran thinking, even asleep or hypnotized, to follow that creature into these woods? She should have gone back to bed and left him to his fate — like he had left her.

She flopped against the tree. Its bark was smooth and spongy, with a sharp scent that made her light-headed. Her head hurt. Her feet hurt. Her knees hurt. The green light showed two dark smudges where they were probably bleeding. "Sidran, you idiot!" She took a deep breath. However betrayed she felt, if she didn't find him, she was lost. And she would never see him from down here.

Varia climbed tentatively onto the lowest branch. Sticky sap oozed out of the bark where her hands and feet pressed against it. Feeling for sturdy branches, she groped her way up the tree. Once she bashed her head into an unseen branch, and nearly fell. She climbed until she couldn't see the mushroom's light, hoping to catch even a glimpse of another light bobbing through the trees. She didn't. Sidran and the star child had been swallowed by the forest.

So had she.

Varia shivered. Fear and movement had let her ignore the cold so far, but now the clammy air enveloped her. She thought of trying to climb back down — but then what? It was no warmer on the ground, and even if she made it down without falling, it was safer up here. Probably. She found a crook in the branches, and eased into it. The trunk sagged gently behind her. She braced herself as comfortably as she could and pulled prickles from her feet. Her feet weren't swelling; those particular leaves may have been safe. She leaned back, listened to the silence, and breathed in the heady scent of the tree sap.

It reminded her of the mints they used to eat on the spaceship. Varia pushed the thought of food to the back of her mind. She was good at that: their field of Earth crops never grew quite enough potatoes or carrots or peas to fill anyone's stomach.

It wasn't supposed to turn out this way. The Kettle had been chosen from among hundreds of known, reachable planets to be the closest match to Earth. It had breathable air, apparently fertile soil and a circular orbit the right distance from its sun, a young, stable star slightly smaller and cooler than Earth's. It even had a single large moon to stabilize the tilt of the planet's axis and moderate the seasonal temperatures.

But astronomers can only see so much through a telescope. They didn't see the eternal dampness, or the fungi that colonized on every surface. There was mould between the layers of onions; mildew so thick in the blankets and pillows, and most of their clothes, that they had to be burned; slime on the rocks of the creek where they got their water; and an endless film of smothering mushrooms to be raked off the garden so their own crops could grow.

When Varia's parents and the other colonists had looked through the telescope at their new home, they had seen adventure. Promise. Hope. Escape from the crowding and pollution-sicknesses on Earth. When Varia looked up, she had seen Draco.

From Earth, he looked like a long, starry necklace. He was mischievous, shining brightly for an instant, then fading into blackness while she searched for his next star. Dad traced the dragon's winding body patiently with his finger, over and over, until her five-year-old eyes could follow it. Start at the diamond-shaped head, leap up, then twist back around the Little Dipper. Twist again, and follow the tail to the Big Dipper's bowl.

Dad had pointed a telescope at a dim star in the middle of Draco's back. "That's where we're going," he had told her. "To Sigma Draconis, also called Alsafi, to ride on the dragon's back." His muscles were tense with excitement. "Thousands of years ago, one of Draco's stars was the pole star, the one at the top of the sky that all the other stars circled around. People used it to find their way in the dark. They said it was the gateway to heaven, and Draco was the guardian of the gate."

"We're going to live next door to heaven," whispered Varia, staring up at Draco. It only lasted an instant, but she was sure she saw him close his eye in a twinkle of a wink.

Dad had given her a long, tight hug.

When they left Earth the next day, Varia barely noticed what they were leaving behind. All she could think of was the day she would meet Draco face to starry face, and just maybe, if she felt very brave, ask him to take her to visit heaven.

It hadn't worked out that way.

The nearer they got to Sigma Draconis, the less Draco looked like himself. His stars moved apart, or together, until she couldn't even tell which ones were his. None of the Earth constellations looked the same out in space. And from this planet that circled Alsafi, she couldn't see Draco at all. Not even the ridge on his back. She felt like a flea that couldn't bite hard enough to get the dog to notice her.

Even worse, she learned that Alsafi meant cooking tripod. Her new sun was named after three sticks lashed together to hold a pot over the fire! Mom chuckled and said they should hope it meant there would be lots of food for them. Varia didn't find it funny.

Beautiful, starry Draco was lost to her forever — until tonight, when he suddenly flew into her dream. With a star child on his back. She'd often seen the star child's constellation, whenever the clouds lifted long enough for the stars to show. It hung in the southern sky with its arms and legs spread out in mid-leap. Varia hadn't known until tonight that the child was leaping onto Draco's back.

"And now look where I am," she muttered through chattering teeth. "Why did that star child come down here anyway? More important, why didn't it bring Draco?" She squinted upwards, but the only thing falling from the sky was rain.

She wiggled closer to the trunk in case it was drier there. Draco would be able to find Sidran and carry them both back to their sleeping hut in a minute. He might even agree to carry them around the rest of the planet to look for the lost lander. The one Connie and the other kids had been on. She imagined the warmth of Draco's starry back, the wind streaming through her hair as they glided over the treetops, and the lost settlers cheering at their approach. She closed her eyes, or maybe they were already closed — it was too dark to tell.

Then another thing happened that Varia would never have believed. Cold and alone in a dark, dripping forest, high in a smelly tree, Varia fell asleep.

Chapter 2

*A BRAID OF SILVER VINES GLISTENS among wet leaves. Varia parts
the branches and lunges. The braid snaps to the side. Varia opens
her hand. She is holding a purple leaf. She half smiles and scans
the forest. A humpback bush gleams silver through the branches.
Varia tiptoes toward it, but her feet slid on slimy mushrooms and
she slides through slick, spiny foliage.*

"Draco!" she yells. Her voice sputters like the rain.

*The silver bush explodes into a hurricane of leaf-wings and
stick-claws and seed pod-scales and round, glassy raindrop-eyes.
Twiggy fingers encase her body, and Draco's dragon heart thumps
against her back.*

Suddenly the heartbeat stops. " Draco?" Varia falls . . .

Water streamed down Varia's face. She tried to wipe it off,
but couldn't lift her hand. She tried to sit forward, but something
held her hair. She blinked her eyes open to raindrops glistening
on bright green, triangular leaves, and her heart fell. The forest.
Sidran. The star child. It must be well into the morning. People
would be frantic. She was frantic herself. Why couldn't she lift
her hands? Why couldn't she move?

"Varia! Sidran!" The voices came from a long way off.

"I'm here!" At least she could still yell.

It took a few minutes for the searchers to reach her. "How on the Pot did you get up there? Come on down." It was Dad's voice.

"I'm stuck." The Pot was another term she detested. But she wasn't going to object now.

"Hang on. I'm coming up."

As if she could do anything else. Rustlings and mutterings rose toward her. Suddenly, he was there. Wet hair was plastered over his forehead, his unruly beard was full of twigs, and there was a fresh scratch across his cheek. He looked wonderful.

"We were so worried!" Dad reached for her, wobbled, and hastily grabbed the branches again.

Varia nodded and blinked.

Dad worked his way closer and poked at the clear, shiny stuff that cemented her to the tree. "I don't know how this sap managed to dry in this rain," he muttered. He pulled his jack knife from his pocket. "It's as hard as stone. I'll have to cut the bark out around it." What a good thing they had tools from Earth, Varia thought, not for the first time. Her father sliced the soft bark from the tree, leaving it hanging from her skin and nightgown. Fresh sap oozed around each slice and stretched in long strings when she lifted her bark-soled feet.

"It will be easier if I cut your hair," Dad said. Varia bit her lip and nodded with her eyes. Dad grabbed Varia's hair close to her scalp and sawed it with the knife. Her head jerked free, splattering water over Dad's face. "Thank you," she said in a tiny voice, glad she was too stiff to turn around and see how much hair she was leaving behind.

The bark on Varia's hands made it impossible for her to hold branches as she followed Dad down. Instead, she hooked her elbows and wrists awkwardly around them. It was a relief when strong arms reached up and lifted her down. One of the hands had glossy pink stumps where two of the fingers should have been.

It was Sidran's father. Mom amputated the fingers after his hand got smashed under a tree two summers ago.

"Hi, Samuel."

"That's a nasty cut on your forehead," Samuel said.

"I tripped."

Dad scowled. "What were you two thinking? Coming out here on your own — and in the dark! You're lucky you ran into that tree first, before you found something worse."

"I was trying to rescue Sidran," Varia began, then stopped. In the daylight, the whole story seemed preposterous. How could a constellation fall out of the sky and lead Sidran into the woods? She wondered if she had dreamed it all, and sleepwalked into the woods alone.

"Rescue him." Samuel stiffened. "From what?"

"From . . ." Varia shrugged. "The forest. I was trying to make him come back."

"So it was his idea. I knew that boy would cause us trouble," growled Dad.

Samuel bristled. "If Sidran came out here he must have had a good reason."

"What good reason could he possibly have to — "

"She was obviously in on it too, or she wouldn't have been awake when he left. She probably pulled him out here to look for dragons." Samuel glared at Varia. "Well?" he prodded. "Where's Sidran?"

"I lost sight of him when I fell."

"I'm astonished you could see him at all," Dad said. "We found you by following the trampled plants. But in the dark?" He scowled again. "Worse than foolish! And worse than thoughtless, after we've already lost so many."

"It wasn't my idea," she muttered. "And there were glowing mushrooms." She pointed at the dull, rust-coloured globes squatting at the base of the tree. Dad looked at them and frowned. Varia looked away. Glowing mushrooms were at least plausible. He would never believe a star child.

Samuel scanned the trees. "Sidran?" Except for the dripping of rain, the forest was silent. No birds chirped; no small animals scurried under the bushes.

"I can show you where I last saw him," Varia offered. The sap on her feet picked up leaves and dirt as she walked, and a fat mushroom wobbled on the end of her toe. Dad snapped some branches off the fallen log and helped her cross it. Rain rolled down the back of her bare neck where her hair had been. At least the bark "shoes" protected her soles from the prickly plants.

"See?" She pointed at the leafy mat. "My footprints and Sidran's. That's where I fell, and he kept going." It did look like only two sets of prints. Didn't the star child make footprints? Or had the star child been a dream? But if it had, how had she followed Sidran?

Samuel followed Sidran's prints into the forest. Dad hung back and inspected the ground where Varia had tripped. "No tree root; no fallen branches," he muttered. He bent over and picked up a tangle of vines. When he stood up, his cheeks were red blotches on suddenly white skin. He held out the vines. Varia froze. It wasn't a tangle; it was a braid.

"Did Sidran do this?" Dad demanded, shaking the vines at her.

"He didn't have time," Varia stammered. "I was right behind him." And Draco's silver braid had definitely been a dream.

Samuel rushed back to the clearing and grabbed the vines. "What game are you playing? Where's Sidran?"

Varia felt small. There was only one answer, and they wouldn't believe her. "It was the star child," she whispered. It had to be. She braced herself for a new onslaught.

Instead, Dad and Samuel just stared at her. Dad's whole face was now red. Samuel's eyes were so round she could see white around his pupils.

"Sidran was following the star child," she said. "I was trying to make him come back."

"The star child!" A smile flickered over Samuel's face. "I knew Sidran had a good reason to come out here."

Dad sputtered. "I don't know about any star child." He looked down at the vines in Samuel's hand. "But we do know the plants are dangerous. Maybe they braided themselves together to trap Varia."

"Plants can't — " Samuel interrupted.

But Dad was already tugging Varia along the path. "We've got to get you home to your mother so she can check you out."

"What about Sidran?" asked Varia. "We can't just leave him here."

Dad glared at her. "Maybe your star child will bring him home."

Varia shivered. If it had tripped her, why would it help Sidran?

Samuel glared at Dad. He straightened his back. "Maybe it will."

Dad sighed and put his hand on Samuel's shoulder. "Hugo can help you search some more. But right now Varia needs to get home."

Samuel nodded. He followed with his eyes down.

Varia stumbled over her heavy feet as she followed Dad. But now that she could see what was on the ground, she glad the bark was there. There were assorted mushrooms, black lichens drooping from dead branches, thick blue mosses, vine curtains, and bushes with spiky thorns on their leaves. Just what you would expect to find on a dragon's back. She peered into the trees, but the only thing glistening was the rain.

Varia yanked her hand back from a spiky bush. These bushes grew along the creek at the settlement too. Gretel, the team's botanist (and Sidran's mother), said the spikes were probably there to protect the plants from hungry animals that had once lived here.

Varia cringed at a sudden thought. What if she had it backwards? What if the spikes were there so the hungry plants could eat the animals? What if Dad was right about the plants tripping her on purpose? Reyk and Thora hadn't been able to tell what had attacked them.

Maybe Sidran had been following a trail of glowing mushrooms, and she had imagined the star child. What if the mushrooms had led him to their feeding place and then turned off their lights? What if Sidran was lying unconscious somewhere past the sticky tree, half digested by a predatory plant? But if that was the case, and there was no star child, how did Samuel know about it? And if the star child really had braided the vines to trip her, why was Samuel so happy that Sidran had followed it?

A shower of water spilled onto Varia's head. She looked up. Her head had grazed a cluster of round seed pods. Dragon scales. The vine had jagged, silvery leaves. She stopped walking. "Look, Dad. Dragon wings."

Dad glanced at the leaves. "They do look somewhat bat-like," he said. Books always described dragon wings as "bat-like," but if Varia was writing them, she would say bat wings were "dragon-like." Dad walked on.

Varia turned sideways to avoid a sagging bush with wide, curved needles. Dripping teeth and dragon claws. The trailing, black lichen above them: congealed smoke from a dragon's nostrils. The plump, pink fungus fans that sprouted all over fallen logs: dragon feet. Was Draco teasing her, leaving all these tracings on his planet after being invisible for so long? Or were the plants playing games? She ducked away from a coiling tendril. Dragon's eyebrow.

"We found Varia," Dad reported to the crowd when they finally reached the settlement.

Hugo looked down from the top of the signal tower, where he was tinkering with the crackling transmitter. "But not Sidran."

Samuel shook his head and stalked toward the sleeping hut. Gretel followed him, wringing her hands. Varia was suddenly conscious of her bark armour and jagged hair.

Mom pushed her way through the crowd and clasped Varia in a smothering hug. Tears flowed from her puffy eyes. But in a moment she regained her composure. "We'll ask questions later," she said, gripping Varia's and Dad's shoulders and steering them toward the kitchen.

Chapter 3

MOM WAS THE COLONY'S MEDICAL DOCTOR. Every adult on the spaceship was a doctor of something — zoology, geology, astronomy, botany, agriculture, nutrition, electrical and structural engineering, psychology, and more. Dad was the psychologist. Reyk had been the physicist, and Thora the mycologist, the expert on fungi. Unlike most of their skills, however, Mom's were in constant demand on The Kettle.

She improvised bandages, splints, and poultices, but she couldn't ease their chronic coughs, headaches, and fatigue. She also hadn't been able to cure Reyk and Thora when they stumbled back from the woods screaming that they were on fire, and trying vainly to put it out by submerging themselves over and over in the creek. Then they got swollen blisters all over their skin and shouted at Earth people that weren't here. Finally their hands and feet turned dry and black, and literally fell off before they died. Varia hadn't been allowed near them, but she remembered the nauseating stench of rotting flesh. Their symptoms matched those of a horrible Earth disease that Mom said was caused by eating grain infected with a fungus called ergot. "Saint Anthony's Fire." The reader told her what it was, but it hadn't told her the cure.

The worry lines around Mom's mouth as she helped Varia out of her bark-laden clothes and handed her a blanket. The look on her face was the same one she'd worn that awful cold afternoon last fall when Varia had left the window open during her baby brother's nap. Adriel had been born on the ship shortly before they got here, a month before he was due. In the cold air he got sick, and spent every night barking like a seal until the weather mercifully warmed up. Mom had been livid, then exhausted and irritable.

Mom set to work immediately in her most efficient hospital manner. She filled the wash tub, made from the nose cone of the lander, with hot water, sent Varia's and Dad's clothes out with Nara to be soaked in the creek, and ordered Varia to soak in the tub. Varia's head began to ache.

Baths were rare treats here where water came out of the creek and hot water came out of a kettle on the stove . The settlers drew numbers to determine the order for using the bath water, and Varia had never come in higher than eighth. But it was hard to enjoy this one.

Mom tugged the tangles out of Varia's hair with a broken comb, snipped off the remaining long strands, then scrubbed her scalp fiercely with ashes from the stove. Varia wrinkled her nose at the smell. If only the shampoo from the ship hadn't run out.

Mom's mouth grew thinner and her cheeks redder as she attacked the sap on Varia's neck. Finally she stopped with a big huff. "At least you don't have spots." She turned away and took several deep breaths.

Varia sank deeper into the washtub and picked half-heartedly at the sap on her foot. Since it had hardened in the rain, she doubted it would soak off in the tub. It didn't, although bits of the grass and leaves broke off it and floated to the top. She picked the mushroom off her toe and tossed it onto the floor.

By the time the bath water cooled, it was clear that the sap would not soak off — although the black mildew that grew persistently around the edges of Varia's toenails was gone, for now. Dishwashing kept it off her fingernails, but it was a permanent feature on everyone's feet. Mom had read everything in the reader on destroying fungi, but to no avail. Chlorine bleach, copper sulphate, and other chemicals they didn't have; prolonged drought and hot weather were impossible to arrange, and how could they know which other fungi might kill these ones, or what their side effects might be?

The settlers agreed that if they ever got to a point where they didn't have to work every minute just to survive, and if they could figure out how to avoid the unknown danger in the woods, they would try to find a drier part of the planet. Maybe they would also find the other lander. No one said it, but hope of that was growing thinner. Even though Hugo made sure the transmitter faithfully sent out its whining homing signal, the receiver was ominously quiet.

Mom handed Varia a towel and helped her climb out of the tub and pull her shirt and trousers over the bark that remained stubbornly glued to her skin. Dad strained the floating grass and ashes out of the bath water, added a kettle of hot water, and climbed in.

Mom pressed her fingers against the sides of Varia's throat. "No sign of swelling. Do your ears hurt?"

"No."

"Say 'aaah'." She opened the window shutters and adjusted Varia's head so the daylight lit her mouth. "Do you feel like you're on fire?"

"No!"

"Do you know who I am?"

"Mo-o-o-m!" Obviously.

Mom studied the pink skin on her hands, then her feet. "Good circulation." A relieved smile flickered over her pinched face. "My best medical opinion is that your limbs are not about to wither away."

Now Varia understood. Whatever Reyk and Thora had contracted, she had avoided. Even if she had acquired a wooden shell, she wasn't going to die.

Mom stood up and took off her doctor's smock. She folded it sharply and slapped it onto the table. "All right, young lady," she snapped. "Let's talk this out." And the lecture began. "What on the Pot did you think you were doing? You could have been killed!" She gulped. "Sidran may have been. Dad and Samuel could have been killed looking for you!" Dad submerged his head and blew bubbles in the water while Mom's voice rose. "We've already lost two adults, we almost lost Adriel, and without the other crew, there are barely enough of us to do all the work as it is."

"Work!" Varia sputtered. Was that all she meant to her mother? Someone to do the work? Her eyes darted around the room as Mom's tirade picked up. She had done lots of work. She had packed mud into the spaces between the reeds and the log frames of the buildings. She had broken sticks off trees and tied them together with grass to make shutters. She had tied a bundle of straw onto a long stick to make the broom she then used to sweep creeping insects off the dirt floor. She had picked much of the long grass that had been woven into the mats they slept on, and the blankets they slept under, and the clothes they wore. She had washed pretty much every dish they ever ate from. But was that the only reason Mom would miss her if she disappeared?

Varia pressed her fingers hard between her eyes. Her forehead throbbed fiercely, and she just wanted to lie down. Mom ranted on. The settlers couldn't afford to spend time nursing her instead of working in the fields. They had to get the crops off before winter. Varia had already cost them half a day, and looking after Sidran would cost more time, if by some chance they found him alive. Had she forgotten everything they had to do?

Varia hadn't, but Mom detailed it anyway: cut more weaving grass and dry it, weave more boots and cloaks and blankets, dig the onions, carrots, and sweet potatoes and shell the hard peas, thresh the barley, cut and stack firewood, repair the cracks in the walls, and finish the addition to the kitchen so they could all sleep comfortably near the stove this winter. It was a matter of survival! They had to stay alive, that was all that mattered, to stay alive. How could Varia be so foolish? And thoughtless? Mom began to cry.

"It was Sidran's fault!" Varia exploded into the break in the words. "Not mine! I yelled and yelled at him to come back, but he wouldn't listen!"

Dad stepped out of the tub and wrapped a towel around his waist. Pieces of bark still clung to his hairy forearms. Varia could see his ribs under the muscles of his chest and shoulders. He put his arms around Mom, as if she was the one who needed comforting, and she leaned into the curly hair on his wet chest. Her face was blotchy and her grey-streaked hair straggled over her eyes. She looks so old, thought Varia. And so mean.

"Sidran was following the star child," Varia continued recklessly. "The star child who jumped out of the sky and hypnotized Sidran into following him, then left me behind in the woods." She didn't care any more how foolish she sounded.

She wasn't going to be blamed for someone else's stupidity, especially when she had been trying to help.

"The star child!" Mom looked shocked. "But that was only a dream!" She looked at Varia strangely. "My dream."

"It was my nightmare," Varia snapped. Tears pushed at her eyes, but she blinked them away.

Dad looked back and forth between them as he tied the drawstring in his trousers. Mom walked to the door and opened it. Cool air flooded in. "Nara," Mom called. "Come here a moment, please."

Nara stepped inside, carrying a big basket of wet clothes. She set it down on the floor and tucked her hair back into her scarf with a chapped finger. She was the team's geologist. She did the laundry because it gave her a chance to study the stones in the creek. Yesterday she'd found a glassy, black one that was either volcanic or melted by a meteor impact.

"Any news about Sidran?" Mom asked. Nara shook her head and looked sympathetically at Varia. "No luck with the tree bark, I see. It won't come off your clothes without ripping them either, even with that rough piece of pumice I found." Another volcanic rock.

Mom crossed her arms. "Varia says Sidran followed the star child into the woods."

Nara grabbed Mom and hugged her tightly. "Then he'll be all right for sure!"

"You dreamed it too," said Mom, pulling away.

Nara beamed. "Isn't it exciting?"

"Exciting!" shrieked Varia. "That star creature kidnapped Sidran and left me glued to a tree, and now I feel like a wooden spoon." She glared at the two women. "I've seen it. I know what it's like. Trust me: Sidran isn't coming back."

Mom opened her mouth, but before she could say anything, a shout resounded from outside. "I'm back!"

The grown-ups ran outside. Varia waddled after them. The clouds parted, and the bright sun glinted off the tower's metal bars. She shaded her eyes with her hand. The bark cast a big shadow, but it was heavy. She moved into to the shadow of the trees behind the sleeping hut.

Sidran stood beside the tower in a circle of sunshine. He wore a dripping nightshirt and bare feet like Varia, but he was grinning from ear to ear and carrying a mound of trailing, white clouds that looked like he had plucked them straight out of the sky.

"Look!" He held it up. "The star child showed me this fluff!"

He handed around tufts of the white stuff. Varia hung back. If it was from the star child, she didn't want any. Besides, she didn't want Sidran to see the bark — especially since her adventure had turned out so badly, while his had evidently been a grand success.

The crowd oohed and aahed. Sidran babbled on. Yes, he had caught the star child — his name was Specto — and yes, he was hot to touch, but not too hot, and Specto had marked the trail to the fluff field so they could go back later for more. It was for making warm cloth. No, there weren't any poisonous plants on the trail, and yes, it was wonderful how the star child had come to them, and before he forgot, Specto wanted all of them to come to his special tree tomorrow morning and eat breakfast with him. Sidran would take them there himself.

Sidran scanned the crowd. "Varia!" he cried when he spied her huddling in the shadows. "You found your way back! I thought I might have to rescue you."

Anger surged.

Sidran pushed his way through the crowd and dug in his pocket. "Specto said this is for you." He pulled out a crumpled leaf. Inside was a pink fan fungus, the dragon-foot kind she had noticed on the walk home. "Don't touch it — it stings. Specto said to boil it in water and it would unstick you." He frowned. "I don't know what he meant by that." He saw the bark and his eyes grew wide. "Bulrushes! I wonder how he knew."

Varia put her hands behind her back. The star child knew she'd been stuck in the tree? How could it know that unless it had deliberately tripped her, knowing she would go towards the glowing mushrooms? And Sidran knew she was following him and had ignored her. She was so flabbergasted by the cruelty of it that she could think of nothing to say.

Mom hurried toward them. "Thank you, dear," she breathed as she took the package from Sidran. She cradled a piece of fluff in her other hand. "It's just what we need." She put her arm around Sidran's shoulders and steered him back to the crowd.

"Nice haircut!" he called over his shoulder.

Varia turned her back to them and waddled towards the sleeping hut to lie down. Mom holds that package as if it contains jewels, she thought disgustedly, while she treats me like an old rag.

Mom caught up with her at the door. "Sweetheart, I'm sorry for yelling. I was so worried when you disappeared. I didn't know the star child was involved. I thought he was only a dream. Of course it's okay to follow him." She gave Varia a hug. Varia was glad her arms were stiff and she couldn't hug back. Why were they all so in love with that constellation? "But now you're back, and Sidran is back, and no worse for wear."

"I'm worse for wear," said Varia.

Mom kissed her forehead. "It will be okay now."

Varia pulled away. "Mom?"

"Yes?"

"Did you catch the star child . . . in your dream?"

Mom smiled and closed her eyes. "Yes, I did."

"What happened then?"

Mom folded the fungus back into the leaf. "He made me warm. Not like a stove, which only warms one side of you, or the sun, which can burn. It was more like a hot bowl of soup that warms your middle and spreads out through the rest of your body. It was like that. When I caught him, his warmth spread through me, and then it flowed out of me and into everyone I touched. For a doctor, that's a beautiful thing." She opened her eyes. "Why? What happened when you caught him?"

Varia shrugged. "I woke up."

Mom smiled again. "I'm going to boil this up right away," she said, "and then we'll melt that bark off you." Mom looked completely happy. So did Sidran. So did everyone else. Varia just felt cold.

The boiled fan worked. The sap and bark slipped right off when Mom poured the pink water over her skin. She cleaned Dad up too, and when they soaked the clothes in the leftover water, they too came out clean. It was Dad who noticed that the cut on Varia's forehead was gone.

"Maybe it was only a bump," protested Varia. "I didn't see it, after all." She rubbed her knees through her pants. They didn't hurt either.

"I saw it," said Dad. "It was bleeding from here to here." He drew a line on her forehead with his finger, and Mom turned Varia's head and squinted at it.

"There's nothing there now," Mom said, her voice trembling. She picked up a strip of bark and gazed at the sap that still clung to it.

For once, Varia was glad to return to her chores. She blinked back tears as she walked away. None of this made sense. The star child was being so generous and good. But when she caught it, in her dream, it had seared her hands, and she had flung it away. It was the burning pain that woke her up.

Chapter 4

Something green flashed beyond Varia's closed eyes. She opened her eyelids a crack to see what it was. Instead, she saw Adriel. He grinned at her upside down, his curly black hair hanging off the top of his head.

Mom spoke. "Varia, get up. We're meeting Specto in five minutes." Adriel flopped, tummy first, onto Varia's chest. She rolled him off the blanket and pulled it over her face. She was definitely not getting up for that.

Mom picked up Varia's pants from the floor and tossed them onto her mat. "How many times have I told you to hang up your clothes! They're going to rot away before winter."

"Grass clothes don't rot that quickly," Varia mumbled under the blanket. Adriel yanked it off her face. "Peek-boo!" She pulled it back and held it there while he tugged at it.

"If you had hung up your Earth clothes, you could have worn them today."

Varia peeked out at her. Mom was wearing her only remaining Earth outfit: baggy, too-big jeans and a red knitted sweater that hung shapelessly over her thin shoulders. She pulled the blanket back over her face. "They wouldn't fit me anyway."

Varia's covers suddenly disappeared. Mom stood above her, blanket in one hand and Adriel's arm in the other. Mom's eyes slid over her knobby joints and stick-thin arms and legs. Varia sat up and folded her legs inside her nightshirt while she turned her pants the right way out.

"You're right," said Mom. "They wouldn't." Another accusation.

Varia pulled the baggy pants over her legs and fumbled with the knot. "I'm not the only one who's thin. Everyone is."

Mom dropped the blanket on Varia's mat and tied a grass bow around the end of her braid. Her finger flashed green. Varia gasped. Mom had on her emerald ring! That ring was a gift from her mother just before they left Earth. Mom kept it tucked away in a little grass bag under her mat. Varia had never seen her wear it.

Varia could hear Sidran and his parents getting dressed on the other side of the grass curtain that delineated their part of the sleeping hut. The outside door opened and closed.

"Thin is one thing," said Mom, "but you're way too small for your age." She turned to Dad. "It was that half-gravity on the spaceship, I know it. They said the children would grow normally again once we got onto a planet, but they were wrong."

"She's as healthy as any of us," Dad replied wearily. They'd had this conversation before. "Even if she is small for her age, we can't change how fast she grows. Adriel is growing."

Mom pursed her lips. "With the amount of food we produce, it's a miracle."

"What is my age?" asked Varia. She paused in buttoning her shirt and looked back and forth at her parents.

"We don't have time to figure it out now," said Mom. "We have to go and see if Specto can tell us how to grow more food."

"You never have time," said Varia. "How can you say I'm small for my age if you don't even know how old I am?"

"I'll work on it while we eat," said Dad.

Varia stood up and tied the drawstring in her pants. "I don't want to eat with that star child," she said.

Mom sighed heavily. "It doesn't like me," Varia insisted. "If you make me go, I won't eat breakfast."

"You go, Candace," Dad said. "I'll take Varia to the kitchen and we'll make some porridge."

Mom sighed again. But she picked up Adriel and slipped through the curtain.

Varia snuggled against Dad's warm side as they walked across the dewy clearing to the kitchen. "Thank you." A trickle of water worked its way into a hole in her boot. Bulrushes, she thought. Another job.

"I wasn't going anyway," Dad said. "I want to do some research and find out what kind of alien that star child might be."

"But first figure out how old I am."

Dad squeezed her shoulder. "I'll try."

The big porridge pot was missing from the shelf over the wood stove they made out of the lander's shell. "The cups and bowls are gone too," said Varia, glancing at the dish shelf.

"We'll use this." Dad plunked a small pot on the stove next to the slightly steaming water kettle, and ladled in three scoops of water.

"I was five years and two months old when we left Earth," said Varia.

"And five days," added Dad. "Stand back." He pulled open the stove door and pushed in another piece of wood.

Varia measured out a scoop of coarsely ground barley from a basket on the food shelf. "So, how many years were we on the spaceship?"

Dad scratched his head. "That's where it gets tricky. Alsafi is 18.8 light years from Earth. That means it would have taken us 18.8 Earth years to get here if we were travelling at the speed of light."

"But we didn't go that fast."

"Not quite. It took us almost two Earth years to reach our maximum speed, and a Kettle year to slow down. People watching us from Earth would say it took us about twenty-three years."

"So I'm more than twenty-eight years old? No wonder Mom thinks I'm small!"

Dad chuckled. "No. That's only from Earth's viewpoint. Did you put in the yeast?"

"What? Oh." Varia grimaced. She picked up a spoon and added a tiny bit of the smelly, brown stuff Luella, their head cook and nutritionist, kept in a covered bowl beside the shelf. "An excellent source of vitamin B-12." Varia mimicked Luella's voice. After six seasons, she still didn't like yeasty porridge. "Why am I not twenty-eight?" she asked.

Dad picked up a reader from a small ledge under the window and sat down at the table. "Well," he said, flipping open the cover to show the view-screen, "when a spaceship travels close to the speed of light, time slows down for everyone inside it. So for us the trip only took a few years. But how many . . . " He sighed.

Dad tapped the reader's keyboard. "One of our goals on the flight here was to adjust to the Kettle's shorter day. One Kettle day is only twenty Earth hours long, instead of twenty-four. So the ship's computers automatically sped up the clock for us by 1 second a day. They adjusted the gravity on the ship too, and the composition of the atmosphere. After about, oh, six-and-a-half years, we were living on Kettle time, gravity, and air."

Varia stirred the porridge. "So we were on the ship for six-and-a-half years."

"Actually more than that. About eleven mixed years, part long Earth years and part short Kettle years, and some in between. Wang would know." Wang had been on the other lander.

Varia carried the pot to the table and handed Dad a spoon. "They took all the bowls." She sat down and leaned her head against the padded back of the chair. These chairs were the only things in the whole settlement that felt right. Her scratchy, shapeless clothes, her hard sleeping mat, the holey boots she wove herself — nothing else fit properly.

She watched Dad eat from his half of the pot. "So you don't have any idea how long the trip was in Earth years?"

Dad pursed his lips. "Between seven and nine? Maybe?"

"So I'm five plus seven to nine. That's twelve to fourteen Earth years. Plus a year-and-a-half here, which is just a bit more than one Earth year, right?" Dad nodded, swallowing. "That makes me between thirteen and fifteen Earth years. Probably." Well, it was more than she knew before. Connie had been three Earth months younger, and Sidran almost one Earth year older. All of the kids had been within four years in age — so that in a few years, after the colony was well-established, they could start having children. That was the theory, anyway, before they landed on a fungus-land and lost the other lander.

Dad pushed the pot toward her and opened one of the two readers.

She leaned forward and swallowed a spoonful of porridge. Good. Not too yeasty. Dad had left her more than half of it.

Slow down, she told herself. When you're done, you'll just have to get up and work. She ate another spoonful and leaned back in the chair again.

The chairs had come straight out of the lander, one for each of them except Adriel, who had travelled strapped onto Mom's chest. He still ate sitting on somebody's lap. They had removed the five-point seatbelts to use the straps for hauling logs. The table was made of wood planks laid across six stumps, three at each end. The men had thrown it together last fall, and sanded it smooth over the long winter using the grainy, non-slip treads from the lander's steps.

Dad frowned at the screen. "Found anything?" Varia asked

"Lots of known life forms, but nothing like the star child."

"Look under 'constellation'," Varia suggested.

Dad snorted. "Constellations only exist in our imaginations. Stars that look side by side to us may be light years apart. Specto is either an alien life form that just dropped in, or an indigenous life form that we haven't encountered yet. Given how much he knows about the forest, I suspect he lives here."

"What about the dreams?" asked Varia. "Didn't you see him fall from the sky?"

"I have many dreams," Dad replied. "I never mistake them for reality."

Neither did I, thought Varia, until that one. She leaned over so she could see the reader's screen. Pictures of strange creatures scrolled past her eyes, while a red arrow on a star map jumped around to show where they had been discovered. None of them looked like a constellation.

"You're sure he glowed?" Dad asked.

"That's how I followed them."

Dad snapped the reader shut and strode out of the kitchen. Varia gulped down the rest of her porridge and slid into Dad's chair. She opened the reader up again, hardly believing her luck. She had a reader all to herself, and no one was around to give her a job. She jumped quickly through the menus for survival information, past the maps and scientific information, and into the deeply buried "entertainment" menu. Varia sometimes thought she lived for the times she could read stories. They gave her something to think about beyond the musty, dreary Kettle.

The screen filled with a list of dragon books. She'd read them all on the ship, but she was happy to read them again. She clicked on the bookmark she had inserted in *The Voyage of the Dawn Treader* last spring when the snow melted and the unending work started again. She had barely begun to explore the unknown Eastern Seas beyond the Lone Islands when a loud clunk on the table beside her made her jump. The dishpan, bent out of an aluminum cupboard divider in the lander's storage bay, wobbled at her elbow.

"Dish time," said Luella.

Samuel plunked two aluminum buckets full of water onto the floor. Sidran followed him in, sloshing water out of another one.

"Refill the kettle and put it on the stove when you're done," said Luella automatically as she left.

"Okay," Sidran replied just as automatically.

Varia bookmarked her new place in the story and returned the reader to the shelf under the window, making sure its solar panel faced the light. The window, one of two salvaged from the lander, was built into the south wall of the kitchen. The other one was in the weaving hut, the smaller building next to the kitchen. Two of the women were going there now. I should have given them my boot to fix, she thought.

Varia poured hot water into the dishpan and added some cold from the bucket. She quickly plunged in her hands to claim the job of washing. Their slippery grass towels didn't absorb anything, only smeared the water around. Sidran flicked a towel at her while she sprinkled a handful of ashes into the water and began to scrub. Varia would have preferred to let the dishes air dry so she could be alone with her thoughts, but Luella liked the table to be clear when she came in to grind the grain and mix the sourdough starter.

The starter, a bubbly mix of barley flour and sweet potato cooking water, had a sharp, pungent odour that made Varia sputter every time Luella opened the lid. "Be glad we have it," Luella had snapped at her once. "Sourdough makes your bread rise. Without it, our bread would taste like boot soles." Lately, however, the sourdough had been changing. It smelled so sharp that even Luella held her breath before opening the lid, and the bread rose twice as fast as before. "It's picking up foreign yeasts from the air," Varia heard her whisper to Mom.

Their crops were changing too — just slightly, but enough to make them look alien. The porridge didn't taste much different, but the bread was tougher and the soup tasted musty. Luella and Mom both worried that this was the cause of everyone's increasing coughs and headaches. They ate it all anyway. It was that or the unknown plants from the forest. Samuel had carefully sorted out the best-looking seeds and tubers for next spring's planting, and they could only hope that next year's crops wouldn't be worse.

"You didn't have to follow me," Sidran broke into her thoughts. "Specto knows all about the woods. You should have known that from your dream."

"He didn't get to the woods in my dream," she retorted. "And you shouldn't have ignored me. But don't worry; I'll never try to rescue you again." She tossed a bowl at him, splashing water onto his shirt.

"I don't need to be rescued." Sidran caught the bowl and swished the towel over it, leaving dirty fingerprints and most of the water behind. "Specto said there was nothing dangerous in that part of the woods. If I'd turned around to help you when you didn't need help, I might have lost sight of him."

Varia scowled. "You could at least have waited when I called."

"Specto didn't stop," Sidran said. He rubbed the back of his hand over his runny nose, then wiped it on his pants. Varia edged away from him. "In my dream," he said quietly, "the forest was full of things to build with. The star child showed me where they were, and I carried them back and made machines that could help us do our work." He laid down the bowl and picked up another one.

"Now you can build a fluffy blanket," Varia snapped.

"Yeah," he answered doubtfully. "Maybe the machines will come later. Hey, you brought something back too." He held up a long, grubby finger. "I had a sliver, and your mom pulled it out with some of that leftover sap. She's crazy over that stuff. She spent all afternoon yesterday following everyone around with a piece of bark to see if they had any cuts."

Varia flung her head around to face him. She missed the sweep of her long hair. It was much harder to make a point with it cut short. "I don't want any of that sap on me ever again. I don't want to see that — that creature ever again either, unless he's back up in the sky where he belongs. And stop smearing dirt on those clean bowls!" She grabbed the bowl out of his hands and dropped it back into the water.

Sidran's green eyes flashed in his freckled face. He wiped his hands on his shirt. "You're just sore because he didn't bring his pet dragon."

Varia dropped several more bowls into the water. "If Draco had come," she retorted, "I wouldn't have spent the night glued to a tree, where your precious Specto stuck me. If Draco had come, he would have helped me find the other lander."

"We might still find it," Sidran said quietly. His unruly red bangs flopped into his eyes as he looked down at the bowl cradled in his oversized hand. "Dad says that as long as the tower is transmitting our location, we have hope, even if they aren't transmitting back. We just have to stay alive until they come."

Varia didn't answer. The other team obviously hadn't received their signal, because they hadn't replied. Unless their transmitter was broken. And even if they did get the signal, why would they be able to travel more easily than Varia's group could?

"Specto will help us survive," Sidran went on. "So next winter we won't be as cold and hungry as last time." He paused. "Blankets and bandages will be useful, even if they're not exciting." He started stacking the bowls on the dish shelf.

Varia picked up a dirty cup. She tried hard not to remember last winter. "What is this stuff?" she asked, sniffing the strange liquid at the bottom.

"Star water," replied Sidran. "Specto gave it to us."

"What for?" she asked doubtfully. She emptied it into the big porridge pot before washing the cup in the dishpan.

"He says it helps our bodies adapt to the fungus — the rust on our crops, and the mildew. He agrees with your mom that it's making us sick. He says with star water, we can start over."

Varia emptied several more cups into the pot and plunked them into the dishwater. "Start over how?"

"You can come tomorrow and ask," Sidran said. "He'll give you some. It doesn't taste bad — just hot and flowery. And I haven't coughed once since I drank it."

Varia swallowed hard to stifle her own cough. She would love to feel better. And why shouldn't it work? The tree sap and fungus fan had worked. But would the star child give it to her? What if it burned her again? "I'll wait and see what happens to you," she said. She carried the porridge pot to the back door and dumped the star water onto the ground before pouring in water from the dishpan. "My dad and I want to figure out what's really going on before we do anything we might regret," she added, scraping the sticky porridge off the sides of the pot with a spoon.

Sidran shrugged and dried the rest of the cups in silence.

Chapter 5

AFTER THE DISHES WERE DONE, VARIA wandered next door to the weaving hut. She much preferred working in the fresh air to crouching in the dim light forcing her fingers to do things she was sure they weren't designed to do. Still, she was curious what the women were doing in there now when there was still weaving grass to cut for winter.

Gretel sat on the floor staring at the reader on her lap. Next to her, seated on a stump beside the window, Nara combed a tuft of Sidran's fluff with two flat paddles studded with shards of small bones. Varia's eyes widened. Gretel must have let her smash the bone specimens she'd found in the field. She obviously thought this fluff was pretty important. Luella and Beatrice each held one end of a combed piece of fluff, and were twisting it in opposite directions to make a lumpy piece of yarn. Adriel was climbing onto a stump, sitting down on it, then sliding off and doing it again.

"What are you reading about?" Varia asked Gretel.

Gretel glanced up. "Spinning wheels. We're going to make one so we can turn fluff into yarn."

"You won't get much yarn out of that little bit of fluff," Varia said doubtfully.

Gretel laughed. "We're going to get more this afternoon. Your mom already gathered the sacks. She also wants to get more of that sap you found, and some of those fungus fans."

"How will you know where to go?" Varia reached out her hand to steady Adriel, who was teetering on the edge of the stump.

"Sidran is taking us. Specto marked the trail."

"Spec — the star child isn't going?"

"No. He said as long as we've drunk star water, we'd be safe."

"Oh." Varia left the hut feeling confused. A minute ago, no one could have persuaded her to go back into the woods, but now that others were going, it sounded intriguing — certainly more interesting than picking peas or digging potatoes. And she could point out the sticky tree.

Mom was by the creek, cutting bunches of weaving grass and tying them into bundles. The answer was no. "I need you to look after Adriel. You can shell peas in the hut while he has his nap." She frowned. "Besides, you haven't drunk star water. It's not safe for you."

"I survived without star water last time."

"You were only on a small part of the trail. Sidran said you fell behind quite early on."

Varia scowled and stomped to the field to help Dad pick peas. She yanked the dry pods off the vines and threw them at the waiting sacks. Sidran wasn't in any trouble for abandoning her. He was the new hero, while she had to stay home and do the boring jobs — including, it later turned out, washing and drying the lunch dishes while he got ready for the trip. She could hear his know-it-all voice long after the last grass sack disappeared from view.

"Specto broke branches for us, see? And there's a pile of stones, and the marks on that shelf fungus show us that we have to turn . . . "

If the trail was that clear, Sidran needn't have gone either, Varia grumbled. Out the kitchen window, she watched Dad drag a large sack full of dry pea pods into the sleeping hut. Mom had left her a basket for the peas, and an empty sack for the broken pods. They would be used to plump up the sleeping mats. If it were sunny, Varia could shell the peas outside the door of the hut, and at least watch what was going on in the field. But a fine drizzle had been falling since morning, and the peas would mould if they got wet. Not that the pods weren't already mildewed. The white powder than flew into the air when she snapped one always made her eyes itch. It would be a long, miserable afternoon.

Adriel squatted on the kitchen floor, playing with a pebble. "Time for your nap," Varia mumbled when the dishes were finally done. He ignored her, so she picked him up and carried him to the sleeping hut. Adriel kept the pebble clutched tightly in his fist as she untied his grass diaper, pulled out the damp moss by the driest-looking corner, replaced it with fresh, dry moss that Mom kept stacked in the corner, and re-tied the diaper. They knew the moss wasn't poisonous, because Mom wore a piece of it next to her own skin for several days before using it on Adriel.

"Stay here," Varia told him. "I'm just going to get rid of your wet moss." Adriel grinned and sat up. Varia opened the door, raced to the edge of the woods, and tossed the dirty moss away just before it fell apart. She wiped her fingers on a damp leaf. "Now, lie down on your mat and I'll sing you a song," she instructed as she went back inside. But Adriel wasn't there.

"Where's Adriel?" she asked, peeking around the curtain that separated their sleeping area from Sidran's family's space, then the one that led to Nara and Hugo's, and on to the end of the building. She expected to find him hiding in a corner, waiting for her to play "Gotcha!" But he wasn't. She ran to the door. Adriel stood across the clearing, staring up at the signal tower. "I can't leave him alone for one second," she grumbled. Giggling with delight when he saw her running toward him, Adriel climbed onto the first rung of the tower.

The signal tower was the ribs of the lander, turned on end once the shell and everything inside had been stripped away. The tower's base, which had been the back end of the lander, made a wide hexagon that even a tall man like Samuel could lie down in. The beams curved together at the top of the tower, which had of course been the lander's nose. The small, square transmitter, the receiving dish, and two wide solar panels were bolted to the top. Horizontal bars ringed the six vertical beams. When Varia reached him, Adriel was wobbling on the third bar.

"Not safe!" Varia scolded, reaching for him. Water dripped off the bars under his bare feet. Adriel's lower lip trembled. He glowered at her, then grabbed the next rung. Varia wrapped her arms firmly around his chest and lifted him off. He screamed in protest and strained for the tower, kicking Varia in the stomach. Varia staggered on the muddy ground. She fell forward into one of the tower beams. Adriel wailed.

Blood streamed down his leg. Varia held him close and tried to think. Mom wasn't here, so she had to treat the wound herself. She pressed her hand against the cut to stop the blood from flowing, the way Mom always did. She wasn't going to touch any mouldy bread. But what about tree sap?

"Do you need help?" Dad called from the field, where those who hadn't gone to get fluff were working.

"No," she shouted back.

Varia carried Adriel to the kitchen and laid him on the table. The wound was a long scrape, rather than a deep cut. She washed Adriel's knee, which made him cry harder, tied a clean towel around it, and carried him into the sleeping hut. He lay still inside his blanket, sucking his thumb, his eyelashes long and dark against his tear-stained cheek. Varia lay down beside him and hummed softly until his thumb fell out of his mouth.

She opened the door and waved at Dad to let him know everything was okay. He waved back and returned to work. That was good. Now he wouldn't guess she was about to slip away. She made sure Adriel was still asleep, then climbed out the window and skirted the settlement just inside the woods until she reached the trail to the sticky tree.

Chapter 6

Specto's broken branches were clearly visible, as well as the pile of stones and the arrow drawn on the side of a large, pale green shelf fungus growing on a fallen log. Most of the time Varia didn't need the markers; she could just follow the trampled plants. They didn't hurt me last time, she reminded herself, and this time I'm wearing long pants and boots — even if one of them has a hole.

The dragon plants were still there, teasing her. Scalloped wings fluttered. Eyebrows lifted, fingers pointed, tails dangled, scales flashed. Shiny eyes peered from shadowy bushes, and invisible wings swished over treetops.

Suddenly, she was at the prickly plants, then the sticky tree with the clump of rust-coloured mushrooms at its base. The other night, she thought they'd walked for miles. But it was the same tree: high up on the trunk, her black hair hung in wet, dark strands like silky moss. New bark was already growing in around it. It was a healing tree, she reminded herself. She felt a twinge of pride. Accident or not, if she hadn't climbed the tree and gotten stuck in it, they would never have discovered what it was good for.

Varia studied the tree. She had planned to pull off a strip of bark, then run home with it before the sap dried. But how could she peel it off without a knife? She jabbed a stick into it. Sap dribbled out, and she wiped it off the tree with the end of the stick. That would be enough. She turned around to head back when she saw a flickering light in the shadows. The star child.

Go back, part of her screamed. Remember last time! But another part of her wanted to know what it was doing. She dropped the stick and crept toward the light, hiding behind tree trunks and bushes.

The star child flitted in and out of sight. Varia passed a marshy pond ringed with leafy reeds. Small bees, or rather the four-legged pollinating insects they called bees, buzzed among the reeds' yellow blossoms. Beyond the pond, the ground sloped downwards and the trees thinned out around several boulders, dark and shiny in the rain. Varia crept behind one of them. At the bottom of the hill, the ground was pebbles and gravel, with a single bright patch of large, yellow flowers. A jumble of boulders lay at the edge of the gravel, under a rain-furrowed cliff. Above the cliff, and on the far side of the gravel, the rock-strewn shrubby hillside led back up into the forest. In the other direction, the valley disappeared into the trees.

Varia crept closer and peered out between two smaller boulders. The star child looked like a filmy piece of fabric fluttering over the rocks, its stars seeming to blink on and off depending what colour was behind it. It circled the flowers, flitted among the boulders, crawled back to the pool, then disappeared down the long ravine.

What was it looking at? Varia wanted to go down and find out — but Adriel might wake up early if his knee hurt. Just a quick look, she decided. The bright flowers turned out to be tall reeds growing around a small pool. Instead of leaves, large, glistening flowers grew right out of the stalks. The reeds were topped with single, large clusters of petals that gave off a strong, dizzying odour. She backed away — into something mushy.

Beneath her boot was a squashed orange and blue striped bee, big enough that its head and tail end were both intact. Varia lifted her foot and scraped it against the gravel. Tiny bones protruded from the gooey sludge. Another bee crawled past her foot and lumbered up the thick stem of one of the reeds. Like the small bees that flew around the settlement, it had four legs, two sturdy wings, and no stinger. As it brushed against a flower on its way to the top, a stripe of glistening nectar brushed off onto its fuzzy coat. Gretel would be fascinated — but if she took one back, they would know she'd left the settlement.

Varia walked around the ring of flower reeds. The pool was fed by a trickle of water that bubbled out of a crack in the ground. That was what the star child was looking at. Down the valley there were more yellow spots, presumably more flower pools like this one.

It was too bad she had to go home, but Dad would be furious if he knew where she was. She would only stay for one super-quick look at the boulders. A flaky, grey lump bulged out from one of them. A fat bee crawled out of it and down the rock. It was an enormous hive, and the bees must be too fat to fly in and out. She caught her breath. Next to the hive, almost hidden between two of the boulders, was a shadowy hole.

Varia had read about caves. Dragons often lived in them. She felt cautiously into the hole as far as she could reach. Nothing. "Stay asleep, Adriel," she whispered, and slipped inside. It was indeed a cave. Rays of light filtered through a crack in the ceiling. The yellow-brown walls were smoothly sculptured, like the creations Varia remembered making with play clay on the spaceship. Here and there they were streaked with sooty smudges. She rubbed her finger across one, and it came away black, although there was no sign of wood or anything else that might have burned. Stone icicles hung from the high ceiling. Stalactites, she remembered from her reading. Draco's teeth.

She traced a shaft of light to the far corner of the cave. The first thing she saw was a dark, bubbling pool of water, which might have been three hands or three people deep — from where she was standing, it was impossible to tell. The second thing she saw was the stone.

Silence flowed around her as she tiptoed to the pool. The stone was faceted, like the emerald in Mom's ring. But it was not merely green. It glittered pink and yellow and blue and violet, and when she swayed back and forth, the colours mingled. She picked it up in both hands. Her palms burned with cold. But she held it firmly, willing to forgive anything of this treasure. When she passed it through the shaft of sunlight, it sent a cascade of stars rippling across the cave walls.

How had this giant jewel gotten here? Had it crystallized out of the dampness and the dissolved minerals in the walls? Grown slowly through silent centuries? Was it a dragon's tear? Or a starry mushroom spore from Draco's collision?

There were no jewels in the water. Instead, through a cloud of tiny bubbles she saw a tangle of sticks, naked branches sticking out at crazy angles. A shiver jolted her. She would have dropped the stone if she had been able to open her frozen fingers. That was no bush. It was bones. A skeleton. The skeleton of a dragon. Wings and tail and ribs and teeth and hollow eye sockets.

Varia stared at it, unable to move. A real dragon, here, on this planet that didn't have animals. A dead dragon. A drowned dragon. And in her hands, a mysterious jewel, which must have been the dragon's treasure. All dragons had treasure; she knew that from the stories. Why, oh why did everything turn out wrong? First Connie and everyone else on the other lander disappeared. Then the star child burned her. And now, when she finally found the one thing she most desired, it was dead.

Suddenly Varia only wanted to be back home with Adriel. Why had she sneaked into these hateful woods anyway? Tears welled in her eyes. She blinked at the jewel in her hands. A tear splashed onto it and froze. She started to put it down, but couldn't bear the thought. Leave this beautiful stone in this forsaken cave? What good was a treasure to a dead dragon anyway? Varia eased the jewel out of her frozen fingers and caught it in the bottom of her shirt.

Wincing as the icy jewel bounced against her stomach, she fled out of the cave and up the hill, past the pool, and toward the sticky tree. When she reached it, she knelt and rolled the jewel down beside the mushrooms to give her stomach a break from the cold.

"You found it," came a reedy voice above her head. It actually sounded like many voices running together. Varia looked up. The star child sparkled in the sticky tree. One eye blazed against a triangle leaf that showed through its face, making it look like a storybook pirate. Its hair-stars fluttered even though there was no wind, and its mouth stars widened as she stared at it. Was it a smile or a snarl?

"It's beautiful," the star child's voices chorused. Rainbow colours swirled in her mind.

The jewel. Varia nodded.

"And dangerous." The colours darkened ominously. The pointed leaves behind the star child's mouth looked like fangs.

"How can a jewel be dangerous?"

The star child's lights flared, then settled back down. "Not time yet."

Not time for what? The star child held out its hands. There was no sap on them. "Throw," it chorused, and the colours in Varia's mind arched like a rainbow.

Varia suddenly realized what it wanted. Her head cleared in the flash of her anger. "You can't have it!" she exploded. "I found it and it's mine!" She plucked a mushroom and hurled it through the star creature. "Catch this!" Then she scooped up the jewel and raced for home. Whatever made that star-alien think she would just hand over her treasure?

Adriel was still asleep when she slipped in through the window. She rolled the jewel under her mattress and bunched up her nightshirt over it to hide the lump. Then she wrapped herself in her blanket. She was safe — as long as the star creature didn't blab to anyone about seeing her in the woods. But it took many minutes before her heart stopped pounding and her legs stopped shaking, and many more before the feeling came tingling back into her fingers and stomach. It was only when she noticed the red stain on Adriel's bandage that she realized she hadn't brought back any sap for his scraped knee.

Chapter 7

MOM WASN'T ANGRY WHEN SHE SAW Adriel's scrape. "You used to run away from me all the time when you were small," she said with a wry smile. "And you did the right things." She softened a chunk of dry sap with leftover fan fungus water that she kept in an emptied pill bottle, then hardened it again on Adriel's knee with creek water. "It's messy, but it works," she said, placing the leftover supplies into her first-aid bag where the bandages and antibiotic cream used to be.

In the ensuing weeks, Varia mended her boot sole and shelled sacks of peas. She dug onions, garlic, sweet potatoes, and carrots, and picked cabbages and dill. She beat piles of weaving grass with a stick at the edge of the creek to soften their fibres, spread them out to dry, and carried them into the weaving hut. She piled mounds of firewood, carried buckets of water, raked a field of compost, scrubbed mould out of corners, held reeds steady while the men lashed them together for the walls and roof of the kitchen addition, and washed countless dishes.

She did not return to the woods, and she did not eat breakfast with the star child. Since their encounter in the woods, she was sure he wouldn't give her star water even if she asked for it, which she was not about to do in spite of her worsening cough.

She also didn't tell anyone about her second trip into the woods, or the skeleton, or the jewel. She would have told Connie, but Connie wasn't here.

Varia did accept the sweater of white fluff yarn that Mom knitted for her. It was from Mom, after all, not from the star child. Besides, the frozen jewel under her mat made it hard to sleep at night without an extra layer. And the sweater felt as soft as the fluffy clouds looked. It was softer than Mom's Earth sweater, which felt scratchy next to her bare skin, softer than the hairy heads on the weaving grass, even softer than Adriel's cheeks. Not that she gave Sidran the satisfaction of hearing her go on about it like everyone else did.

It was the day after the first snow fell that Varia noticed the shrinking. She had noticed small changes before: Mom's greying hair darkening into chestnut brown and the worry lines in her face smoothing out. Dad was the only one who still needed a hot poultice for his shoulders after a day of chopping wood, and the only one beside Varia who still complained of headaches. Samuel swore that the stubs of his fingers were growing longer.

But that morning after breakfast, standing beside the dishpan with Sidran, Varia's gaze wandered out the window — and she realized she was looking over the top of Sidran's head. Her first thought was that she had finally started to grow. Mom had told her that girls often spurted up before boys of similar age. But her clothes fit the same as ever, while Sidran's were rolled up at his wrists and ankles. And he had trouble drying the bowls because they no longer fit in his hands.

"We're all getting smaller," Sidran said matter-of-factly. "Did you just notice now? Specto says it's part of starting over."

"Starting over by shrinking?" Varia asked, genuinely puzzled. "I can understand why our parents might want to be young again. When I'm thirty or forty and all worn out, I might too. But I'm still trying to grow!"

"Why?" asked Sidran. Now he looked puzzled.

Varia stared at him. "We're supposed to grow," she said. "It's natural."

Sidran put a bowl on the stack and took a wet one from Varia. "Nothing will change when we're big," he said, "except there will be even more work."

"And who's going to do the work if you all turn back into babies?"

Sidran rubbed at the bowl. "I don't think it will get that far. I think we just shrink until our bodies get used to the fungus, then we grow again. I think — "

"You think!" Water dripped from Varia's dishrag onto her foot, but she didn't care. "Don't you know? How can you trust that star thing if you don't even know what it's doing?"

Sidran plunked the bowl down. "Because I do know. Not exactly what he's doing, but I know he's helping us. Even you're wearing a fluff sweater. The sap's amazing. And yesterday he showed Luella a kind of mushroom we can eat."

"I'm not eating any slimy mushrooms," Varia retorted. She grimly scrubbed the sides of the pot. "When I'm grown up I won't do anything I don't want to."

"If things don't change, you won't have a lot of choice," Sidran replied.

"If you think shrinking will give you more choice, you're dumber than I thought." Varia carried the dishpan to the door and flung the water outside.

"Varia!"

Mom and Nara stood outside the door with armfuls of weaving grass dripping onto their clothes. Adriel stood behind them dragging his own bundle of weeds. Behind him, stems and leaves dotted their melting footprints.

"Sorry," muttered Varia. "I didn't see you."

"Next time, look," said Mom, shaking the water off her sleeves. They were rolled up. So were her pants. So were Nara's. Neither of them was much taller than Varia, if at all, and Mom might be a tiny bit shorter. How could she not have noticed? Only Adriel wasn't smaller.

"Since you've finished the dishes," Mom said, "come help us in the weaving hut. We need more boot soles."

"Dad wants help stripping bark," Varia said, struggling to keep her voice steady. This was all backwards! She had looked forward to being as tall as Mom, but because she grew, not because Mom shrank!

"He didn't tell me that. But go and help him, and join us when you're done."

Varia left Sidran to rinse out the dishpan and re-fill the kettle, and raced to the edge of the field. He, at least, was the same. She sagged with relief. He hadn't really asked for her help, but she needed to talk to him.

Varia watched him hack the bark off the large log. She was grateful for his strength, his wide shoulders, his big hands that clutched the axe handle so firmly. She was even grateful for the grey hairs that curled among his black ones. She began gathering bark chippings to take back to the kitchen for kindling.

"Dad," she began casually, when she felt she could trust herself to speak. Her voice sounded higher than usual. "Have you noticed that everyone is shrinking?"

Dad laughed harshly. "Yes," he said, and buried his axe in the log.

"Well?" asked Varia. "What are we going to do about it?"

Dad shrugged. "There's not much we can do. They're all adults — except Sidran and Adriel, and their parents, or mothers anyway, approve."

"But how can they let themselves be changed like that? Sidran says they don't even know how small they're going to get."

Sweat glistened on Dad's forehead. "They think it's our only chance for survival. You've seen how the fungus is taking over our crops. They think that star water is some kind of miracle potion that will keep them healthy."

"What do you think?"

Dad sighed and picked up the axe again. "Other doctors besides your mother have experimented on themselves. Me — I like to wait until I know it's going to work."

"So we just stand by and watch them shrink?"

"You can try to talk them out of it if you like, but you won't get very far." He raised the axe and sliced off a large chunk of bark. "Here," he said, handing it to her. "Take the big pieces to the weaving hut. Your mother wants to try gluing bark onto boots soles to make them stronger."

Varia snatched it from his hand. "So you've just given up. You don't care what happens to them."

Dad looked tired. "I care very much," he said. "If I had anything better to offer, I would."

"We'll stay as we are," said Varia.

"That might not work much longer," Dad said softly. A gust of cold wind parted Varia's hair. Dad pulled her into his arms.

Later that afternoon, she helped her small mother lug sleeping mats through the swirling snow to the kitchen. The bins of vegetables had already been carried to the sleeping hut. It would feel good to sleep in the heated kitchen. "Where does the star child sleep now that it's cold?" Varia asked.

"In the woods." Mom held the door open with her foot while Varia wrestled her end of the mats inside. "Quickly, now. He says stars aren't bothered by cold — they just melt out a patch of summer." Mom and Varia piled the mats beside the table. The men were still tying the last bundles of reeds onto the roof of the addition, and bits of grass and snow dripped in where they worked. Varia left Mom to help Luella with the soup, and crossed back to the sleeping hut alone.

The dragon's jewel could freeze out a patch of winter under a blazing sun, Varia thought as she rolled it up in somebody's torn shirt and hid it in a dark corner of the hut before carrying her own mat to the kitchen. The winter cold would certainly not harm this jewel. She pictured the star child holding it in his fiery hands. Which one would win?

"Why doesn't the star child let you eat breakfast inside?" she asked Mom later. "Why does it make you eat outside with it?"

"He's waiting until all of us want him to come in."

Varia kept her eyes on the ground. She didn't want it to come inside. It hadn't told anyone about meeting her in the woods, or about the jewel, she grudgingly acknowledged. That was decent of it. But it had tried to steal her jewel. And how could she watch everyone drinking that star water, knowing what it was doing to them?

Some of the changes weren't so bad, actually. Mom no longer rubbed raw onion on her shoulder to ease her bursitis. Her voice had become high and light. She looked like Varia's sister. But soon, Varia would look like the older one. And then who would look after whom? Would Varia be in charge? Would she tell Mom to watch Adriel while she took her turn making barley bread with a shrunken Luella in the kitchen? Or would she find herself taking instructions from a little girl who used to be her mother?

That night, Varia overheard her parents whispering. "How long is this going to take?" demanded Dad's urgent voice. "You've become like my daughter!"

"Maybe until we're the same age as Specto," Mom replied.

"How old is he?"

"As old as the stars."

"Oh, come on. How can any living creature be as old as the stars — you or that alien? And if he really is that old, why do you call him a child?"

"He is old and young at the same time." Varia's father snorted, and Mom shushed him. There was silence for a moment, then Mom's voice continued. "Think about it. When you look at stars, you don't see them as they are now. You see them the way they looked when the light left them. The farthest stars look the youngest of all, even new born. But by now, they are actually very old. Just like the star child."

"But he isn't far away. He's living in our forest."

"He's still up there. Haven't you seen him?" Varia had, still frozen halfway through his leap onto Draco's back. Dad grunted.

"What's down here is just part of him. His spirit, maybe, like an image or a projection. Or maybe that's his image in the sky. I don't really understand it either. But he is here, moving and talking and doing things, at the same time as he's up in the sky."

Dad didn't say anything. Varia could imagine him regarding her mother skeptically from under one raised eyebrow. She knew that he would dismiss Mom's words with a gruff "nonsense!" if only her mother weren't getting younger before his eyes. "What about Adriel?" he finally asked. "He's still growing, even though you take him with you every morning."

"I've noticed that," replied Mom. "I think it's because he's already a child."

"Well, that's a relief," said Dad, "if it means you won't get too small." He sighed. "Still, I don't like this. From over here it just looks like the star child is taking you away from me."

"From over here it looks like you're refusing the only help we have."

"It's just too . . . strange."

"And you're too stubborn."

"I just want to know you're going to be all right."

"I want to know you will too."

Varia bit her lip under the blanket. She hated this planet and its impossible choices. Stay yourself and die from fungus poisoning or put yourself at the mercy of a weird alien who wants to turn you into someone you're not, with no guarantee that it will help.

A great loneliness swept over her. She and Connie could have talked about this and figured out what to do together. Here she was caught between Mom and Dad, with no one else to turn to. But at least she was here. Where was Connie? She rolled over and tried to fall asleep.

Chapter 8

WINTER WAS COLD ON THE KETTLE, though it was better this year with sweaters, mitts, bark-boot soles, and fluff liners inside their boots. It was also dark, as the sun rose late and set early. But there was less work to do, so Varia and Sidran had time to use the readers when their chores were done.

At night, they either went to bed ridiculously early or burned smoky reed candles in the kitchen. Last winter, a few settlers had carved chess and checker pieces from wood scraps, and woven boards from two-toned grass. So they played games and sang old Earth songs until the air got too smoky. Adriel's favourite was "Mrs. Murphy's Chowder". He bounced along the floor in time to their clapping, laughing at the sound of the rhyming words: silk hats, door mats, bed slats, democrats... Varia found the words strange and exotic.

The most urgent early winter chore was peeling, chopping and hanging the vegetables to dry in nets above the stove so they would keep through the winter. The ceiling was already festooned with clumps of onions and garlic, and bouquets of starry dill and curly cabbage leaves, when they started on the sweet potatoes.

Varia sat at the table with the others, scraping grey strings off sweet potatoes with Earth knives. "What is this hairy stuff?" she grumbled. "Last year's sweet potatoes didn't have it. Ouch!" The knife sliced into her finger as her potato rolled across the table. Mom jumped up to fetch her first aid bag from the corner.

Samuel scowled from his chair by the window, his toes dangling just above the floor. "It's a fungus," he said. His voice sounded like Sidran's. "Fungi don't get their nutrients from sunlight the way plants do. Instead, they feed off other things: dead leaves, rotting logs, insect bodies, and other plants." Varia wrinkled her nose. Samuel continued. "It's quite common to find fungi on the roots of plants. You know those mushrooms we had to keep raking off the field? They're the fruit bodies that grow from those stringy fibres."

Sidran rolled her potato back to her and she stopped it with her good hand. It was three times the size of last year's. "If the fungus is eating the potatoes, why are they so big?" Varia asked as Mom smeared sap on her finger. "Shouldn't they be smaller?"

Samuel nodded. "The plant does feed the fungus, but the fungus also feeds the plant. It breaks down nutrients from the soil that the plant wouldn't be able to get otherwise, and absorbs water that the potato plant can use. Plants often grow bigger with a fungal partner. Some grow much bigger."

"They're also changing colour," said Nara, who was chopping a potato into slices and handing them to Gretel to string onto strands of grass. "See? They have violet-coloured veins."

"And the onions are thick and tough," complained Luella. "I could hardly cut them."

"Even the cabbage leaves are a different shape," Mom pointed out, pressing Varia's finger into a dish of water to harden the sap. Varia looked up at the ceiling, where the cabbage leaves lay in a net suspended from the rafters. It was true. Their edges were ruffled like the frill on a dragon's shoulders.

Hugo scattered a handful of peas on the table. "These peas are too big for the pods," he said. "They're crammed in so tightly that they're square instead of round."

Dad looked up from grinding the rust-coloured barley. "Maybe we can use them for dice," he suggested. "I know some great games with — "

"We can't eat dice," Luella snapped. She turned on Samuel, waving her chopping knife in the air. "It's all very fine to tell us why our plants are changing, but we need to know what effect these fungi are having on us. Is our food still safe to eat? And will our crops even grow next year?"

Samuel looked at her for a long moment. "I don't know," he said quietly. "Thora was the mycologist."

"But you've been reading," persisted Luella. "What have you learned? What about this rust on the barley? That's our staple food. If we can't grow barley . . . "

Samuel sighed. "I've learned that rust fungi need two hosts to grow — at least on Earth."

"And that means?"

"It means the fungus grows alternately on two different plants. This one grows on barley and something else. If we get rid of the other one, the fungus can't grow."

"So what's the other plant?"

"I'm working on it."

"How does the fungus get on the plants anyway?" asked Varia.

"Spores," said Sidran. "Everyone knows that."

"I've never seen one," Varia retorted.

"Spores are very tiny," explained Samuel. "They blow around in the air or float on water or get carried by insects and animal bodies."

"You're breathing them in right now," said Sidran. "They're going to grow in your lungs and ears and between your toes."

"Don't be disgusting," said Varia.

"They only grow if they land in the right places," said Samuel. "Fortunately, most of them don't grow on us."

"Star water protects us from fungus anyway," said Sidran, scraping a neat peeling of strings off his own sweet potato.

"Only if you drink it," Mom said shortly. She pulled Varia's finger out of the bowl and tapped the sap to make sure it was hard. "Okay, Varia, enough cutting for today. Go and read."

"Hooray!" Varia skipped to the shelf by the window.

Samuel snapped his reader shut. "You too, Sidran. Take this one."

Varia pulled out her mat and sat cross-legged on it with the reader. Sidran did the same next to her. Varia looked through the menu of choices. She had already read about gemstones. She'd found diamonds, amethysts, rubies, sapphires, and emeralds, but nothing that resembled her jewel. Some sapphires reflected light in a star pattern, but they were plain blue. Opals had rainbow colours, but weren't faceted.

She'd also read everything about dragons. The ancient Babylonians considered them symbols of primordial chaos. To Europeans, they were dangerous, fire-breathing monsters that had to be destroyed, usually by a knight in armour. A magic sword didn't hurt either. Chinese dragons were conglomerates. They had the antlers of a deer, the head of a camel, the neck of a serpent, the belly of a frog, the scales of a fish, the claws of a tiger, the eyes of a phantom, the claws of an eagle, and the ears of an ox. And the wings of a bat, Varia added — although most Chinese dragons didn't have wings.

Dragon lizards weren't dragons at all. Flying dragon lizards had a set of membrane-covered false ribs that they could spread out like wings, and glide on from tree to tree. Bearded dragon lizards had spiky scales around their chins. When they felt aggressive or wanted to mate, their "beards" puffed up and turned black. Water dragons were large lizards with long tails and powerful hind legs for swimming. They could hide underwater for many minutes at a time. Komodo dragons were the largest lizards of all — big enough to swallow a pig whole.

Some kinds of female lizards could lay eggs and hatch them even if there were no males for them to mate with. That was interesting, Varia thought. If they had brought one of those to the Kettle, it could have had babies. They could have filled the planet with lizards. But even if they had, which was against colonization rules, she didn't think lizards would be much of an improvement over the insects. She wanted the friendly animals. Like dragons.

She opened a picture of a dragon and watched it soar in circles above its forest.

Sidran glanced over from his mat. "Why don't you read about something real?" She ignored him. It was too bad he said that, because otherwise she might have told him about her discovery. Once she almost told Dad, and Gretel, but the words faded away guiltily before they reached her tongue. If she told, she would have to admit leaving Adriel and sneaking into the woods. Worse, Mom might make her give her jewel to the star child.

She decided to read about pterosaurs, prehistoric flying reptiles. They looked like primitive dragons with elongated jaws and no arms, although their wings weren't dragon-like or bat-like. Pterosaurs ate fish and other small creatures. Well, the dead dragon certainly hadn't, not on this planet — unless it ate insects or the animals that left their bones in the dirt. Maybe they all died at the same time. Or maybe the small animals died out from a plague or something, and the dragon starved to death. Maybe it fell into the water and was too weak from hunger to pull itself out.

Gretel had no idea what killed the animals that once lived on the Kettle. But she had told Varia about several mass extinctions on Earth. The dinosaurs, including the last of the pterosaurs, had died off suddenly. Some people thought a meteorite, possibly a comet, had smashed into the Earth, creating huge tidal waves and super-heated forest fires, and blocking the sun's light with dust. The planet had been plunged into a long winter, and many things had perished. Only animals that hibernated or laid patient eggs underground survived.

Pterosaurs and their eggs hadn't survived. The reader showed a picture of a fossilized pterosaur egg with curled-up bones inside it. The little animal had been almost ready to hatch when it was suddenly buried in mud. There was also a picture of a desert in a country called Chile where people had found a rookery of pterosaur eggs. Varia tried to imagine a rookery of dragon eggs on the Kettle. Maybe in the warm, gravel valley beside the cave. Dragons from all over would fly there to lay their eggs and take turns watching over them. But their eggs wouldn't be drab and leathery like the ones in the picture. Dragons' eggs would be beautiful, so the valley would sparkle like a treasure trove. The eggs would look like — like giant jewels.

Varia's heart skipped a beat. Had she found an egg? Impossible. As impossible as finding a dragon. Yet she had found a dragon. And her jewel didn't resemble any known stone. Had she found — and taken — the dead dragon's egg? Maybe that was why the star child said it was dangerous. As well, she realized with mounting excitement, it meant that the star child thought it could hatch!

Birds sat on their eggs or covered them to keep them warm. If she warmed up her icy jewel, would it hatch into a baby dragon? She plunked the reader back on its shelf and raced out of the kitchen, pulling on her boots as she ran.

Chapter 9

VARIA UNWRAPPED HER TREASURE IN THE corner of the summer sleeping hut, now the storage hut. She traced its rigid colours with her finger. "You little frozen dragon," she whispered. She wrapped it up again and tucked it under her shirt, next to her stomach — and gasped. It was far colder than the chunk of creek ice Sidran had dropped down her back last week. But at least this one wouldn't melt and drip into her underwear.

The question, of course, was how to accomplish the hatching. She couldn't very well walk around shivering with a lump inside her shirt. She couldn't bear the cold for more than a few seconds at a time anyway. Somehow she had to get the egg into the kitchen and near the stove — or even into it; in some stories, dragons hatched in fire. But no one could know it was there.

She was still mulling over this problem the next morning, while she helped Nara and Gretel plump up the sleeping mats with the empty pea pods and bunched-up strands of leftover weaving grass.

"We're done," Gretel announced finally, after the last mat was sewn up again. "And we still have stuffing left over."

"We could make pillows!" Varia exclaimed. Losing her pillow to mould had been one of the worst moments among many on this planet. Sleeping on a pillow again would be a treat. It would also be a perfect place to hide her egg.

"We could use this bit of fluff too," said Nara, holding out a sack. "It would be softer than grass by itself."

"I'll make mine," Varia offered quickly. "And Adriel's and Sidran's too." If they have their own, they won't want mine, she reasoned. Mom already insisted that they not share bedding, so she wouldn't have to worry about keeping her pillow apart from the rest. She would just roll it in her blanket when she wasn't in the kitchen.

Varia practiced on Sidran's. His pillow ended up with one side wider than the other, but didn't look too lop-sided once she stuffed it. Adriel's turned out better. Both halves were about the same size, if not exactly square, and she embroidered her best impression of a rabbit on it with light-coloured grass threaded through a sharp shard of tiny bone. Adriel had recently discovered pictures on the reader, and his favourite one had a rabbit in it.

Her own pillow turned out very well. She even figured out how to weave in a zigzag design around the edges. It was a simple matter to drop the egg into the fluffy stuffing when she went into the storage hut to fetch cabbage leaves for Luella. Then she laced the pillow shut with a strand of grass, and tied it with a knot she could easily undo. The pillow made a perfectly sized nest, although there wouldn't be much room beside the egg for her head.

Adriel took his pillow everywhere, hopping with it or sitting on it, or cuddling it while he napped in a corner of the kitchen. Sidran leaned his elbows on his pillow, lying on his stomach beside the stove while he read. Or he lay on his back and practiced tossing and catching it with his feet, or balanced it on his head while chasing Adriel back and forth across the clearing.

Varia held her pillow facing the stove when she was reading or weaving, and left it wrapped up in her blanket when she went outside. At night she held the egg close. She discovered that putting her head on the cold pillow eased her headaches, but holding the egg against her chest made her cough. She didn't sleep well. No matter where she put the pillow, she woke up shortly with one part of her body frozen. Then she had to move the pillow and try to get back to sleep before another part of her froze.

The worry didn't help either. Now that the jewel had become an egg and was going to hatch a baby dragon, it couldn't remain a secret indefinitely. Should she wait until it was ready to hatch and surprise everyone? Or should she tell them right away and get it over with? Sidran and Gretel would jump at the chance to help hatch it.

But then the star child would find out, and make them stop. Or take the egg. But it couldn't — especially since she realized that if she had a dragon to ride, she might be able to find the other lander. And even if the star child didn't interfere, she would have to tell everyone how she found it. Sidran would stop teasing her once he saw the skeleton, but they might not believe her about the egg even yet. Better to wait until she was sure.

The cold days dragged on. The settlers only met the star child briefly in the mornings to drink their daily dose of star water, then returned to the kitchen to eat their musty porridge. They brought back other things in their empty cups, though. A mushroom that the star child said was edible. Some dry leaves to boil into a bitter tea for calming an upset stomach. Nuts to grind and add to the porridge for protein. Strips of bark to make lavender dye for the sweaters.

Varia did chores in the mornings and spent the afternoons reading about eggs. She learned how chickens, crocodiles, and maiasaura grew inside their eggs. She learned that turtle eggs hatched into male or female turtles depending how deeply they were buried in the sand. She learned how to make fluffy cakes and chocolate eggs — if she'd had egg beaters, milk, chocolate, and chicken eggs. She found pictures of exquisitely decorated jewellery boxes made out of ostrich eggs, and intricately patterned Easter eggs in colours she could only gape at. She learned that chicken eggs had to be kept at a carefully regulated temperature in order to hatch at all.

Her poor egg was exposed to a whole range of temperatures, from the cool kitchen wall to her body temperature under the blanket to as close as Varia dared sit beside the stove. But these erratic changes didn't seem to bother it. When she slipped into the storage hut and unlaced the pillow, it was more beautiful than ever. Colours drifted over its surface as if the heat had liquefied them. How strange, she thought, that a creature that breathes fire should start out so icy. She was sure now that she could feel the egg vibrating under her blanket, and wondered if the little creature inside was purring like the cat Connie had smuggled onto the ship.

One morning, Varia tried to sit up and couldn't. The morning light stung her eyes, her throat felt raw, her blanket was much too thin, and attempting to talk or take a deep breath sent her into a fit of coughing.

Mom flew to her side, lifting her with cool hands. She tipped a hot liquid bit by bit into Varia's mouth, then covered her with a fluffy, blue-striped blanket.

Varia had no idea how long she lay shivering on her mat. She heard people tiptoeing around the kitchen and speaking in hushed voices. Periodically, Mom unwrapped her and wiped her with a damp cloth. She tried to swallow the thin porridge Mom spooned into her mouth, but her throat hurt so much she often couldn't. Once in a while, Dad picked her up in her blanket and carried her to the outhouse. The egg never left her arms. Even with her fever-clouded head, Varia remembered to hold her pillow tightly so no one would discover the egg. Sometimes she rested her burning head against it and let its coolness drift her into sleep. Most of the time she just lay still and felt the rhythm of its purring against her body.

"Varia." Mom lifted her shoulders, making her suddenly dizzy. "I'm taking you to see Specto. I don't know how to help you, but he will." Varia felt her sweater being pulled on over her head. "Dad will carry you in your blanket. Leave the pillow on your mat." Varia let the pillow roll out of her arms before Dad picked her up. She was too weak to protest, or even to care.

The cold air cut her throat and lungs like a knife. Mom pulled the blanket over her face and she felt herself being bounced against Dad's chest, up and down with his steps, and side to side with his own hacking cough. Finally he stopped, and sat her gently on the snowy ground with her back against a tree. He pulled the blanket off her face. Varia opened her eyes and looked into the face of the star child.

Its stars were pale against the snow, and grey branches showed like crooked bones through its body. The light hurt her eyes, so she closed them. A damp warmth like steam misted over her face.

"Drink this." The voices tripped into her head.

"She's too weak." It was Mom's voice. "Let me help her." Varia felt Mom's hands tip her head back and press a hot cup against her lips. She opened her mouth and the hot liquid trickled in.

Varia sat up, sputtering and choking. Her tongue sizzled. Her eyes streamed. Her lungs felt tight and desperate for air.

Mom, Dad, and the forest disappeared into a dark red void. All she could see was the star child's eyes burning into hers. She saw its words rather than heard them.

"Do you have it?" A picture of the frozen egg rolled into her mind. The picture grew and pushed against her skull.

Varia's thoughts snapped into focus. If the star child could find its own way through her thoughts, it wouldn't be asking her. She conjured an image of the cold jewel lying forgotten under a bush.

The intensity of the star child's gaze lessened. The words came more softly. "You will leave it there?"

Varia forced herself to breathe. The lie was necessary. "Yes." Her chest tightened again, but she held back the cough. The red void started to fade. "Wait!" she cried. The red grew stronger again. She conjured a picture of the missing lander, and Connie. "Can you help us find this?"

The star child's eyes flickered. The red faded. Words tumbled into Varia's mind. "No time. No need. Not now." And then a jumble of yellow leaves and mushrooms and bones and what looked like a shining lake. The images swirled together and flowed away, bringing her back to Mom and Dad and a tree in a snowy forest.

Varia felt hot and sweaty, then cold and shivery. Mom raised the cup to her lips again. The flowery liquid cut like lava across her raw throat and churned in her stomach. She struggled onto her knees, pushed aside Mom's hand, and vomited onto the snow. The cup with the star water landed upside down on top of it. The world spun and went dark.

When she opened her eyes, she was lying on her mat in the dim evening light. The others were sitting at the table eating soup. Varia rolled onto her side and watched them. Dad looked like a grandfather surrounded by his grandchildren. Not only did he have the only beard, but his beard was greyer than she remembered. His feet were the only ones resting on the floor. His voice was the only baritone in the soft conversation. She wondered how many days she had slept.

"You're awake." Mom rushed over with a cup. "Don't worry; it's just hot water."

Varia let Mom tilt it into her mouth. It trickled down her chin. "Sorry," she mumbled. Sorry for the spill, sorry for the disappointment.

"Try again." This time Varia got it down. She managed to finish the whole cup before she sank onto her mat, feeling terribly weary, but somehow not as bad as before. She hugged the lump inside her pillow. I saved you, she thought, for better or for worse. Because that star child really doesn't want you to hatch. The egg didn't feel cold at all as she fell back to sleep.

That day was the turning point for Varia's illness. Mom fed her more water, then thin porridge, then thin soup. Soon Varia was able to feed herself, then walk to the outhouse leaning on Dad's arm, then sit at the table for meals.

One warmer afternoon, Varia followed Dad to the edge of the forest to watch him chop wood. The sun was a red ball shining weakly through the clouds. Varia sat on a tree stump, resting from the walk, while Dad heaved a section of a log up onto his chopping block. He leaned on it for a moment to catch his breath before picking up the axe. He swung the axe up over his head and brought it down in a wobbly arc. One corner of it stuck in the wood. He wiggled it loose and tried again. This time he missed the log all together. Varia stiffened as the blade swung past his leg. His hands trembled.

Sidran rushed over to them from the field. No, it wasn't Sidran, Varia saw when he got closer. It was Samuel. Every day they looked more alike. "Need some help, Nat?" he asked. Dad let the axe dangle at his side, uncertain. Samuel took it from him. "I'll finish up."

Varia heard the log crack into splinters as they walked away. Dad kept his eyes on the ground. Blue veins ridged the loose skin on the back of his hand.

He's getting old way too fast, thought Varia. Her heart felt tight. "Do you think that star water helped me?" she asked.

"Didn't look like you kept much of it down."

"But I'm getting better."

"Maybe you would have anyway."

Varia tugged on his arm to make him stop, and looked into his eyes. "It would probably help you," she said. "I think it's just me the star child doesn't like."

"Are you saying you want me to drink it?"

Varia looked at little Samuel, who had finished Dad's log and was whacking at another one. "No. Just that if you wanted to, I'd understand."

Dad coughed. "I like the world to make sense. Big carrots from small seeds. Not growing backwards because of some mysterious substance called star water, when everyone knows stars are made of fire. Besides," he added wearily, "someone has to stay adult enough to look after the settlement."

It looks like they're looking after you, thought Varia. But she just squeezed his hand and walked with him back to the kitchen.

Varia grew stronger as the days lengthened and the snow thinned. She started washing dishes again. By the time the snow melted and everything was muddy, Varia was strong enough to sweep out the kitchen and weaving hut. In between those jobs, she rested, read, and collected supplies for a sack she kept hidden in the storage hut. She squirrelled away a torn grass blanket, a parcel of barley, dried vegetables filched one piece at a time, a short piece of rope, and a bowl and spoon she had whittled out of wood last winter while waiting for her turn with a reader. She wasn't quite sure what a hatchling dragon would need. The only thing she knew for sure was that the dragon could not hatch in the settlement where the star child would find out. Somehow, she would have to take it back to its cave.

One evening, Dad settled down to read with his bare feet soaking in the dishpan. "Pleiades," he muttered when Varia leaned over his shoulder. "A Greek story about a group of sisters who were turned into a cluster of stars to protect them from Orion, the hunter."

Sidran and Samuel sat opposite each other at the table, playing chess. They looked like brothers, with their red hair framing their serious, freckled faces, and their short legs dangling from the chair seats. The women were knitting at the table, the men were playing games and Adriel was already asleep on Mom's mat. Varia lay down on her mat and cleaned her teeth with the frayed end of a fat twig, a trick Mom had learned by reading about people in an Earth country called Nigeria.

There was nothing Varia particularly wanted to do, so she slipped under her blanket and pulled the pillow close. Right away she knew something was different. The egg thumped, very softly, against her chest. She sat up and looked around the kitchen. No one paid her any attention. Slowly she lay back down and clutched the pillow tightly to keep from shaking. I've got to get to the cave, she thought. Visions of herself walking alone one more time through the dark forest flashed into her mind. If only Connie were here!

She wondered how long it would take her dragon to break the egg, and if it would suffocate inside the fluffy stuffing if she didn't get it out in time. She pretended to sleep until Sidran finished his chess game and Dad closed his reader and the settlers finished their interminable preparations and got ready for bed. The tapping reverberated through her whole body. Why did no one else notice it? She waited without moving a muscle until everyone was in bed and the only sounds — besides the tapping in the egg and the thumping of her heart — were quiet breathing and intermittent snores. Then she slipped out of her blanket, picked up her pillow, and tiptoed between the mats to the door, where she quietly pulled on her boots and coat. If someone woke up, she would say she was going to the outhouse — but she was relieved when no one did. She slipped outside and closed the door.

The sky was clear, and there was a rare moon above the trees. The silvery light it cast on the ground made it easy to see her way across the clearing to the storage hut. With the door open, she made her way around the bins of food to where her sack hung behind a cluster of empty ones on the wall. She lifted the sacks — and the whole clump came off together and fell to the floor.

Varia picked up the empty ones and hung them back up. Bulrushes! She'd dumped everything! She felt around on the floor, dropping everything she found into the sack. The egg thumped insistently. "I'm hurrying," she told it.

The pillow fit inside her sweater, and Varia tied the rope around her waist to contain it. She pulled on her fluff mittens and went outside. The shadow of the signal tower lay across the clearing like a ghostly cage on the moonlit snow. Varia hugged the pillow tightly and set off into the woods.

Chapter 10

EVEN IN THE MOONLIGHT, IT WAS tricky picking her way through the dark woods. Twigs snagged on her mittens, so she took them off and tucked them inside her shirt with the pillow. More than once she slipped on the icy ground.

She was relieved when she smelled the sticky tree, and found the glistening forest pool, surrounded now with dry, bent flower stalks. She picked her way among the silver rocks on the hillside. The ring of strangely tall reeds in the valley stood like frozen sentinels, and the spring made a shimmering line along the valley floor.

Varia had to feel her way into the shadows to find the cave entrance. A shower of icicles crumbled onto her as she entered. Another row glittered along the crack in the ceiling. She put down her sack and pulled out the pillow. The thumping was very fast. She untied the knot in the thread with her stiff fingers and rolled the egg carefully onto the floor. Then she put her mittens back on, wrapped herself in the blanket, and curled up around the egg with her head on the pillow. It was the first time she had actually used it as a pillow. It felt luxurious, even as the cold from the cave floor seeped through her blanket.

She closed her eyes and listened to the egg's jerky rhythm. Thump-tap-tap-thump-thump-tap . . .

She woke to the sound of a tiny chirp. Stone gleamed softly above her. Her leg and shoulder throbbed from pressing against the cold stone. She felt for the egg. Something sharp poked her finger. Eggshell?

She sat up. A tiny hatchling glistened in the shaft of moonlight that now hovered at the edge of the pool. Its slender body shimmered with translucent scales. It had sturdy back legs and short, wiry arms, and large, glittering eyes that protruded over a narrow snout with a small horn on the tip. A long, arrow-shaped tail flicked back and forth — and yes! Two short, delicate wings folded tightly up behind its shoulders. "Sweet dragon," she murmured.

The dragon turned and looked at her. Moonlight shone in its eyes. Varia sat perfectly still.

"Suwee drogon," it squeaked.

Varia's mouth fell open. It had imitated her! She put her hand on her chest. "Varia," she said slowly and clearly.

"Waria," squeaked the dragon after a moment. It put its hand on its chest.

Varia laughed. The dragon jumped. Something green flashed in its hand.

Was it a piece of eggshell? Varia wiggled closer. The dragon's shining eyes were fixed on her face. She was so close now she could have picked the little creature up. I'd have to be careful not to crush it, she thought. And avoid those sharp little claws. Her heart gave a sudden lurch. The dragon was holding Mom's emerald ring in its three-fingered hand. How was that possible?

She looked over her shoulder. Her blanket and pillow lay in a heap on the floor. Behind them, in the dim light, she could see the dark patch that was her sack, surrounded by smaller dark things. I must have picked up the ring by accident in the sleeping hut, she thought, and pulled it out in the cave when I got my blanket. She looked back at the dragon.

"Suwee drogon," it said again.

Varia smiled. It was sweet — but she still had to get the ring back. She pointed at it and held out her hand. "My ring," she said.

The dragon held out its empty hand. "Moi rong," it squeaked.

Maybe she could distract it. She tucked her mittens inside her shirt and crawled backwards. She felt around in the sack until her hand closed on a strip of what she guessed was dried carrot, then crawled back to the dragon. It pushed one hand through the ring like a bracelet, then pulled it out again.

Varia tore the piece of carrot in half. She waited until the dragon looked up, then took a bite. She held out the other piece. "Yum."

The dragon took the carrot and bit it. "Yom." The ring plinked to the ground.

Perfect. "Yum," she said again, sliding her hand toward the ring.

"Yom." The ring was almost in her hand when the dragon choked. Pieces of carrot flew out of its mouth. It staggered backwards, slipped, and flopped into the pool. The thin film of ice on the water tinkled as the dragon fell through.

Varia lunged and grabbed it out of the cold water. Its wings slid over its slippery back like flimsy shreds of cloth, and she had to adjust her grip to keep it from slipping out of her fingers. She could feel its heart thumping against her palm. She stroked a shard of ice off the dragon's head with her thumb. Its skin felt smooth going down, but prickly coming back up as she wiped its snout, neck, stomach, and legs. She wasn't sure how to dry the rumpled wings that lay across the back of her hand. They looked so delicate that she was afraid she would snap the thin bones or tear the skin if she tried. The dragon leaned into her hands and began to vibrate.

"You do purr!" Varia held the dragon against her chest and covered it with her other hand. She rocked back and forth and hummed "Puff the Magic Dragon." The dragon's eyes closed. What will I name you? Varia wondered. Funny she hadn't thought about that before. "Draco" was too fierce. "Puff" wasn't special enough — and besides, that song had a sad ending.

The dragon lay still with its head resting in the crook of her thumb. She could feel its chest rising and falling with its rapid breaths, warm on her skin. It's asleep, she realized. A wave of tenderness swept over her. "I could hold you forever," she murmured.

But even as she said it, she knew it wasn't true. The rock beneath her was cold and hard, and the parts of her pressed against it were getting numb. As well, she had to get home before anyone noticed she was missing.

She uncrossed her legs and stood up. When the pins and needles in her feet settled down, she kicked the blanket into a heap, laid the dragon down on the thickest part, and covered it so only its snout was exposed. She picked up her pillow and a piece of eggshell. The rest could stay where it was. She turned back to the pool. The ring was gone.

Varia's heart sank. She knelt by the water's edge and looked down, but it was too dark to see anything.

I'll fish it out when I come back, she decided as she left the cave, with a piece of string and a bent twig on the end to hook it with. Like a fishing rod in stories. Or I could jump in and get it. Ha! She couldn't swim, and even if she could, the thought of picking through the mother dragon's bones felt wrong. As it would feel wrong to dig up Reyk or Thora's bones. Or Connie's, if... She pushed the thought out of her mind. I'll fish it out tomorrow, she repeated to herself. Or maybe the little dragon will get it for me, just like it will help me to find Connie — alive — when it's bigger.

The moon hung low in the sky and the clouds were blowing in again, but the darkness was fading to grey. She didn't feel tired at all. The trees and rocks were now dark shadows against the sky, and she could see a few dark shadows scattered across the ice on the pool. Frozen bees?

How different everything was from yesterday, she thought as she climbed the hill and picked her way back through the forest. If only Connie were here. She would have cried at the newness and tenderness and magic of this night. How was she, Varia, going to keep from shouting her secret for everyone to hear?

Uh-oh. The star child flickered in the branches of the sticky tree. What would it do if it found out she had lied? If it saw her coming from the cave, it might investigate. What if it found the dragon and took it away? Or worse. She stopped. Maybe if she waited it would just go away. It didn't.

It was watching her, she realized after a while. Varia took a deep breath. Okay, then: onward. Maybe the star child didn't know about the cave. The star child's warmth blasted her as she passed the tree. The warmth felt good, but she wouldn't stop. She could feel its eyes boring into her back. She would hurry back to the little dragon as soon as she could — during Adriel's nap — and make sure it was okay.

Varia took off her boots outside the kitchen and opened the door softly. Dad sat at the table reading; everyone else was still in bed. He glanced at her empty sleeping mat. "Up early!" he whispered.

"I couldn't sleep," Varia offered. It was true.

"I couldn't sleep either." Dad rubbed the back of his neck. "But I think I'll try again now. You should too."

"What are you reading?" Varia asked quickly. She was still too excited to be tired.

Dad turned the screen so she could see it. "An old Greek story about a sculptor named Pygmalion. He carved a statue of a woman that was so beautiful he fell in love with her. He wanted her to come to life so badly that she did."

Like my dragon, sort of, thought Varia. "What was the statue's name?" she asked.

"Galatea."

"That's perfect!"

"I suppose so." Dad yawned. "For a statue." Or a dragon, thought Varia. Who could be a girl.

"Dad?" Just one more question before they went to sleep. "What was it like when I was a baby? For you, I mean. How did you feel when I was born?"

Dad flicked off the reader and closed the lid. He smiled and held out his arms. Varia climbed onto his lap and leaned her head against his shoulder. There are some nice things about being small, she thought. Dad spoke softly against her hair. "It was the most special thing that ever happened to me. Looking at your tiny face and holding your delicate body was like receiving my very own miracle."

"Mm-hmm." That sounded exactly right.

Dad chuckled. "The first time I knew for sure I was grown up was when I looked into your shining, newborn eyes. For the first time, I cared more about someone else than I did about myself."

Dad's whiskers brushed her forehead, scratchy and perfect. She thought about baby Galatea's tiny, delicate wings. She would do anything for the little dragon. "Is that what it means to be grown up?"

Dad whistled softly. "A weighty question for this hour of the morning!" He rubbed circles in her shoulder. "It's also knowing that you can look after yourself and contribute to your community. You have to understand that you are only one among many, and that your own wishes aren't always the most important." He glanced at the sleeping children on the floor. "You're really asking about your mother, aren't you? I'm trying to figure her out too. She looks like a nine-year-old, but she still knows everything she used to, and does almost as much. Except for her size, she's the same person." He sighed. "No, not completely the same. She runs everywhere, and sleeps like a rock."

Varia grimaced. "We need to find the other lander," she said. "Maybe they're in a nicer part of the planet, and if we went there, no one would need that star water."

Dad sighed. "Except that they haven't made contact so we have no idea where they are, and we would have to walk to this unknown place, and we don't even know if they're still alive."

Varia sat up. "But if we found them, we could join them."

Dad didn't answer right away. "What would they think if they saw us now? Except for you and me, they wouldn't even recognize us."

A jolt ran through Varia. She stared into Dad's eyes. "Is that the real reason you aren't drinking the star water? In case they find us, so you can explain what's happened?"

Dad shrugged.

Tears sprang into Varia's eyes. She buried her face in Dad's neck. "You still think they might find us," she whispered. "I thought I was the only one who hadn't stopped hoping."

Dad stroked her hair. "Don't hope too hard," he said. "They might not."

Varia pulled away and looked into his eyes. "No, Dad," she said. Her voice trembled. "We'll find them." She stood up, threaded her way to her mat, and lay down facing away from him. Mom lay curled up beside her. I wouldn't know her either, thought Varia, in that stranger's body. She buried her face in her empty pillow. How could things be so wonderful and so horrible at the same time?

Dad's footsteps shuffled across the floor. He coughed and lay down heavily next to Mom and Adriel.

Oh, little Galatea, thought Varia. You have to help me. You just have to.

Chapter 11

THE NEXT MORNING DRAGGED ON FOREVER, even though Dad let Varia sleep until the others had gone out and he had finished his breakfast. "So you don't get sick again," he said. Actually, Varia felt better than she had in weeks. But she was relieved to eat alone. How could she possibly carry on a mundane conversation when her heart was bursting with excitement over Galatea?

The real world crashed back in when Sidran arrived to help her with the dishes.

"Don't touch that towel!" Varia grabbed it away from his muddy fingers. She poured him a bowl of warm water and stood over him while he washed his hands. Then he knocked over his pile of cups onto the dusty floor so Varia had to wash them all over again. She felt like a nursemaid. Sidran's babble about adapting star maps from Earth for their new sky irritated her even more than usual. She took a deep breath, rubbed the eggshell in her pocket, and didn't chase him out the door.

School and reading had ended with the arrival of the warm weather, and Varia's light workload had ended with her return to health. After the dishes were done and the floors swept, she helped Dad spread compost onto the field. The first step was to haul it on a wooden toboggan from the soggy compost heap at the edge of the forest. Clumps of mud stuck to the bottom and made it hard to pull, but dragging it was still faster than carrying it one shovel-full at a time.

Others were out in the field too, turning it over with shovels and carrying rocks to the pile at the edge of the forest. Luella and Samuel sorted out the best chunks of sweet potatoes and the roundest peas to start the new crops. Nara and some of the other women washed sacks in the creek. Adriel dabbled in the dirt with sticks and pebbles. He would need a wipe before his nap.

The compost was dark and crumbly, and smelled warm and musty — thanks to hardworking micro-organisms and fungi, as Samuel liked to say. It was the smell of spring, of new things growing and of old things returning to life. And it promised new food.

Varia was utterly sick of pea soup and sour-tasting bread. She'd begged Samuel not to plant dill, even if it did mask some of the vegetables' mustiness. She could hardly remember the taste of strawberries, lettuce, radishes, and green beans — summer treats that didn't keep over the winter. Tiny green leaves were already pushing through last year's red-tinged strawberry leaves. She hoped they would grow quickly. And unchanged. She dumped another load of compost and tossed it around with her shovel so Dad could rake it into the soil. Sweat rolled down his forehead, and the veins stood out on his arms.

Varia's arms ached too, and her winter-softened palms blistered. A dragon keeper shouldn't have to do menial work. When Galatea was bigger, she could help. Varia would sit on her back and direct her while she dug with her tiger's claws or her shovel-ended tail. If Sidran designed a plow for the dragon to pull, she would let him ride on Galatea's back with her.

Dad clanged his rake on another rock and Varia pushed her shovel into the dirt to help him pry it out of the soil. It was funny how rocks floated to the surface every spring.

Sidran's whooping interrupted her thoughts. He and Samuel were digging out the bushes with the silver berries at the edge of the woods, in case they were the alternate fungal host for the barley rust. Sidran waved something in the air. Varia gratefully dropped her shovel and trotted over, rolling her stiff shoulders. Adriel toddled over too, grinning through the dirt smeared over his mouth and nose. Gretel ran over from the river, drying her hands on her shirt.

"I found a leg bone!" Sidran shouted. The dirty stick he held up was as long as Varia's foot, and lumpy at both ends. Sidran rubbed the dirt off on his shirt and handed it to his mother. He and Adriel scrabbled in the dirt with their hands.

"Here's another one," he cried a moment later. In a few minutes, they had a dozen pieces of oddly shaped bone.

Gretel took the fragments. "This is the biggest animal we've found yet." She arranged the bones on the dirt, using twigs to fill in for the missing ones. "Six limbs again." She rubbed some dirt off with her finger. "See the extra socket in this elongated shoulder bone?"

If only all of these animals had laid eggs in caves, Varia thought wistfully as they dispersed back to their work.

Finally it was lunchtime, then more dishes, then at last, Adriel's naptime. Mom agreed with Varia that Adriel would nap better in the quiet storage hut than the noisy kitchen, now that the daytime weather was warm enough. She looked surprised and grateful for Varia's offer to sit with him and weave patches for the torn sacks and clothes. Varia felt a twinge of guilt, knowing why she really wanted to disappear into the hut, but the excitement of seeing her dragon again quickly quashed it.

While Mom gave Adriel a quick bath in the dishpan, Varia carried the broom to the sleeping hut. She couldn't sweep the hut's dirt floor the way she did the wood ones in the kitchen and weaving huts, but a broom was handy for shooing away insects, brushing litter out of corners, and smoothing out the dirt where she was going to bury the eggshell.

She measured out one hand length from the corner by the window and scraped out a hole with the eggshell. Even in the dim light it sparkled. She covered one eye and looked out through the eggshell at the shuttered window. Rainbows shot out from the cracks in the shutters. She tilted her head and they danced across the walls. If she looked through the shell from the other side, as if looking into the egg, she couldn't see anything. Interesting. So Galatea had been able to see out of the egg. If she'd known, she might have taken the egg out of the pillow more often! Connie would love this eggshell. One day I'll show it to her, Varia promised as she smoothed the dirt over her treasure.

She returned the broom, then carried over Adriel's mat and a bundle of weaving grass. Mom carried Adriel.

"Sleep well," she said, laying him on his mat. "See you when you wake up." Varia lay down next to him. He snuggled against her shoulder. When he fell asleep she counted to two hundred, tossed the weaving grass aside and slithered out the bedroom window. She was a slow weaver. No one would expect her to get a lot done in one afternoon.

"I'm coming, Galatea! I'm coming!" she sang as she skipped through the glistening woods. The ice was melting, and the ground was squishy and wet. The thought of seeing the little dragon infused her with energy. Her very own, delightful to own, no-more-alone Galatea!

The star child wasn't in the prickly tree. It better not have harmed her dragon! She ran the rest of the way to the cave, snapping off twigs to use as a hook to fish out the ring.

The shaft of daylight drew a sharp line across the middle of the cave floor and lit up the yellowish walls. Her sack and its contents were scattered across the floor where she had left them, but the eggshell was gone. So was Galatea. Varia rushed to the water's edge. There was the old skeleton, with Mom's ring hanging crazily on one of the wing bones. But where was the baby dragon?

"Waria!"

Relief washed over her. "Galatea? Where are you?"

"Waria." The voice came from above her head. The little dragon peered down through the ceiling crack.

Varia left the cave and scrambled up the boulder. In the sunlight, Galatea glittered in all the colours of her eggshell. A mud-covered bee, nearly the size of the little dragon herself, was skewered on her claws. Its four legs and two wings were jerking spasmodically, and a gooey, yellow liquid oozed out from the punctures. Varia clamped her lips together.

Galatea waved the bee at her and chirped. It sounded like a question. She better not be trying to share, Varia thought. Her lunch turned over in her stomach. Galatea cocked her head, waved the bee more insistently, and chirped again. "Oh, I get it!" Varia grinned. "Bee."

Galatea's eyes turned dark purple. "Bee." She gave a satisfied nod and bit a chunk out of the bee's head. Yellow goo billowed out of the opening. Its legs went limp. Galatea's belly, already distended, expanded further when she swallowed.

Varia's stomach churned again. "I brought you a present," she said, digging in her pocket. "Want some bread?" She squatted down and held out a piece she had saved in her pocket from lunch.

"Prosont." Galatea inspected it carefully, then darted out a blue tongue and licked it. Her eyes rolled. They turned yellow. She clutched at her throat and wiped her tongue against the rock. "Yom," she said weakly. "Yom." She took another bite of the bee. As she chewed, her eyes slowly faded to lavender. One of the insect's legs wobbled in and out of her mouth.

"Yuck!" said Varia, making a face that she hoped would look disgusted even to a dragon.

"Yock," said Galatea. "Bee yock." She flicked the leg into her mouth with her long tongue, looking very pleased with herself.

Varia laughed. "True, but not in the way you mean it!"

Galatea made a raspy noise, as if she was trying to laugh too.

"I'll teach you more words," offered Varia. She patted the stone beside her foot. Should she call it a stone or a rock or a boulder? "Boulder," she said finally. Rocks and stones were things she could pick up.

"Boulder," repeated Galatea. She patted the rock with the bee. It left a blob of yellow goo.

Varia turned away. Galatea was cute, but her manners were atrocious! Adriel was a pretty messy eater at first too, she reminded herself. She walked to the edge of the boulder and looked down into the valley. The ice on the pool had melted, and bees were floating near the edge.

Varia felt a twinge of disappointment that Galatea was so self-sufficient. But it was a good thing, really, because Varia couldn't be with her that often. And why should she like people food? She was a dragon, not a human. What did dragons eat in stories? Oh yes — sheep. And princesses. She gulped. Bees were okay.

Galatea appeared at her side, picking her teeth with a tiny claw. "All done," said Varia. Adriel said that after every meal now.

"All don," squeaked Galatea.

"Good."

"Goood."

It's funny how she lengthens the "o" sounds, thought Varia. It must be because she has a long snout. But it's wonderful how eager she is to talk. She pointed to a low plant growing out of a soil-filled crack in the boulder. "Plant."

"Plont."

Although Galatea repeated the word, she didn't seem very interested in plants. She skidded down the side of the boulder on her rump, flapping her pale green wings for balance. She led Varia to the edge of the cave's pool, gave a loud chirp, and tumbled into the water.

"Not again!" Varia bent over to rescue her. But before she could, Galatea grabbed the ledge and pulled herself out. She stood up, tottered, and lurched violently to keep her balance. Water sprayed onto Varia's face. "Hey!" she said, wiping it off.

"Hoi!" Galatea chirped again and jumped back into the water. It didn't look like she needed rescuing.

"Splash," said Varia when Galatea's head reappeared. Or should she have said "water?" Teaching someone to speak was harder than she'd thought.

"Sploss." Galatea paddled in a circle and chirped again.

"Swimming," said Varia. "In the water."

"Swomming. In da water." Galatea lay on her back and pushed herself along by waving her tail. Translucent scales drifted behind her and gathered at the water's edge, pushed by bubbles and the little dragon's wake. Varia had never learned to swim. She'd never had anywhere to learn except the cold, shallow creek by the settlement. Until today, she'd never wanted to. Galatea made it look so easy. Maybe she'd try it, one of these days.

But first, she better retrieve Mom's ring. She found the rope she had used last night, and reached in her pocket for her assortment of twigs. She tied one of them onto the end of the rope, and dropped it in. It floated on the surface. "Bulrushes," she muttered, yanking it back out. She'd have to make the hook heavier somehow.

Galatea climbed out of the water and shook herself off. "Hoi!" Then she climbed onto Varia's lap. Varia cupped her hands around the dripping dragon the way she had the night before. The water seeped through her pants onto her skin, but what was a little water between friends? Galatea chirped. "Love," said Varia, snuggling the little head against her neck.

Galatea nipped Varia's shoulder.

"Ouch! What was that for?"

Galatea looked up at her. "Love," she squeaked, licking the blood off her needle-sharp teeth.

Chapter 12

DRAGONS HAVE A FUNNY WAY OF showing love, Varia thought as she walked back through the trees. The dragon's bite reminded her of the kitten Connie had smuggled onto the spaceship when they left Earth. She hid it in her backpack and made a bed for it in a closet. It took two days before anyone found it. They went looking because of the scratches on Connie's hands.

The star child wasn't in the sticky tree when she got there. Maybe it hadn't discovered the dragon yet — although if it went anywhere near the cave, it soon would. She stopped at the tree to smear sap on her shoulder. She didn't need Mom to see the punctures and ask questions. She held her shirt off her shoulder to let the sap dry while she walked home.

She crouched behind a bush at the end of the trail to make sure it was safe to proceed. Mom and Gretel stood conversing outside the weaving hut. Hugo was carrying an armload of wood into the kitchen, and the others were in the field. Varia slunk through the trees to the back of the hut and climbed in the window. By the time Adriel finally woke up, she'd patched two carrot sacks and was starting on the third.

Adriel napped reliably and long every afternoon. Varia started taking bundles of grass and torn clothes with her to the cave. As long as she produced a pile of patched garments when Adriel woke up, Mom was happy to let her sit with him every afternoon.

"Last year you never wanted to stay inside and weave," Mom commented once.

Varia looked down on her mother's head. "I guess I'm growing up."

Mom looked a little surprised. But it was true. Varia was finally growing — and not just compared to everyone who was getting shorter. Her sleeves and pant legs were way too short. Since the snow melted, she felt stronger too. Coughing less. Running more. Was it all from that tiny bit of star water? Or was it something else? It felt a little strange, with the others so small. But she wasn't changing as much as they were. Connie would still know who she was.

Galatea grew much faster than Varia. After three days she no longer fit inside Varia's hand. After eight days she could sit on Varia's lap and lean her head on Varia's shoulder. Fortunately, the bees were awake and crawling by the time the little dragon finished the dead ones in the pond, and the smelly yellow flowers were open and waiting for them.

In the settlement, it was time to convert the storage hut back into a sleeping hut. Varia had to spend several of her precious afternoons carrying food to the kitchen, rinsing bins, shaking out sacks, and taking down empty ceiling nets — all quietly enough not to wake Adriel. Once that was done, she swept out the hut and carried the sleeping mats over from the kitchen. Finally, she hung the curtains to make rooms.

Galatea would forget who she was if she didn't get back to the cave soon! "I need to make my sleeves and pant legs longer," she told Mom the next morning.

"I'll help you after lunch," Mom offered.

"I'll figure it out. Just tell me what to do."

"If you like." Mom turned back the edge of Varia's sleeve. "First, you pull out the string that holds the edge down, then undo part of the sleeve so you can weave in the new grass. Make it longer than you need it. Then cut the grass so it's even, fold the edge over twice, and sew it down."

"Okay." Varia smiled too as she carried a sleepy Adriel into the hut. Mom wouldn't expect her to get something that complicated done too quickly.

She skipped down the hill to the cave a short time later, her hands full of weaving grass. Galatea paced beside the pool, studying the flowers. "Waria come bock!" she squeaked as Varia skidded to a stop and dropped her bundle on the ground. Galatea scurried to her and wrapped her arms around Varia's knees.

She's grown so much! thought Varia, stroking Galatea's head without even having to bend. Her scales were thicker and had harder edges than before, and her wings were longer. But she was still a baby. Her whole body wiggled with excitement as she hopped around Varia's legs. Her little wings flapped up and down, and she was making her vibrating noise.

"Of course I came back." Varia knelt down. "I missed you. Varia missed you." Galatea purred louder.

Galatea's eyes flickered to blue and back to pink. "You mossed Waria." She resumed pacing. "Waria gone. Bees gone. Poor you."

Varia grinned. They would have to work on pronoun use. "Poor Galatea," she said. "But Varia is back. I am back. I am happy to be back." She frowned. "What do you mean, the bees are gone?" She glanced around. "There's one, crawling down the rock."

Galatea looked at it. Her shoulders drooped. "One bee. You eat mony bees. You need mony bees."

Varia sat down and hugged her knees. This was a problem she didn't know how to solve. The only place she'd ever seen them was here. "I wonder where your mother found more of them," she said.

Galatea looked at her. One eye turned yellow. "Waria is your moder. Waria will foind bees."

Varia blinked at her. "I'm not your mother. I just . . . oh dear." She stood up. "Come with me."

Galatea followed her into the cave, to the edge of the bubbling water. Varia knelt down and Galatea squatted beside her. The skeleton was still there, still wearing the ring. That's, er, that was your mother. She laid your egg and I . . . found it."

Galatea stared into the water. The furrows in her forehead wavered in her reflection above her dark eyes. "Your moder sploss," she said. She bent over and buried her head in the water.

Varia watched the little dragon rock from side to side. Ripples spread out around her head, and the edges of her wings ruffled as if there was a breeze. She stayed under for a very long time. Varia wondered if she should pull her out.

Suddenly Galatea sat up. Water streamed down her body, but she didn't shake it off. "Your moder knowed," she squeaked, and ran out of the cave.

Varia found her swimming circles in the pond outside. Her scales were sticky with the yellow stuff from the flowers when she came out. "Hoi!" she squeaked, shaking the smelly water all over Varia. She took a step toward Varia, as if to climb onto her lap. Then she turned away. "Your moder knowed. You moik bees," she called over her shoulder, and trundled up the hill into the forest.

"Wait!" cried Varia. She picked up her weaving grass and ran up the hill after the dragon. But Galatea had disappeared.

What on the Pot was that all about? Varia puzzled over the afternoon's events as she made her way home. Had that skeleton really been talking to Galatea? And had she said she would "make" bees? But the question that really nagged at her mind was what Galatea would think of her now that she knew Varia wasn't her mother. Would she even be there next time Varia went to see her?

Chapter 13

IT WAS A GOOD THING GALATEA cut Varia's visit short, because Adriel woke up crying and flushed as soon as Varia sat down to begin weaving her shirt cuffs.

"It looks like the same thing you had," Mom said after examining him. "I was beginning to wonder if you really needed to sit with him every afternoon. I thought we could just leave the door open, now that it's warm out, and when he woke up he could come out by himself. But it's a good thing you were there today."

"Good thing," Varia echoed as her heart sank into her stomach. If she couldn't sneak away and visit the cave, Galatea would have another reason to forget all about her.

Adriel's fever got worse, and Mom hung a hammock for him in the kitchen. On dry mornings, Mom bundled him up and carried him out to see the star child. On wet mornings, she brought back steaming star water in her own mug and spooned it into Adriel's mouth. Varia watched him swallow it. Maybe his drink was cooler than hers had been. Maybe he was already used to the taste. Maybe the star child liked Adriel.

"That star water isn't helping," she pointed out several days later when Adriel was still sick.

Mom sighed. "The sickness has to run its course."

"I'm healthier than I was before," said Varia. "Without star water."

"Maybe your sickness became an inoculation," Mom suggested. "It happens on Earth. People who got cowpox, for example, didn't get smallpox, which was a much more serious disease. Maybe your body has developed antibodies that are protecting you from other pathogens. Maybe it will do the same for Adriel." Mom sounded very hopeful.

"Maybe," Varia replied. She wondered if the changes had more to do with Galatea, since her growth spurt had started the day after Galatea hatched. How hatching a dragon could have this effect, Varia had no idea. But she felt better than she had since they landed.

Varia's weaving improved now that she was actually doing it. Mom helped her lengthen her cuffs, and Nara showed her a decorative edging that she'd invented. After Varia finished, she started making a new, bigger pair of boots for Adriel.

No one spoke of the possibility that Adriel wouldn't get better. Varia had; he would too. But everyone moved around the kitchen quietly and spoke in hushed tones — the way they probably had when she was sick. Varia didn't like it. She stayed outside as much as she could, fetching wood and water with Sidran, and helping Dad weed the fields. Working helped keep her from fretting about Galatea. But after the first day, the trees around the clearing might as well have been prison bars. It was all she could do to keep from running down the trail to the cave.

Spring became summer, and Adriel slowly improved. But Mom kept him napping in the kitchen. Varia could hardly contain her frustration. She'd been away from Galatea so long that sometimes she wondered if the dragon was real, or if she'd only imagined her. Only the two small buttons of sap on her shoulder reassured her.

Finally, one morning they woke up to such heavy rain that there was no point even trying to work outside. Everyone crowded into the kitchen. The game boards came out; so did the readers. Varia tried to play checkers with Sidran, but Adriel climbed onto her lap and plucked her markers off the board. He ran off with her weaving grass and hid it under his mat. He upset the bowl of sugar peas so she had to wash them all over again. He made a game of tumbling out of his hammock as soon as Varia tucked him in.

"Mom, he has to sleep in the hut," she said through clenched teeth.

Mom agreed. Varia carried his mat and her weaving grass over through the downpour, while Mom carried Adriel. Varia got him to lie still for his diaper change by pretending they were both rabbits, and made his blanket into a burrow so he would go inside. Then she closed the shutters to make it dark like it would be in a real rabbit burrow. It took several repetitions of "Little Rabbit Fufu" before he finally dropped off. Varia breathed a huge sigh of relief, but she forced herself to sit quietly for a few more minutes to make sure he was really asleep. Finally, she slipped out. The rain poured down in sheets, but she hardly noticed as she raced through the trees.

She found Galatea — twice as large as last time — with her head submerged in the cave pool, oblivious to the rain dripping through the ceiling crack onto her back. She rocked from side to side and her wings rippled in an unfelt breeze. The tip of her tail wove a slow figure eight.

Varia waited beside the cave wall. What was Galatea's mother telling her this time? How could bones talk anyway? If she knew how to listen, could she learn secrets from the bones in the garden? And most important, would Galatea remember who she was?

Galatea didn't see her at first. She lifted her head out of the pool very slowly, as if a weight hung from her neck. "Moolor," she moaned.

Varia shuffled her feet. Galatea's shoulders straightened and her drooping wings snapped into place on her back. "Hoi!" she cried, spraying water all over as she bounded across the cave. "Waria! Golotya mossed you!" Her voice alternated between a croak and a squeak. She grabbed Varia around the middle and rubbed her head into Varia's stomach.

Varia hugged her back, and her nose twitched at the dragon's familiar metallic scent. "I missed you too!" Galatea's scales felt rough and hard through Varia's shirt. But the wings under Varia's fingers felt soft, smooth, and tough over ridges of muscle and bone.

"You come bock," said Galatea, gazing up at her with shining blue eyes. "Golotya is hoppy. Oi is hoppy."

"I'm happy too." Varia smiled at the dragon's pronunciation. She stepped back and looked at her. She was so tall! And she'd figured out pronouns. And her name. "You must have made many bees," she said.

"Mony," Galatea croaked in her new voice. "Come look." She took Varia's hand in her scaly one and pulled her out of the cave. Rain streamed down Varia's face and hair and off her grass-covered shoulders as Galatea pulled her past the pool and down the valley. She scurried past two more pools, also ringed by the tall flowers, then turned and climbed the hill into the woods.

Varia followed. The hillside was so slippery that she had to hold onto shrubs to pull herself up.

"Moi moder knowed," said Galatea, pushing through a stand of ferny leaves at the top. "Oi moik mony bees. Mony droizu."

"What's droizu?" Varia held her arms close and squeezed through the leaves.

Galatea hopped up onto a log. "Bees eat droizu. Yock." She flicked her tongue at a clump of blue mushrooms. They came loose and fell onto the leaves in front of Varia's feet.

Varia grabbed a branch and pulled herself past the mushrooms onto the slippery wood. "I don't know that word droizu."

Galatea looked proud. "Moi moder knowed da word droizu."

"Your mother tells you words?"

"Moi moder tell me moik droizu in da water." Galatea stretched her neck toward the trees and hopped off the log. Varia followed her into a small clearing. A sticky-sweet smell wafted toward her. Sure enough, the clearing held another small pool, ringed with yellow flowers like the ones in the valley. Galatea patted a sticky blossom. "Droizu." She reached her hand inside and pulled out a sticky bee. "Yock." She bit off its head.

Varia left her to finish and walked around the pool, shivering in her wet clothes. Grey water shimmered in rainbow colours through the tall reeds. The flowers — the droizu — crawled with fat, striped bees. Their grey hive hung off the smooth bark of a tree at the edge of the clearing. Bees crawled up and down its trunk and over the slick ground. Varia scuffed the dead leaves by her toe, and they smeared under her foot. A rotten smell invaded her nose.

Galatea hopped around the side of the pool, streaked with shiny nectar and holding a wiggling bee in each clawed hand. "Waria loves droizu?"

"Nice droizu. Nice flowers," she said because Galatea looked so eager, and smiled when Galatea ruffled her wings. "How did you make them?" she asked, looking again at the dead plants around her feet.

"Waria come look." Galatea beckoned from the far edge of the clearing. Varia followed her through the trees, avoiding as many unfamiliar plants as she could while keeping the dragon in plain sight. They came to another pool. This one was like the one in the woods above Galatea's cave — shallow and surrounded by knee-high grass topped with tiny, yellow flowers. Raindrops stirred the surface of the water and bounced off the carpet of low, green plants in the clearing.

"Sploss," croaked Galatea, and jumped into the pool.

Varia watched her swim in circles, leaving behind translucent scales and an oily-looking film. This was all very strange. And very cold. She thought of her warm sweater hanging on the back of her chair in the kitchen. "I thought you were going to make more flowers," she said.

"Swomming moik droizu," Galatea said as she paddled past.

Varia sat stiffly down in the shelter of a tree to wait. After a short time, Galatea climbed out of the pool and into her lap. Her head rested on Varia's shoulder. The water from the pool soaked into her clothes, but she was already so wet it didn't make any difference. Varia held her close. Her dragon breath was warm on Varia's neck.

"You're almost too big to sit on my lap," Varia said, feeling a pang as she said it. But she kept the dragon there anyway, stroking the smooth, metallic-scented scales. Galatea nuzzled Varia's ear. Then she bit it.

"Galatea, NO!" This was the second time. Varia pushed Galatea onto the ground and jumped to her feet, cupping her ear in her hand. "Bad dragon! No biting Varia!"

Galatea stared up with wide eyes. Her blue tongue lolled out the side of her mouth.

Varia took her fingers off her ear. Yes, there was blood. "Biting hurts Varia. Ouch!"

"O," said Galatea in a low voice. "Golotya mooop." She hung her head. Her shoulders drooped until her snout touched her belly.

Moop must mean "sorry," thought Varia, pressing her fingers over her ear again. She sighed. It was just a play bite — no worse than the ones Connie's cat had given her. "Okay," she said. "I forgive you. You won't bite me again, right?"

Galatea looked at Varia out of the corner of her eye. It was a sickly yellow-green. "Oi wont boit Waria agoin roit," she croaked.

"Good." Galatea was a good dragon. She just needed to be taught how to behave. Varia took her hand off her ear and patted Galatea's snout. Galatea sniffed Varia's fingers. Carefully, she licked away the blood. Her tongue felt slippery and warm. She finished one finger and moved to the next one, then the next. Varia smiled. Galatea's tongue slid across her palm. "Nice, gentle dragon," said Varia.

Galatea mumbled something and turned back to the pool. Varia held her hand out to let the rain wash off the dragon spit. She stiffened. Had Galatea said "yock"?

Suddenly Varia suddenly felt chilled right through to her bones. She pressed her dripping hair over her bloody ear like a bandage, and hid her cold hands in her armpits. Rain ran into the collar of her shirt, and her sleeves stuck to her arms. She would put on dry clothes in the sleeping hut when she got back — even if they were dirty and full of holes. "I have to go home," she said. "My brother will wake up soon."

Galatea trotted to the edge of the clearing. "Whad is broder?" she asked.

"Hmmm. You wouldn't know that," said Varia. She thought for a moment as she followed Galatea through the trees. "I have a mother." Galatea nodded over her shoulder. "I am my mother's child," Varia continued.

"Waria is Waria's moder's choild. Golotya is moi moder's choild."

"Right. But my mother has another child. Look. One child is Varia." Varia held up one finger. "And the other child is Adriel." She held up another finger. "One mother, two children. Varia and Adriel. Adriel is my brother."

Galatea snorted and slithered under a low branch. Varia pushed it aside and followed her down the hill. She checked her ear again when they reached the valley. It wasn't bleeding any more; the cold rain must have stopped it.

She needed to hurry. It was time to get home. But Galatea wasn't in any hurry. She dragged her feet, pausing between steps. Her head drooped and her tail thumped the ground. "What's wrong?" Varia asked. She crouched in front of Galatea and lifted the dragon's head.

"Waria hos broder." Galatea's voice cracked. "Golotya hos no broder. Moi moder hos no anoder choild. Oi is moolor, moolor, moolor." Galatea wrapped her wings around herself, buried her head inside, and rocked back and forth. Her tail beat an anxious rhythm on the stones.

Moolor. The word sounded hollow and immensely sad. "I'm so . . . so moop, Galatea," whispered Varia. Had she done the right thing by hatching the single egg? Or had she doomed Galatea to a life of lonely misery? Varia had lost her best friend and most of the other people she knew, but she still had her parents, and Adriel, and Sidran too, for what that was worth. Galatea had no one except a skeleton mother, even if the bones could somehow talk to her. And she had Varia, but Varia wasn't a dragon.

Galatea clutched Varia's hand. The rain glistened off the tough, green skin of her knobby fingers. "Waria stoi here." She dug in her claws. Varia's heart pounded. A sheet of rain slammed into them, almost pushing Varia over.

"I can't stay," whispered Varia. "I have to go back to my family." How cruel that sounded.

"Waria no go home." Galatea sobbed out the words. "Waria is Golotya's broder."

"I have to go back," said Varia, close to tears. "They don't know I'm here. They'll worry and come looking and . . . " Galatea hung on. What would her people do if she took Galatea home with her? What could they do? Galatea was big now, and she could even talk. "Come back with me," Varia said. "Come and live with my brother and my mother and everyone. You can be part of our family."

Galatea let go of Varia's hand. Varia flexed her fingers. Galatea gazed up at her with blue eyes, her mouth hanging open, her teeth glistening. "Oi come bock wid Waria." She bounced on her heels and waved her tail in circles above her head. "Oi live wid Waria's moder and Waria's broder Oidriel." She grabbed Varia's hand again and yanked her toward the cave.

Varia laughed. Let her family be angry with her. It wouldn't last long. Once they saw Galatea, they'd understand. They reached the cave and ran up the hill. "Sploss!" cried Galatea when she saw the small pool. She jumped in, pulling Varia with her. Water splashed over the top of Varia's boots. What did that matter? They were soaked anyway. Varia aimed a big splash at

Galatea, who shot one right back. "Puff the magic dragon . . ." Varia sang at the top of her voice as they marched through the trees. Galatea snapped at little bees.

There was a glow in the sticky tree. Varia stopped mid-step; Galatea slipped and fell onto her rump. "The star child," Varia whispered. It must have heard her singing.

Galatea got to her feet, squinting at the light. She hissed softly. Varia tried to ignore the clenching fear in her stomach. Should they go back or forward? What would the star child do when it discovered she had lied? But it would find out about the dragon soon enough, if it didn't know already. And Adriel would wake up soon. Varia took Galatea's hand again. "Come on," she said.

The star child floated out of the tree and landed squarely in the middle of the path. Rain turned into sizzling halos of steam around its stars. The trees behind it quavered in the mist. I wonder what holds it together, thought Varia. I wonder if I could walk right through it. Galatea huddled against her, gripping the back of her pants. The star child's glow intensified. Its eyes blazed and clouds of steam rose from the ground around its feet. Galatea buried her face in Varia's back. Varia felt Galatea's warm breath through her shirt, and sharp claws pressing into her skin.

"It won't hurt us," Varia whispered, trying to keep her voice steady. She took a deep breath. "When I say 'now', we'll run as fast as we can." Galatea's scales rattled against her leg. Her tail beat the wet ground. Slap-slap-slap . . . "Now!" cried Varia.

Galatea pulled back, and Varia sat down hard on the soggy trail. Galatea peered over her shoulder. Her wide eyes were night black. The star child's eyes blazed. Varia's face felt flushed through the cold rain. She shook her hair off her face, took Galatea's hand, and yanked her to her feet. "Come on!"

Galatea's answer was a swift bite and a crashing of bushes. Varia spun around. The dragon was a blurry streak in the trees. "Galatea!" she yelled. Blood oozed out of four neat puncture marks on the side of her hand.

Suddenly the star child was all around her, its hand clamped hard over hers. The heat was suffocating. Varia struggled, but the star child held her firmly, its eyes burning black spots into her retinas. "YOU LIED!" The voices spurted from the jagged mouth stars and snarled into her head. Varia closed her eyes and tried to twist away. Her hand was puffing up — it felt like one huge blister. The voices accused her in a scream of dark colours. "Ignorant — Presumptuous — Foolish — DANGER DANGER DANGER!" She needed to get free — her hand would be charred to the bone if it didn't let go soon. The colours swirled faster, pushing against her skull. Her head felt like it would burst.

Suddenly the pressure vanished. Cool rain pattered onto her face, her hand, streamed down her burning ears, washed away her sweat. The only sound was gentle dripping. The only light was the orange sunshine diffused through low clouds. The steam drifted away. The star child was gone.

So was Galatea.

Varia held up her hand. It was puffy and flushed, but not burned. A row of four pale scars beneath her little finger showed where the tooth holes had been burned shut. Cauterized, like Mom had done to Samuel's fingers when she amputated them. Samuel had screamed, and Mom had cried. The awful smell had stayed in the kitchen for a whole day.

Varia sniffed her hand. Nothing. She ran her finger over her four new scars. They were small enough that Mom might not notice them, once the swelling went down. That was good, because otherwise she might think Galatea was dangerous when Varia finally took her home. Obviously, the star child was the dangerous one.

She stamped her foot in frustration. She had to help Galatea. She had to go home. She squeezed back tears. She was right — the star child did hate her. It hated Galatea too. What if it hurt Galatea? What if it killed her? No, she wouldn't even think it. The star child hadn't hurt Varia, only scared her. It wouldn't hurt Galatea. If only she could believe that.

It surprised her how frightened Galatea had been, right from the moment they'd seen the glow in the trees. Had Galatea seen the star child before? Or had her mother seen it, and warned her? And of what? Varia's heart tightened. Hide, Galatea. Listen to your mother. I shouldn't have . . . shouldn't have what? I'm so moop.

She turned toward the settlement. Why did the star child have to choose this day to sit in the tree? Hot tears trickled through the cool rain on her cheeks. She'd explain tomorrow. Apologize. She wiped her eyes and walked faster. If Mom and Dad found out she'd left Adriel, she wouldn't get the chance.

Adriel was already waking up as she slipped in the window. "Vawa all wet!" He squirmed away from her cold hands when she changed his diaper. Then he ran away, and she had to chase him all the way around the tower. He was better, all right. She laughed. Running felt good. The cool rain felt good on her hand too, and was taking away the puffiness. She caught Adriel beside the outhouse and swung him in a circle. At least something was good in the world. Someone was happy. By the time they went inside, they were both so soaked that no one could tell she'd been away.

Chapter 14

"Next time you see your star friend, ask him how to make raincoats," Dad said, coming in after supper with an armload of dripping wood. He laid the pieces on the net above the stove to dry.

"Or umbrellas." Luella squeezed out her long hair over a bucket.

"At least the crops are coming up," said Samuel. The main outdoor job these days was raking the mushrooms off the fields, and muddy boots were piled high on a mat beside the door.

But the star child had other things on its mind. The next morning, Varia and Dad's breakfast in the kitchen was interrupted by the small settlers rushing back from their star water picnic.

"There's something in the forest!" Sidran announced as he kicked his boots off. One of them bounced off the back of a chair. Adriel laughed and tried to kick his off too. Mom grabbed him and pulled his boots off for him. "We're supposed to stay in the settlement unless we're with Specto."

Varia's heart skipped a beat. Did this mean Galatea was okay?

"I think we should trap it." Sidran tossed his boots onto the mat by the door. "We could dig a big hole and cover it with branches and grass so the animal falls in, like they did in *Swiss Family Robinson.*"

"Then what would you do with it?" asked Samuel.

Sidran shrugged and flopped into his chair. "Depends what it is."

"The star child didn't say what it is?" asked Dad, pushing his empty bowl into the middle of the table with the ones the others had brought back.

Mom took her seat. "He just said it was an animal. But it's dangerous and we're not to go near it if it comes into the settlement." She put Adriel on the floor and he toddled over to the corner to his pile of sticks and rocks.

Varia jabbed her spoon into her porridge. That was a low blow. Now the others would never let Galatea come to live with them.

Gretel bounced in her chair like Sidran. "I hope it comes just to the edge so we can see what it is."

"We better not leave any food around to attract it," said Hugo with a frown. "If it's dangerous, we don't want it going near the children."

Dad cleared his throat. "Or the rest of us either." He winked at Varia and she gave him a small smile and hunched her shoulders forward. How much did he know? Since yesterday's visit with Galatea, her body had taken another leap forward — almost as if she was mimicking Galatea's super-fast growth. She didn't think anyone else could tell, because her clothes were loosely made. But she was acutely aware of the new way her shirt brushed across her when she walked, and she'd seen the changes when she got dressed under her blanket. It felt a little scary, but exciting too. She wondered what Mom would say when she noticed.

"We could build a cage in the woods and put food out as bait," said Sidran.

"It probably won't eat our kind of food," muttered Varia, remembering what had happened when she tried to feed bread to Galatea.

"No, it probably won't," agreed Gretel.

Varia pushed her bowl away.

"Thanks!" Sidran grabbed it and wolfed down what was left. Varia looked away. The other settlers ate less as they got smaller, but not Sidran — probably because he jumped around so much. He was worse than Adriel.

"Did the star child say what was dangerous about it?" asked Dad.

Varia put her scarred hand in her lap. The swelling was gone and the scars had faded almost to skin colour — but Mom had sharp eyes.

"He didn't say anything specific," answered Gretel. She furrowed her brow. "It must have wandered in from another part of the planet. If it's a carnivore, it might think we're food."

"Specto also said we must only drink water from flowing streams, not from pools," said Nara. "But we only take water from the creek, so that's okay."

"Probably in case the animal fouls the water," said Samuel.

Mom sighed. "I wanted to get some more sap from that tree, but I forgot in all the excitement. Now we won't be going there until Specto tells us it's safe."

"How will we get star water?" asked Luella. "I missed that part."

"Specto's going to bring it to the edge of the settlement, with the mushrooms and things," Mom said. Luella sat back, satisfied.

Varia wrinkled her nose. Luella had started adding strange ingredients to her stews — fortunately after first removing two portions for Dad and Varia. Varia was sure she would gag on plum-coloured cauliflower fungus sprinkled with crushed, dried lichen, or slimy black mushroom sauce thickened with pasty roots from the dragon-wing plant.

"Ask him to bring you some sap too," suggested Dad. Mom nodded.

"We should make spears," said Sidran. "Then if it comes near and tries to eat us, we can stab it." He mimed thrusting a spear.

Gretel looked horrified. "We don't want to hurt it!" Varia shot her a grateful look.

"But we should be able to defend ourselves if we have to," said Mom, looking slowly around the table. "I can treat minor wounds, but anything major . . . "

"And we can't afford to lose anyone else," said Hugo. "Spears will work if we're attacked, but how about a net to trap it if it just wanders too close? Then we can drag it away without hurting it."

"It might be hard to get a net over it," said Dad. "But we have the rock pile beside the field. What about a big slingshot? Flying stones would scare it away."

Nara tapped her fingers against her cheek. "We don't have anything stretchy enough."

Sidran jumped up. "A catapult! I saw plans for one on the reader. It only needed logs and rope. We have those."

Hugo laughed. "I made one of those back on Earth when I was a Boy Scout. I'll help you put one together."

"Spears are a good idea too," said Dad. "Just so we're prepared for anything. I'll whittle points onto some sticks and harden them in the fire."

"We could even use sharp bone fragments for the tips," suggested Mom. "You must have some we could use, Gretel." Varia looked at her in horror. What was happening here?

"I don't." Gretel looked back and forth between them. "Specto told me to save them."

Varia jumped to her feet. "I don't think we need weapons at all," she said. "We don't know for sure it's dangerous. It probably won't even try to hurt us. But if we come at it with spears and rocks, we might scare it into doing things it wouldn't normally do." She turned her hand so the scars were hidden against her leg.

One by one, the settlers shook their heads, even Gretel. "Specto said it's dangerous."

Fear clutched Varia's stomach. "Specto said to stay away from it. He didn't say to make weapons."

"No, but he wouldn't have warned us if he expected us to sit around and do nothing." Hugo thumped his hand on the table for emphasis, and everyone else nodded.

"But we won't use them unless we absolutely have to," said Gretel.

Dad stood up beside Varia and put his hand on her shoulder. She winced. The bite-marks under her shirt prickled where he pressed them. "They're right, sweetheart," he said. "We can't take chances." He walked to the door. "I'm going to cut some sticks."

"Take Adriel," said Mom. Dad turned back and dug through the pile for Adriel's boots.

Sidran skipped to the door. "C'mon, Hugo. Let's find our logs for the catapult." He sagged as he noticed the mound of dirty dishes on the table. "After dishes, I mean."

"Just go. I'll do them for you," snapped Varia. Drying a few dishes would be better than having to listen to his murderous plans.

"Wow! Double thanks!" Sidran pulled on his boots and ran outside. Hugo raced after him.

Samuel stood up and stretched. "Well, time to get to work. We still need our crops." Dad and Adriel followed.

"Some of the weaving grass is getting long enough to cut," Gretel said to Mom. "We can start making ropes for the net."

"Come help us when you're done here, Varia," said Mom as she walked out with the other women.

Varia sat rigidly until she was alone with the dishes. Then she wiped them all onto the floor. The star child had wrecked everything! And lied about Galatea! Galatea wasn't dangerous — as long as they didn't scare her, which was exactly what they planned to do. But at least she knew Galatea was still alive.

She sloshed water and ashes into the dishpan, picked up the bowls, and attacked them with the cloth. She had to tell Galatea the bad news. The little dragon would be so disappointed. But now everyone would be watching the woods and it would be even harder to slip away. And how could she possibly help make weapons to use against Galatea? She dried the dishes as slowly as she could.

The weaving grass was about waist high on Varia. Normally she liked cutting this early grass. It was much easier than cutting the fall grass, which was twice as high and twice as tough. Today, though, she hated every part of it.

"We've got enough sacks and blankets," Varia complained as she held a bundle of wet grass so Mom could tie it. "And you put bark on the bottoms of everyone's boots, so we won't need to fix the soles so often."

"We need the grass for the net," said Mom in her bossy little girl's voice. "Now carry this bundle over there and help me tie the next one."

Why do I even have to listen to a little kid? Varia grumbled to herself. But she did it. "Why can't we wait and see what the animal is like before making plans to destroy it?" she asked. "Are we going to cause mass extinctions here the way people did on Earth?"

Gretel lowered her sickle and looked Varia in the eye. "We're not making anything extinct," she said. "We're only making weapons to defend ourselves if we have to. And if worst comes to worst and we do have to kill it, we're not wiping out a whole species. Wherever it came from, there have to be more of them."

Varia clenched her fists. "There aren't," she said in a tiny voice. "The star child only said one."

"There have to be others," repeated Gretel. "It had to have parents."

Varia thought of Galatea trudging into the cave, her head down and her tail dragging on the stones, to sit beside her mother's watery grave. "We can't hurt it," she said. I have to tell them, she thought, so they stop this madness. But how can I make them believe me instead of the star child?

Gretel put her arm around Varia's waist and leaned her head on Varia's shoulder. Varia stiffened. I know she means well, she thought, but it should be the other way around. It doesn't feel right. She pulled away.

Gretel sighed. "For my doctoral thesis back on Earth, I studied wild Komodo dragons in Indonesia."

"I remember reading about those," said Varia. "They attack cows, and people, and they have poisonous saliva." She scowled. "Nothing like the animal that's here — probably."

"We hope not," said Gretel. "I was doing egg counts and checking the composition of the shells to see if they were being harmed by pollutants in the water." She looked up into Varia's face. "I had no intention of hurting the animals, but my crew and I carried guns just in case. Tranquilizer guns and real ones. Just in case," she repeated.

"Did you kill any?" asked Varia.

"No. And we won't kill this animal either. Except as a very last resort."

Varia felt a little better. But she still would not tie rope into nets. Unless, of course, it was the only way Mom would let her sit with Adriel while he napped. After all, with a dangerous beast on the loose, they couldn't leave him alone.

"You're sure you'll be okay?" Mom worried during lunch. "Would you like someone to sit with you too, in case it climbs in the window?"

"I'll keep the window closed, and nothing will get in." Galatea wouldn't come to the sleeping hut unless Varia brought her, and right now that didn't seem like a good idea.

"But I have to bring Galatea here. That's the only way they'll believe me," Varia imagined telling Connie while she did the lunch dishes.

She saw Connie's blue eyes widen, and the fresh scratches on the back of her hand as she clutched the squirming kitten hidden inside her shirt. "If you do, they'll take her away!"

"If I don't, they might hurt her."

Connie stroked the kitten's head where it poked out between her buttons. She bit her lip. "I don't know what you should do."

"I don't know either." Varia shook Connie's image away and stacked the bowls on the shelf. Time for Adriel's nap. Maybe Galatea's mother would have an idea.

She found Adriel playing with the wet stones beside the weaving grass. He let her pick him up, and snuggled onto her shoulder.

"What's that on your ear?" Mom stopped Varia as she started to walk away.

Uh-oh, thought Varia. She'd put sap on Galatea's shoulder bite, but not on that one.

Adriel lifted his head off Varia's shoulder. "What dat?"

Mom pushed Varia's hair aside and rubbed her fingernail across her earlobe. "You have some kind of growth. It almost looks like an earring, it's so shiny and silver."

Varia shifted Adriel and rubbed her ear with a finger on her unscarred hand. She'd felt the bump, but she didn't know it was shiny. It sounded pretty, whatever earrings were. "Anyway, it doesn't hurt," she said, pulling her hair forward. Adriel giggled and grabbed at her ear. "Naptime," she said firmly.

"Maybe I should ask the star child about it," said Mom.

"No!"

Mom sighed. "It reminds me of what Reyk . . . " She stopped. "But I suppose if there are no other symptoms . . . I'll keep an eye on it."

Varia carried Adriel into the sleeping hut, dried him off, changed his diaper and wrapped him up in his fluffy blanket. He was drowsy for once. She lay down beside him and hummed "Little Rabbit Fufu". In a few minutes he was asleep.

This time, Varia didn't bother to take her weaving with her when she left. There was too much to discuss. She did take her sweater off the hook and put it on under her shirt, since the grass shirt was more water-repellent. It was tighter than last time she'd worn it, but stretchy enough that she could still get it on.

She opened the shutters and started to climb out. Something snapped not too far away. Varia froze. Adriel slept on. She could hear voices far off in the field, and someone chopping wood, but nothing else. After a minute, she climbed out the rest of the way and closed the shutters behind her, leaving them open just a crack so she could get back in.

Chapter 15

Varia found Galatea crouched in the cave with her back to one of the walls and her tail wrapped around her legs. She looked different somehow. Serious. Older. Her eyes were a harder shade of purple — or maybe it was just the dim light.

'Oi no lov da star choild,' she growled.

"I don't like it either," said Varia. "And it doesn't like me." She shook the rain off her clothes and sat down cross-legged across from Galatea.

"Waria's moder and broder love da star choild?"

Varia fidgeted with the end of her sleeve. "They . . . talk to it."

Galatea regarded Varia with her clear purple eyes. "Oi no live wid Waria's fomily."

Varia looked at the floor. "No. The star child told my family that you're dangerous, and now they're afraid of you. If you come, they might hurt you — by accident." She couldn't bear to tell Galatea that her people were making weapons to use against her. If Galatea just stayed away, that was enough for now.

Galatea started to reply. Instead, she leaned forward and lifted the hair off Varia's ear. Her warm, metallic breath flooded over Varia's face. Her long, yellow-smeared teeth glistened in a dragonish smile. "Waria is my broder."

Varia sighed with relief. Galatea wasn't mad at her. "Does it look like one of your scales?" She grinned. "Actually, I can't be your brother. I'm a girl, so I have to be your sister."

Galatea leaned back against the wall and stretched her tail. It snaked along the wall. "Whad is 'girl'?"

"A girl is — well, like your mother. She laid an egg, so she's a girl."

"Waria loid an ogg?"

Varia giggled. "No. Humans don't lay eggs. Human girls have babies. Dragon girls lay eggs, when they're old enough."

Galatea nodded. "Waria is my soster, when Waria is old enof."

Close enough, thought Varia. "Are you a girl?" she asked. She had wondered.

For the second time in two days, Galatea's eyes darkened to stormy grey. "Oi is loik moi moder," she said in a low voice. Her breath puffed out noisily — Varia almost expected to see smoke. Galatea reached out a trembling claw and touched Varia's ear-scab one more time. When she blinked, her eyes were purple again. "Come see new droizu," she said, pushing herself away from the wall with her tail.

The rain had lessened to a steady drizzle. Galatea led Varia around the pool with the blackened ground and on to the one she'd swum in yesterday. Varia stopped short when she saw it. A carpet of grey and withered vegetation circled the water. There was a patch of shrivelled mushrooms too; apparently there were places even they wouldn't grow. The stems of the water flowers had thickened overnight, and already their stalks were covered with sticky, yellow buds. The only other source of colour in the grey clearing was the oily, glistening film on top of the water. Was this why the star child had said not to drink water from pools? As if anyone would drink water that looked — and smelled — like that!

"See new droizu?" Galatea scurried around the pool, brushing her snout against the tiny buds. She sneezed. "Soon there be new bees."

Varia walked into the clearing. "So you swim in the water, and the little flowers turn into big droizu, and then the big bees find them and make hives here?" The grey plants at her feet smelled like spoiled cabbage, but with a metallic tinge. She sneezed. It seemed wrong to kill off the plants that grew here. But on the other hand, wasn't that what her own people did at the settlement? They'd pulled, dug, and overturned all the plants in the clearing to make room for their crops. Galatea was a farmer, just like they were. Varia sneezed again. Sort of like they were.

Galatea studied a tiny bee crawling up one of the reeds. "Bog bees no come. Small bees torn into bog bees," she said.

"Oh," said Varia. "They grow from the small ones, like the flowers. Your dragon water is very powerful."

"Drogon water wery powerful." Galatea looked pleased.

"You know," Varia went on, "if the star child saw this dragon pool and how you farm droizu for the bees, it would know you don't eat people, and then — "

"No!" Galatea interrupted. "Star choild no see moi pool. Star choild doingerous."

Varia looked at her sharply. "Did the star child hurt you?"

Galatea turned her back. "Star choild hort my mod-er's mod-er's mod-er's . . . mony moder's moders." Her shoulders heaved.

Varia walked around her and squatted down so she could see the dragon's face. So the star child had been here before, terrorizing the dragons. She held her voice steady. "What did it do, Galatea? Tell me." If the star child had hurt Galatea, Varia would have something to tell her family about who was dangerous.

Galatea wrapped her head in her wings and rocked back and forth. Whatever the star child had done, it must have been something horrible.

"Galatea," Varia said softly. "The star child hurt me too. I know it's dangerous." Galatea buried her head deeper. "I need to know what it did to you in case it tries to hurt my family too."

Galatea's voice was muffled inside her wing. "Moi moder told me. Oi not loik," she said.

It took a long time for Varia to get the story out of Galatea, and even then she wasn't sure she had details right. She had to supply a lot of words when Galatea didn't know them, or only knew them in her mother's dragon language.

The first part was clear. There had once been many dragons and other animals on the Kettle. Varia knew that already. Dragons had eaten many things, not just bees. She hadn't known that. Watching Galatea mime devouring squirrels, or their equivalents, the way she gobbled bees, made Varia wince. But some Earth animals ate others too, she reminded herself. The Kettle must have been a lot like Earth before its forests were cut down and its oceans polluted. She and Galatea had that in common — they only knew the place they had come from through other peoples' memories.

Then suddenly, the story changed. Galatea stopped prancing and huddled on the ground. "Purokoot," she croaked. "Purokoot come from da skoi." She gestured weakly at the clouds.

"What's a purokoot?"

Galatea's eyes darted around the clearing as if searching for words. "Woit," she said. Then she disappeared under a bush.

She reappeared a minute later with a claw full of dry leaves attached to a muddy, dark red bulb with dirty roots. "Caraahm-nop." She tossed it into the air and caught it in her mouth.

"You aren't going to eat that!" Even if it did look marginally better than a bee.

Galatea held it between her teeth while she climbed onto a low tree branch. She turned to face Varia and balanced on the branch, her wings arched and her tail held straight out behind her. She champed down and swallowed. Varia watched in alarm as the dragon's grey eyes turned green, then orange, then dazzling red.

Galatea leapt out of the tree. Orange flames shot out of her mouth. Varia dived out of the way, landing on the ground and filling her mouth with slimy, grey plants. She spit them out and wiped her face on her wet sleeve. Galatea lay sprawled on her stomach with her neck arched and her eyes closed. Sooty smoke curled out of her nostrils. Her mother had obviously taught her a lot of things Varia didn't know about.

"Purokoot come loik dat," Galatea said hoarsely. "Wid mony caraahm." Her eyes wobbled open. She crawled to the pool, trailing wisps of smoke, and lapped at the water.

Caraahm: fire. Purokoot: fiery creature from the sky. Varia felt her stomach tighten. There had been light and heat when the star child spun down onto the Kettle, but nothing like what Galatea described. Children didn't make fire. Only dragons did. Was Galatea talking about Draco? To think Varia had once wished for Draco to come down instead of the star child!

Galatea continued her story in a flat voice. That was the end of paradise. Fire, then ice. A long, long winter. When spring finally, slowly, arrived, no more animals. No more dragons, except one. One mother, one egg, one mother, one egg, on and on and on. The mother never living to see her child, and the child only ever knowing its mother's bones. Always, always moolor.

Galatea stared into the pool, her wings drooping over the dank ground. Varia crouched next to her. Poor Galatea! A tear rolled down her cheek, then another one. Galatea looked up, suddenly interested.

"Tears," said Varia. "Your sad story made me cry."

Galatea pushed her face close to Varia's. Varia's eyes watered again at the smell of sooty, rotten cabbage. She turned her head away, but Galatea had a long, flexible neck. She pushed her snout against Varia's cheek and licked the tears. Varia held her breath. Galatea's hot tongue poked into her eye. Varia squeezed her eyes shut while Galatea licked off her eyelids. It was a good thing Galatea didn't have poisonous saliva like Gretel's Komodo dragon.

"I need to go," Varia said when Galatea finally stopped and turned morosely back to the pool. She would really have to clean herself off this time before the others saw — and smelled — her.

Galatea trudged through the woods with her eyes down, grunting if Varia tried to talk to her.

"You'll feel better after a good sleep," Varia told her when they reached the cave pool. "I'll try to come back tomorrow." Galatea's tail tapped once on the rocks.

Varia watched her drag herself into the cave, then ran up the hill. She stopped at the small pool to rinse herself off. The sweater wouldn't need it; the smelly gunk was only on the grass shirt. She removed the shirt and was just about to dip it into the water when she noticed the rainbow film and the unmistakable metallic smell. Oh yes. She and Galatea had splashed through here yesterday. The plants closest to the pool were already starting to wilt. She stirred the water with her finger to make a hole in the film. Underneath, it looked fine. She wasn't going to drink it — and it couldn't smell as bad as her clothes already did. Besides, what else could she do? The rain was barely a drizzle — it couldn't possibly clean her off by the time she reached home.

The smelly goo slid off her shirt and floated to the edges of the pool. Rather than take off her pants and boots, she just waded through to the other side, holding up the bottom of her sweater.

Before putting the shirt back on, she pulled the sweater aside and peeked at her shoulder. The sap had worn off, but two shiny, silver disks clearly showed where Galatea had bitten her.

Varia's stomach clenched. Galatea had called her "broder" when she saw the growth on Varia's ear. What had she meant? Don't be silly, she scolded herself. People don't turn into dragons. That's only in stories. She pulled the sweater back over her shoulder and slipped the shirt on over top.

Varia ran all the way back, pausing only before the sticky tree to make sure the star child wasn't there. She paused again at the trailhead. Sidran was dragging a long tree branch past the signal tower. Other settlers were working in the clearing. She tried to pant quietly as she slipped off the path and crept behind bushes. Sidran paused for a second, but didn't look up. Varia hoisted herself into the window of the hut, and was braiding grass into rope when Adriel woke up a minute later.

Chapter 16

Sidran grabbed Varia's arm as she left the outhouse at bedtime. "Did you find it?"

Varia shook his hand off. "You're supposed to wait over there," she accused, pointing to a rock several steps back.

Sidran lowered his voice to a whisper. "I know you sneaked into the woods." The glow from the kitchen window lit his determined face. "I saw you climb out the window — and leave it open. And you smelled funny when you came back, like the machine room in the ship." Varia's heart skipped a beat. "No one else noticed because you stayed outside in the rain to wash off the smell."

Varia felt her face burning. Had she really been that obvious? "Does anyone else know?"

Sidran smiled. "No, but if you don't tell me what you were doing, they will." He motioned with his head. "I'm supposed to get wood. Come on."

The rain had stopped, and stars were visible between the intermittent clouds. Varia kicked the dirt behind Sidran. Of all the people in the settlement, he was the last one she wanted to tell. Why couldn't it have been Gretel, who loved animals, or Dad, or Nara, who at least liked her?

Sidran slowed down when they were far enough from the kitchen not to be overheard. "Did you find it?" he asked again.

"Find what?"

"You know what. The animal, of course."

Varia glanced sideways at him. His eyes were wide open and he looked ready to shake her. "Maybe."

Sidran jostled her arm. "Then what is it?!"

"A dragon." It seemed absurd to say this to Sidran.

His voice turned angry. "I mean it. If you don't tell me, I'm telling them you snuck out."

"I did tell you," she said, suddenly desperate. He had to believe her. If he didn't, no one would. "It is a dragon. It has wings and scales and a pointed tail. It even breathes fire. That smell you smelled? Dragon smoke and rotten plants from its farm of giant bees. The shiny spot on my ear is where it bit me."

"Bit you! A dragon! But how did you . . . " Sidran's eyes were round in the starlight.

Varia's heart pounded. He wasn't laughing. She took a deep breath.

Once Varia started talking, the words poured out like water through a breached dam. She hadn't realized how much she needed to talk, to hear someone gasp and worry and rejoice along with her. She hadn't realized how heavy her secret was until Sidran held half of it. He listened with rapt attention, which Varia could sense even though it was too dark out by the woodpile to see the details of his face. It was almost like talking to Connie — except that it wasn't.

"The star child told you to leave it alone and you hatched it anyway?"

"Galatea isn't dangerous."

"She bit you!"

"She was just a baby, and it didn't really hurt."

"Vampire bites don't really hurt either."

"Vampire bites!?"

"I read about them. They suck your blood and then you turn into — "

"Sidran! Is everything all right?" Samuel's voice cut across the field.

"Fine," Sidran yelled back. "Varia's helping me."

"Don't be too long."

Sidran picked up a piece of wood. "So what are you going to do with her?"

Varia chose a wood-sized shadow and bent over to pick it up. "I'm going to ride on her back and find the other lander."

Sidran gasped.

Varia handed him the chunk of wood. "She doesn't know it yet. I'm waiting until she can fly before I tell her."

"Tell or ask?"

"Well, convince. I thought maybe I'd tell her that while we're looking for more people, we can also look for more dragons."

"I thought there weren't any more."

"I know." Varia balanced another piece of wood on the pile on her arm. "But that's just here. We don't have any idea what's on the rest of the planet. Your mother made me think of that. Maybe Galatea has cousins she doesn't know about somewhere far away."

"I wish . . . Varia, do you think I could come too? If she really isn't dangerous, I mean."

"If anyone else comes, I think it should be my dad. So the other team recognizes us when we find them."

Sidran stiffened, and Varia braced herself for his retort. Instead, he sighed. "I never thought of that." They started walking back toward the lighted window. Sidran sighed again. "But I sure would like to see her."

Varia stubbed her toe on a rock. "Ow!"

"Everything all right?" called Samuel.

"Fine!" Varia lowered her voice. "She'd probably like to meet you too. She's so lonely, Sidran. You should see how she droops whenever she thinks about it."

"I wonder what happened to her mother. Most animals don't die when they lay their eggs."

"Odd, isn't it? That's something she never talks about. I wish I could bring her here to live with us, but your star child won't let her come."

"Specto says she's dangerous." This time Sidran stumbled over something, and Varia grabbed his arm, dropping some of her wood. She bent over to pick them up.

"She isn't dangerous unless you scare her." She told him about meeting the star child at the tree, and the bites on her hand, which were now just ordinary faint scars.

Sidran walked more slowly as they neared the kitchen. "I've never seen Specto like that," he said. "He's always gentle, and . . . Varia, you better be careful around that dragon."

"She won't hurt me. I'm the only friend she has." But she remembered the hot tongue in her eyes, and the growing spots on her shoulder. How did Galatea really see her? She shivered.

They reached the door. "Thanks for telling me," Sidran whispered as Samuel pulled the door open for them.

That night, Varia dreamed she was walking through the woods to the cave, carrying Sidran on her shoulders.

He is small, like Adriel, and his chunky legs bounce up and down beside her cheeks. The pool inside the cave is flanked by sticky, yellow droizu. Varia puts Sidran down and pushes through to the filmy water. The skeleton fans its wing bones. She lowers

her head into the pool, feeling her wings and tail ripple in the air
among the plants. Bubbles explore her long, green snout. The
skeleton drifts until its hollow eyes are level with hers. "Moolor."
Its gurgling voice swirls and turns into Mom's ring. Varia's pink
fingers waver in the ripples as she reaches for it.

Snap! The toothy jaw closes around Sidran-Adriel's calf, now
in the water. Varia jerks him out, and the dragon mother sinks
back down. Oozing blood turns to silver spots, which spread
down his leg as Varia tries in vain to lick them off.

The star child appears in a cloud of swirling suns. "Run!"
The cave vanishes and Sidran-Adriel steers her across the field.
Flames lick their heels and swallow the pink-veined lettuce.

"See? Galatea is dangerous," Sidran-Adriel yells.

Varia looks over her shoulder. "No, it's the star child." She
points at the forest edge, where Galatea watches, trembling, from
behind a tree. But Sidran-Adriel can't see her.

Varia tries to swerve away from the fire, but it is too hot and
too close. Galatea's eyes flash orange behind the tree. The dragon
answers the star child's blaze with a crackling flame of her own.
But it catches Sidran-Adriel's hair, and Varia pulls him down
and rolls with him through the burning field.

Varia jerked awake. Dark, cool air enveloped her as she lay
gasping and squeezing her pillow in both hands. The room was
quiet, except for Dad's uneven snores. It was a reassuring sound,
a safe sound. Varia let out a slow breath. The dream wasn't real.
There was no fire, no flight, no fight. Adriel hiccupped, and
Varia tensed all over again as the last moment of her dream
flashed back into her mind. In that instant before she'd woken
up, her overwhelming desire had been to sink her own teeth
into Sidran-Adriel's burning flesh.

Morning took a long time to come. When it finally did,
everyone ate breakfast together in the kitchen. Dad and Varia

drank tea made from strawberry leaves — another short-lived summer treat — while the others sipped steaming star water. Varia scraped every last bit of porridge off the sides of the pot into her bowl. She was so hungry she could have eaten three bowls, yeasty or not.

The morning conversation banged around her head as she shovelled the porridge into her mouth. The weapons were progressing well. Dad had found several spear-sized sticks and peeled the bark off two of them. Hugo and Sidran had assembled logs and branches for the catapult, and Nara reported that the new grass was drying nicely over the stove in the weaving hut, and some of it would be ready for braiding this afternoon.

"I'll help Varia braid it," Sidran said loudly. Everyone stopped eating and looked at him. Varia tried to look invisible. "She can show me how," Sidran added.

"Don't you want to work on the catapult?" asked Hugo.

"That's why I want to make the rope," Sidran said, brightening again. "So I'm sure it's extremely strong."

"I'll help cut the wood for the catapult," Samuel offered, trying not to laugh. "I'm tired of raking mushrooms anyway."

"I couldn't sleep last night," said Luella, rubbing her neck. Varia nodded. Her head felt full of fluff, and the food only partly helped. Luella continued. "I kept imagining some great gorilla-like thing crashing through the door and carrying someone off. I think we need to put bars over the doors and windows."

"It wouldn't hurt to patrol the edges of the settlement too," someone else said, "so we can warn everyone if we see anything." Varia's heart sank. That would make it harder than ever to get away. Sidran gave her a sympathetic look.

"We should do practice drills," Mom said. "Set a signal we can use if we see or hear anything suspicious, and practice running for cover when we hear it."

"A reed whistle would work," said Luella. "We could use it at mealtimes too. One long blast for danger, two short for lunchtime."

Varia glanced over at Sidran. He shrugged. The conversation went on while Varia tried to scrape more porridge out of her empty bowl. Dad slid his over to her, and she cleaned it out too. She shifted uncomfortably on her chair. She had a more pressing concern than getting to Galatea this morning. Her body had made another growth spurt last night, and her clothes were uncomfortably tight. Her shirt pulled across her back and the sleeves felt like they would rip apart if she reached across the table. She'd managed to get the pants on, but there was a ripping sound when she sat down.

Fortunately, this time the changes were big enough that Mom noticed. "Come with me," she whispered as everyone was pushing their dishes to the middle of the table and heading to the door. "She'll be right back," Mom said to Sidran, who looked incredulous at the possibility that he might have to do the dishes alone.

"Nara hung the bigger clothes over here," Mom explained as she rifled through a clump of grass cloth on the wall. She pulled out a shirt and a pair of pants and held them up against Varia. "Not big enough. Let's try Samuel's old ones." Varia shifted her weight to her other foot. "You've grown up so quickly," Mom said. "A year ago I worried you never would. And now the rest of us are . . . " She looked down at her own little girl's body and shrugged. "Oh well; we take things as they come. You're a lovely young woman." She reached up and kissed Varia on the cheek, handing her the clothes as she walked out.

Varia didn't feel lovely. She felt haggard. She peeled off the small clothes and pulled on the new ones. The scales on her shoulder had also grown overnight, she saw, and merged together into one big patch. She hadn't mentioned this bite to Sidran. The one on her ear was enough. It felt bigger too. Mom would worry harder when she noticed.

The memory of her dream hung over her like a thick cloud. Adriel had smiled at her so sweetly at breakfast. How could she even have imagined eating him? She shuddered. And Mom was bound to miss her ring sooner or later. Maybe Sidran could think of a way to get it out of the water. Or maybe she was big enough now to climb into the pool and get it herself — if she dared get that close to the toothy skull. She left her discarded clothes on the floor and trudged to the kitchen.

By the end of the afternoon, Varia was sorry she'd told Sidran anything. He peppered her with questions during dishes, then left his catapult work to walk with her whenever she carried a bundle of grass from the creek to the weaving hut. After lunch he followed her into the sleeping hut and fidgeted noisily in the next room while she sang Adriel to sleep — which made it take twice as long. Varia had been hoping to have a nap herself, since there was no way for her to slip away to see Galatea anyway now that Luella had made up her non-stop schedule for patrolling the edges of the woods. But Sidran insisted on talking, so she joined him on the other side of the curtain.

He had ideas for gadgets to pick the ring out of the water, and ideas to disguise them as weapons so he could work on them. He had ideas for hand and grass signals so they could talk to each other without anyone knowing what they were saying, and ideas for a coded dragon alphabet so they could write down dragon words. Of course, they would also have to figure out how to make paper and ink. Varia lay back on Gretel's mat and pretended to listen until Sidran remembered that they were supposed to be braiding ropes.

"Tie three strands together like this." Varia sighed and gave him the end to hold. "Left string over the centre string, then right string over. Left, right, left, right." She took the end and let him try. "Just put it over the middle string, not both of them. No, I don't think Galatea would like us to take her for a walk on a leash. Remember to pull it tight . . . " Varia had once thought her own fingers were clumsy.

Sidran chattered at her over supper dishes, and then pulled her outside to collect wood with him again in the evening as soon as they were done.

"Sidran's taking a real interest in Varia," Luella whispered to Nara as they left.

"I knew he would eventually," Nara whispered back.

It has nothing to do with that! Varia fumed as she followed Sidran across the clearing. He's just a little boy. Still, she knew that was the plan. Part of the job of colonizing a planet was making more settlers, and with all the other children lost, Varia and Sidran would be expected to do their part. But later, when they were both grown. Not now, when she was somewhere between thirteen and sixteen and looked it, and Sidran was — how old now? Older in fact, but he looked about eight. Which was another good reason to find that missing lander.

Sidran's red hair flopped over his furrowed brow and into his eyes. He tapped a fist against his other hand as he walked. "When you go looking for the lander, you'll have to take food, maybe in a basket. We could make a harness and you could tie it on — or a sack might be easier. Water might be a problem. Oh well, there have to be a lot of streams around with all this rain. Remember, it has to be running water. You can't drink from pools. You'll have to tell Galatea to fly in a pattern to make sure you don't miss any places where the lander might be. Concentric circles around the settlement maybe, or a grid pattern."

"You're amazing," said Varia. "I hadn't even thought about food, or where we'd look. I was still thinking about how to convince her to take me."

Sidran looked sideways at her. "Will you let me ride her another time?"

"If she'll let you."

They reached the woodpile. Sidran sat down on a stump and pushed his hair out of his eyes. He looked up at Varia. "You know what the real problem is?"

"What?"

"We don't know who's right. You or Specto."

"I am."

"You don't know for sure. Maybe she's dangerous to everyone except you. We have to find out."

"And how are we going to do that with all these weapons around and the star child scaring her away?" Varia picked up a rock and threw it at the pile of logs waiting to become a catapult.

Sidran stood up. "Take me to see her at the cave. If you're right and she doesn't hurt me, you'll have proof."

"Take you to see her!" Varia studied the broken mushroom caps among the sweet potato leaves. That dream was awful. But it was only a dream, she reminded herself. Still, there was a warning in it.

"Aren't you afraid?" she asked. "What if the star child finds out and gets angry at you like he did me? And our parents will be furious with both of us."

"I am a bit afraid," Sidran admitted. "But Varia — a real dragon! Maybe Specto just doesn't know what this dragon is like."

Varia could see the pleading excitement in his eyes even in the dim light. And he was right. After he visited safely, the others would be more likely to believe her. "I'll ask her," she promised.

Sidran whooped and punched the air above his head with his fists. Varia glanced toward the kitchen. "They're watching us," she said. "In case we get eaten by a great gorilla-thing."

Sidran chuckled. "Or smelled up by a skunk."

"Or hopped on by a great white rabbit." Laughing, they gathered up armloads of wood.

"We'll have to distract the patrol guards somehow," said Sidran as they walked back. "So you can sneak away to ask."

"You'll think of something," said Varia. She felt happier than she'd felt for a long, long time.

Chapter 17

DAYS PASSED, AND SIDRAN WAS UNABLE to distract the guards long enough for Varia to slip away. This day, he was raking mushrooms, while Varia was stuck learning how to tie the finished ropes into a net.

Nara brought her a flat slab of wood with a peg pounded in at each end and a stick resting on the pegs. She had already tied the first row of net circles and looped them over the stick. The remaining rope was wrapped lengthwise around another wider stick, which Nara called the shuttle. She held a third, stubby stick in her left hand and took the shuttle in her right.

"Loop the rope around this fat stick to make the hole the right size, hold it firmly, and twist the shuttle around the top of the loop. Then pull the knot tight. Varia tried to copy her and felt clumsy all over again. Nara untangled the rope and handed it back to her. "Try again. Hold the loop tightly . . . pull right, then down. That's better." Varia tried again. This time her knot looked sort of like Nara's, and there was a new, lopsided loop in the net. She knotted her way slowly down the row.

"You've got it." Nara smiled. "Now turn the stick over and do it again. When you run out of rope, tie on another piece and keep going." She left Varia to it.

Varia tugged at the two uneven rows of the net she'd managed to tie so far. The knots were solid. This was a fisherman's net, designed to keep struggling fish from escaping. If only there was some way to make it looser, so if they ever did try to use it on Galatea, she would be able to wiggle free. She thought about it as she looped and tied the next row.

A few more frustrating days passed. Varia sat on the warm ground outside the sleeping hut with her half-made net in her lap and the rest of the ropes coiled beside her. Adriel had just fallen asleep. The sun was shining, so she rolled up her pant and shirt cuffs and untied the collar of her shirt to let the warmth into her skin. She wondered if Galatea was lying on her rock soaking up the sun too. What did Galatea think of her when she stayed away for days at a time? Did she worry that Varia wouldn't come back? Or was she too busy farming bees and listening to her mother's bones to notice?

It hadn't rained for several days now, and the crops were getting big and leafy, if oddly coloured. Varia devoured them anyway. Lettuce with pink veins, stringy pea pods with the hard peas removed, squishy radishes with the leaves still attached — they all tasted better than that same old stew they'd eaten all winter, and smelled better than those weird things Luella kept cooking up.

The weapons were growing well in the dry weather too. Dad had produced a spiky forest of crooked spears to be kept outside every door, and was working on a practice target to attach to a tree. Once it was done, Varia planned to see how many spear tips she could flatten against it. The catapult squatted next to the rock pile, an impossible-looking structure of unmatched sticks. Varia had laughed with relief when she saw the first attempts to throw something with it. Although Sidran and Hugo had triple-braided the rope so it wouldn't snap, the machine still faced only one direction, and was too heavy and awkward to turn. Galatea would have no trouble dodging those rocks if it came to that.

Luella had fashioned reed whistles on strings for everyone to hang around their necks in case of danger. The clearing had been ringing with newly invented signals ever since she handed them out. Three shorts: "I need help over here." Two longs and a short: "Laundry is done. Come and get yours." Two shorts and a long: "Time to make supper. Kitchen helpers come now." Random sequences of longs and shorts: Adriel is awake. Luella hadn't wanted to give him a whistle, but Mom convinced her that if he had one, they would know if he wandered into the woods. Five of the settlers, including Mom, had noticed that their whistles played different notes, and now spent all their spare time making up tunes. They were sitting at the trailhead practicing now. The transmitter joined in with an off-pitch whine.

Varia's net had grown too. Her fingers now tied the knots so automatically that she hardly had to look at them. It had been harder to figure out where to cut them so her sabotage wouldn't be detected. She slipped the eggshell out of her pocket and slit two of the three braided strands of grass inside her latest knot. Galatea would be able to rip them open if anyone tried to use the net on her. She hadn't told Sidran about this bit of subterfuge. She finished another slit and hid the eggshell in her pocket as he raced toward her.

"We're going to test the catapult!"

"Do it then." Varia turned the net over so she could start the next row.

"Varia!" Sidran whispered urgently. She looked up. "Don't look up!" She made another loop. "I'm telling everyone so they'll come and watch. Make a scene like you don't want to, and take your net inside the hut. Then you can sneak away."

Varia wrapped the shuttle around the loop and pulled the knot tight. "And when I come back?"

"It's my turn to patrol the trailhead when we're done with the catapult."

Varia forced a scowl and gathered up her ropes. "I'm not interested in your stupid contraption," she shouted. The pipers peered at her through the signal tower.

"Oh, come on!" Sidran scowled back at her. "I bet we can throw a rock as far as the outhouse."

"No!" This was fun. "We don't need a stupid catapult and I'm not interested in seeing you smash anything." She stomped into the sleeping hut and slammed the door. Oops. She ran to the curtain and checked Adriel. Whew. Still asleep. She opened the door again and scowled until she saw Sidran leading the pipers to the field. Then she slipped out the window and into the woods.

The forest was silent in the hot, still air, and the unusually limp leaves felt soft under her bare feet. She ran effortlessly; the air pumped itself in and out of her lungs. I'm not afraid of these plants any more, Varia realized. Whatever got Reyk and Thora wasn't on this trail — or anywhere Galatea had taken her. But she would have to remember to be careful if — when she and Galatea flew to new places.

She stopped at the small pool above the valley. Strange — it should be surrounded by sticky yellow flowers by now. Instead, slender stems with tiny flowers sprouted out of the clear water and new, green shoots dotted the dry ground. Varia parted the unfurling leaves with her toe. They were growing up through the residue of the plants Galatea had destroyed. Maybe Galatea hadn't come back to this pool and the dragon water's effects had worn off.

Then she noticed the soggy hive floating half-submerged in the middle of the pool. Why would Galatea dump a hive in the water? Varia caught her breath. She wouldn't. But the star child would.

Varia ran down the hill. The droizu were still there around the pool by the cave — but there was something new too. On top of a boulder, an enormous dragon spread her wings. It had the same shape and the same colours as Galatea. It had to be her. But how she had grown! Her leathery wings were extended like two roofs, and her muscular legs were tensed, ready to spring. Varia held her breath. Sidran would find this dragon very intimidating. She hoped Galatea remembered her.

Galatea held herself rigid on top of the boulder. Then she tossed something into her mouth, clamped it shut, and jumped. Her wings caught the air. She wobbled upward, making little running motions with her legs, her belly swelling as Varia watched. She jerked her wings down, but instead of lifting her up, the motion flipped her over backwards. She fell sideways and landed hard on the rocks. Her belly deflated as flames shot out of her mouth.

Varia winced. Eating caraahm-nop obviously wasn't the way to fly. "Are you . . . ?" Varia started to run to her, but stopped before she reached her. Galatea was so long, so massive, so muscular. She definitely hadn't been starving for the loss of one pool. Even lying down, her shoulders were nearly as tall as Varia's. One wing could make a tent. Her tail was as thick as the trunk of a medium-sized tree. In the sunshine, she dazzled. Varia started forward to help her up, but stopped again. How could she help such a huge animal? It didn't seem possible that she had once held this enormous dragon in the palm of her hand.

Galatea flapped her wings and swung back onto her feet. Varia felt very small. It was a strange feeling after being so big at home. The dragon's great head peered down at her. Her teeth were as long as Varia's fingers. Varia measured with her eyes. She came up to the middle of Galatea's glittering chest. Smoke curled from Galatea's nostrils. "Ooch." It was a snarl. Galatea arched her neck and slid her snake-like tongue over the shoulder she'd landed on. Bits of gravel came off on it. She swallowed them.

Varia couldn't think of anything to say to this giant Galatea. Galatea arched her neck the other way and looked into Varia's face. Her scalloped scales tapered like armour down her long snout. Varia had never seen them so clearly defined before. Metallic breath gusted into Varia's nostrils. "Waria is moi soster," said Galatea.

Galatea did remember her. But it was easier to think with more space between them. Varia backed away a few steps. "You're learning to fly," she said.

Galatea squashed a crawling bee with her nose. "Oi is lorning."

Varia suddenly remembered the soggy hive in the pool. A low growl escaped Galatea's throat as Varia described it.

"Da star choild do dat. Da star choild make drogon water hort." She yanked back her clawed hand as if in pain.

"The star child's water hurts you?"

"Water is hot. Born moi hond." Galatea held up her hand. One knobby finger was grey and withered.

Varia felt a surge of anger toward the star child. Galatea was right to fear it — although Varia wondered if the star child might now start to fear the dragon. "Did it wreck any of your other pools?"

Galatea's eyes narrowed. "It wrock all da pools close to Waria's fomily."

"It doesn't want you near the settlement." So it wasn't going to be a simple as bringing Sidran for a visit and changing people's minds.

Galatea lumbered to the edge of the clearing and looked up over the treetops. "Oi floi in da skoi. Oi moik mony pools far from da star choild." The last word sounded like a hiss.

Varia's insides felt skittish. This was what she'd been waiting to hear. She walked to Galatea and put her hand tentatively on the dragon's large forearm. "I want to go with you." Her voice squeaked.

Galatea lowered her head. Varia cleared her throat. "I want to go with you."

Once more the dragon's hot breath filled Varia's face. It smelled good this time, the way a dragon's breath should. Varia felt the familiar hot tongue slide over her shiny ear. Something hot trickled down her neck. What was Galatea trying to do? Lick the spot off, or . . . She pulled away.

"Yos," Galatea whispered. "Waria come too."

The enormity of what they were planning made Varia feel wobbly. "Maybe we'll find more dragons," she whispered. No, she didn't need to convince Galatea; the dragon already wanted to go.

Galatea turned toward the pool. "Yos. More drogons."

"W-when do you want to go?" Varia wiped her neck. "I need to pack some food." Sidran's idea of a harness was absurd. Galatea was intelligent, full of her own ideas — and she was Varia's partner. She wasn't a beast of burden to saddle up and give orders to, like a horse. "And I need my boots and sweater, and a sack to carry them in."

"We go when Oi lorn to floi." Galatea rifled through the reeds, pulling out bees. They looked like pebbles in her hands. A whole hive wouldn't be more than a few mouthfuls for her now.

Varia took a steadying breath. It was time. "I need to look for something while we're away." She couldn't quite keep the trembling out of her voice. "Another lander, like the one my people came here in. And the other people that came in it."

Galatea regarded her over the reeds. "More people loik Waria?"

"Yes. My friend Connie. She's like me except her hair is blonde and she's taller — or she used to be. And some others too."

Galatea cocked her head. "More sosters?"

Varia smiled. "I suppose. I'm sure Connie would love to be your sister."

Galatea tossed her handful of bees into the air and caught them in her mouth. She would need an awful lot of pools now that she was so big, Varia thought. Maybe they would find a lake to transform.

Galatea backed up to a boulder and rubbed up and down. A bee crawled onto her flank. They obviously weren't too smart. "We look for Waria's sosters. But forst, Waria tell me. Whad is londer?"

Now it was Varia's turn to tell a story about strange and alien things. She drew the spaceship's outline in the dirt: the twirling ring that gave them gravity, the two landers in the flight bay, waiting to carry them down to the Kettle, the ramjet fusion engine that sucked in stray hydrogen atoms and turned them into speed. Galatea seemed confused about that part, so she didn't go into detail. Sidran could explain it better if Galatea really wanted to know more — she'd have to remember to ask if he could visit before they left. She acted out climbing into the lander and flying away from the ship. "Then we fell out of the sky — "

"Loik da purokoot?" Galatea leapt to her feet.

"No! Not like the purokoot." Varia searched for words. "Not that hot. The lander only made a tiny fire when it entered the atmosphere. It didn't burn anything up." The scorch marks on the clearing didn't count. "And it was only two years — eight seasons ago. The animals were already gone."

Galatea settled slowly onto her haunches. Her wings twitched and her tail swirled.

"I don't know where the other lander is, but I need to find my friends."

Galatea closed her eyes and sat very still. Finally she spoke. "Moi moder saw da londer. Moi moder saw Waria's fronds come to da coiv." Galatea bowed her head. Her tail settled to the ground and lay still.

Galatea's mother had been alive when they landed. And she'd seen people in the woods — which had to be Reyk and Thora. Varia grabbed Galatea's arm. "Did she see the other lander too? Does she know where it is? And the people at the cave. Did she see what happened to them?"

Galatea opened her eyes. "Oi osk." She heaved herself up and lumbered to the cave. Varia followed. She hadn't guessed that Galatea's egg was laid so recently, or that the skeleton was only eight seasons old. Dragons changed very quickly at both ends of their lives. Were there more changes in store for Galatea?

Varia sat in the welcome shade and watched Galatea commune with her mother. After a very short time, Galatea stiffened. She pulled out her head, looked straight at Varia, and shook the water off her head and shoulders at her. This time

Varia didn't mind. It felt cool on her hot skin. "Moi moder not know," Galatea said, looking back into the water. "Bot, se tell me how to floi. Den se tell me yos, toik Waria."

Varia stood up and gazed at her dragon, so strong and so beautiful. She felt her heart swell. Everything she planned was happening. Soon she would fly through the sky to find Connie and the other missing settlers. Everyone in her settlement would be so excited when she returned with good news.

"Oh! Galatea, I almost forgot. Would you mind if one of my friends comes to meet you before we leave?" She didn't need Sidran to convince the others any more, now that she and Galatea had another plan. But it would help if he reassured everyone that Galatea was friendly while she was gone.

Galatea was still staring at the water. She answered without turning around. "Oi is hoppy to meet Waria's frond."

Everything was working out today. "I'm happy too." She stretched her arm up onto Galatea's bowed back and kissed her side. "We'll leave when I come back."

"When you come bock."

Varia turned and left the cave. She could taste Galatea's metallic scales on her lips. She would return with Sidran. Then after she and Galatea took off, he would go home and tell everyone where she'd gone. She felt a bit guilty leaving Sidran to break the news. But he'd think of a way to make them understand. She wasn't leaving forever, after all. As soon as she found the others, she'd be back.

Varia hurried down the path toward home. The star child wasn't in the tree. Sidran was pacing back and forth beside the signal tower when she approached. She waved at him and ran through the bushes to the back of the hut. They would have a lot to talk about tonight at the woodpile.

She heard Adriel crying when she rounded the corner. "I'm here, little bunny," she called softly as she pried open the shutters.

"Vawa!" Adriel screamed.

"I'll be right there." She put one leg through the window and hoisted herself in.

Adriel wasn't alone.

Dad crouched on the mat beside her wailing brother, struggling to hold a red-stained cloth over his forehead while Adriel kicked and pushed it away. Dad's cheeks were florid and his mouth was pressed as thin as Mom's had ever been. Varia was in big trouble. But what scared her more than Dad's looming anger was the way her mouth watered at the smell of Adriel's blood.

Chapter 18

"How dare you!?" It was an accusation, not a question. Dad's shouting drowned out Adriel's wails. "Running off is bad enough, but leaving the shutters open? Even if it didn't get you, that beast could have climbed in and stolen Adriel!"

Adriel arched his back and the cloth came off again. Fresh blood trickled over his eyebrow. Dad held him tightly and pushed the cloth back against his forehead. Adriel screamed.

"I'll lick it off." Varia swallowed the words just before they left her tongue. Why would she say that? Her silver ear and shoulder spots were tingling too. What was happening to her?

Dad gave up trying to fight with Adriel. He picked him up under one arm and stalked to the door. He glared at Varia. "Don't move."

Varia smoothed out Adriel's blanket and sat down on her mat. The prickling in her silver spots was gone, as was her desire to lick off Adriel's blood. Thinking about it made her feel sick. Where had that thought come from? Galatea had licked off her bloody fingers. Maybe she was just re-living that memory . . . or something.

Dad returned and closed the door. He planted himself in front of Varia with his trembling hands balled into fists. Once his anger would have terrified her, but now she only thought how small he looked after Galatea. Varia stared at his baggy knees and dirty feet while he raged. The louder he shouted, the faster he tapped his toes. Varia forced herself to pay attention. What he said was true. They had trusted her to keep Adriel safe. She had left him alone and unprotected. She hadn't been there when he woke up, panicked at finding himself alone, and tried to climb out the window, "just yuk Vawa". She winced at that; apparently she'd been more careless than she thought.

Dad stalked to the window and slammed his hand against the shutter. The reeds buckled. He ignored them. "What if Adriel had tried to climb out again and cut himself even worse? What if he fell out and broke his neck? What if that thing found him alone out there?" Varia didn't try to defend herself. There was no point until Dad had used up his anger.

"Just because you have a grown-up body, it doesn't mean you're grown up inside." Dad paced back and forth. "You've acted like a child, so I'm going to deal with you as a child. Someone else will watch Adriel. You will spend your time where we can keep an eye on you. At night the doors and windows will be barred. If you need to use the outhouse, I'll go with you."

"Dad, no!" How was she going to fly away with Galatea?

"Yes." Dad's cheeks were flushed above his greying beard, but his hands had relaxed. He took a deep breath. "What I don't understand is why you left the settlement at all. The woods are dangerous enough as they are — I thought you'd learned that lesson. And now there's worse out there. What could possibly make you go out there alone, not knowing what you might run into?" He sighed hard and plunked down beside her, worn out. "We don't want to lose you any more than Adriel." His shoulders hunched forward and his hands lay limp in his lap.

Varia ran her fingers over the blue veins that ridged the thin skin on his hands. "That's just it, Dad. I want to find what we've lost."

"You weren't looking for the lander! It can't be within walking distance or we would have found it already."

"No, I wasn't." Varia shifted on the mat and looked over at Dad's lined face. "But I'm going to."

Dad tossed up his hands and sputtered.

"I know it's far away. I also know what the animal is, and in spite of what that star child says, it isn't dangerous. It's my friend." She looked out the window. "You probably won't believe me, but it's true."

Dad frowned, but he looked more puzzled than angry.

Varia put her arm around his bony shoulders and leaned her head against his cheek. "Come with me, and I'll show you. She won't mind; she said I could bring a friend." Dad hesitated. "It's not a long walk, and it's safe, honest. I've been there lots of times."

Dad looked at her sharply. Varia pulled her arm back and met his gaze. He had to find out eventually.

"All right," Dad said finally.

Sidran watched them go from the trailhead. Varia gave him an "I wish it was you but I can't help it" look as she led Dad away. Dad followed close behind her; he hadn't been in the woods since her rescue. As they walked, she told her dragon story one more time — minus the star child's warnings. When they reached the small pool, she explained how Galatea farmed her bees and that the star child was trying to stop her.

"Why does the star child think the dragon is dangerous if it isn't?" asked Dad.

Varia shrugged. "It doesn't know Galatea like I do." Dad didn't look reassured.

By the time they reached the clearing, Dad was pale and sweaty. He stood at the edge of the clearing staring at the giant flowers and bees.

"Aren't they pretty?" Varia inhaled their fragrance and guided Dad around the pool. "You can sit over here by the spring. It's nice and cool. And it's running water, so you can drink it."

Dad sat down. He put his hand over his nose and stared at the boulders as if he expected flames to come leaping out from them.

Varia gave him a hug. "I'll go into the cave and get Galatea. Don't worry! She's big, but gentle."

Varia peered inside the cave opening. "Galatea? I brought you a visitor." Maybe she was shy and hiding behind one of the boulders. Varia scrambled up onto one. "Galatea?" Of all the rotten luck. Of course she wasn't here. She was away at the flower pools eating her supper. Varia trudged back down. At least she could show Dad the skeleton.

Dad sat by the spring, splashing water over his hair. He wiped off his mouth and stood up as she returned. "That's better," he said. "I'm ready to meet your dragon."

"She's gone for supper. But you can see the cave."

Dad examined the stalactites, touched the smooth walls, and rubbed his fingers over the sooty smudges. Now that he knew Galatea wasn't here, he was much more relaxed.

"Here's the pool with the skeleton of her mother." Dad bent over to look in. Too late, Varia remembered the ring. She held her breath.

"Skeleton?"

Varia peered in beside him. "Right — well, they were there." The skeleton was gone. A few small bone fragments lay scattered across the bottom. Even the rainbow scales that usually bobbed at the water's edge were gone. So was the ring.

"Sticks," said Dad. He stood up. His cheeks were red again. "Sticks in a pool." He looked around the cave. "The only things I see are ours — our sack, our dried carrots, one of our blankets. Taken without asking, I assume." He raised his eyebrows. "It's a nice cave, Varia, but I don't see any dragon."

"She's just gone somewhere." Why had Galatea emptied out the pool?

Dad's eyes softened. "You really believe in this dragon, don't you?" He put his arm around her shoulders. She tried to pull away, but he held her firmly. "I know you've been upset about the changes in Mom and the others. And about losing Connie. It's hard on all of us to be separated and not know what happened." He turned her to face him. She looked away. "Sometimes when we really want something, we can deceive ourselves into thinking that we have it. I think you made up this dragon, made yourself believe in it, so you would have a place you can be happy. A friend to take Connie's place."

"I didn't make her up," Varia protested as Dad gathered up the things and put them back in the sack. Sometimes it was annoying having a psychologist for a father. "She's just gone to find more bees because there aren't enough here." A column of bees trundled down the boulder as they left the cave. "She eats a lot of them."

"Interesting specimens," Dad remarked. "Gretel would love to examine one of these." He led Varia up the hill, panting by the time he got to the top. "Listen to me, Varia. Substituting a fairy tale for a friend isn't going to solve any of your problems. We have to deal with life as it comes to us. Right now, we have no way to look for the lander. Right now, your mother is happy as she is. Things may change, but for now we have to accept that."

"I'm going to find the lander."

"We can't."

"Galatea will fly me . . . " It was no use. How could she convince him? She could take him to another dragon pool. But if Galatea wasn't there either, what would that prove?

"You are a very lucky girl," Dad said as they passed the small pool on the hill. He peered into the trees as they walked. Varia rolled her eyes. "Lucky that I found out about this game and put a stop to it before anything happened to you. Lucky you didn't run into that beast."

"Galatea isn't a beast," Varia muttered. She didn't feel one bit lucky. She wasn't going to let Dad get away with this. She would get away, and find the lander, and fly back to the settlement with Connie on Galatea's back. Then he would believe her.

"Funny you should use the name Galatea," Dad mused as they passed the sticky tree.

"It suits her. She's beautiful and alive, just like that statue in the story." Varia squashed a mushroom into the ground with her bare heel.

"It is a fitting name." Dad ignored her surliness. "Pygmalion willed his statue to life, just like you did this imaginary dragon." He turned around on the narrow trail so she had to look at him. "But after the statue Galatea came to life, Pygmalion discovered that she had her own will, and he couldn't control her any more."

He put his hand on her shoulder, and she winced. Would Dad believe her if she showed him the silver growth that was now as big as her palm? No. He would tell Mom and they would watch her even more closely. "Varia, don't let an imaginary dragon control you. Inventing dragons will not help you get through life." He turned back to the trail. "You'll feel better after supper. We'll talk then."

"I'm not hungry," Varia announced when they reached the sleeping hut. "I'm going to lie down."

Dad gripped her arm firmly. "Oh no, you don't. I'm not letting you out of my sight until you give up this fantasy. It's far too dangerous." He steered her toward the kitchen. Varia shook his hand off. She wasn't a toddler that needed to be dragged along by her father. They stared at each other for a moment, both of them surprised by her strength. Then Varia tossed her head and stalked to the kitchen. In spite of her anger, she was ravenous.

They took their usual places across from Mom. Varia refused to look at anyone, even Adriel, whose forehead was now smeared with sap, or Sidran, who was strangely silent throughout the meal. Varia focused on eating and ignored all attempts to draw her into conversation.

"I'll tell you later," she heard Dad whisper to Mom.

After supper, Dad walked her to the outhouse, then the sleeping hut. The others watched in silence. Humiliation smouldered inside her. How could Dad do this to her? She lay down on her mat without changing into her nightgown and covered her head with her blanket. Dad went outside, and Varia heard banging sounds outside the window. Dad was serious about keeping her in jail if he was using up their few remaining nails. She hurled her pillow at the barred window and watched it slump to the floor.

The eggshell was still in her pocket. Its metallic odour was the most welcome smell in the world. Maybe Dad would believe her if she showed him the eggshell. She turned it so she could see through it and put it to her eye to watch the rainbows dance. Even in the dim light that seeped in around the now barred window, it cast starry rainbows onto all four walls of the little room. But to his eyes it would look like nothing more than a pretty stone, and since it was a new specimen, he would take it away from her and give it to Nara. She put the eggshell in her pocket, retrieved her pillow, and lay down again. She would have to escape and hope Galatea would be at the cave when she got there.

Dad finished hammering and came back in. Mom arrived shortly afterward to put Adriel to bed. Varia lay with her back to them, feigning asleep. Mom lay down with Adriel until he nodded off, and Dad lay on his mat, waiting. Then he told Mom everything. His version of everything. Varia fumed silently, staring at the dark wall.

"What if she's not making it up?" Mom asked when Dad was done. This was unexpected. Varia had been sure Mom would believe whatever Dad said.

"Of course she is. I was there. There's no dragon."

"There's something dangerous in the forest," said Mom. "You've seen that growth on Varia's ear, and how big she's getting. It could have something to do with a dragon."

"Dragons aren't real."

"Not on Earth. We don't know much about this planet."

"Bulrushes!" Dad exclaimed. It turned into a frustrated cough. Varia smiled in spite of herself. Dad was having a hard time with this unreasonable planet. First it gave him an alien that claimed to be a constellation, then the shrinking, and now a dragon.

Dad stood up. "Well, I don't believe it." The door opened and closed.

Varia heard Mom change her clothes and lie down again. She heard other people slip in quietly and walk to their mats. Dad stumbled in late. She heard him drop the bar into the holders someone had nailed on both sides of the door. Keeping an imaginary threat out, keeping her in. But she wouldn't be a prisoner forever. She would escape to Galatea — the split second the opportunity arose.

As it turned out, she hardly had to wait at all. The grey predawn light was shimmering around the edges of the shuttered window when she next opened her eyes. Dad coughed on his mat. Varia heard someone lift off the bar and open and close the door. Mom. Adriel was asleep, curled up in the warm place Mom had just left. Dad coughed again and adjusted his blanket, but didn't open his eyes. This was it. Varia grabbed her sweater, stepped over Dad, and slipped out the door. She was free!

Galatea was not at the cave. Varia forced the sweater on and lay down on top of the boulder to wait for Galatea. She couldn't wait too long; when Dad woke up, he would come looking for her. Mom would tell the star child what had happened, and it would confirm that the beast was her dragon. All the settlers would come after them with their weapons.

Black silhouettes of trees surrounded her like a host of lonely skeletons. The stars were fading, and the clouds made lilac streaks across the deep blue sky. A few wispy clouds high overhead shone bright pink. She wondered if Galatea ever watched the sun rise from this rock.

Her stomach growled, and she remembered that she'd be missing breakfast. Dad had taken back the sack with the carrots and grain, and she hadn't had time to bring food. But there was water in the spring. As she knelt to drink, she saw the ring.

It must have fallen off the mother's bones when Galatea carried them off. At least one thing was going right. She picked it out of the bubbling water and slipped it onto her finger before she drank. Mom must have had small fingers, even as an adult, because Varia's little finger was the only one small enough for it. The water wasn't as cold as she would have liked, but it tasted good. She returned to the hill. *Please come, Galatea. I'm moolor here all by myself.*

The clouds stretched across the sky like a brilliant pink flag. A tiny black dot glided slowly across one of them. The dot came closer. It sprouted wings and a head, and as the rays from the rising sun brushed over it, it grew a rainbow aura. Varia leapt to her feet and waved.

Galatea circled the clearing. She looped in huge, lazy spirals, and zigzagged high above the trees. As Varia watched with her hands over her mouth, Galatea folded her wings and plummeted. The instant before she crashed into the rocks, she opened her wings and floated lightly to a stop in front of Varia. Galatea knelt down. "Come floi."

Chapter 19

VARIA CLIMBED BREATHLESSLY ONTO GALATEA'S BACK. The dragon was even bigger than yesterday. *So am I,* Varia noticed as she pressed her toes into the ridges between Galatea's scales and swung her leg up. The old, man-sized clothes that Mom had given her only days ago sat well above her wrists and ankles. And the sweater was so tight it was hard to move her arms.

She settled into the hollow of Galatea's back. The hard ridges on her scales pressed into Varia's skin, and she wiggled to find a comfortable position. Breathing rapidly, she pressed her knees into Galatea's sides and clasped the dragon's shoulders. "Ready."

Galatea unfolded her wings and leapt into the air. Varia felt the air flowing past her in waves as Galatea pumped them into the sky. The muscles on her back bunched and straightened under Varia's hands. "Oi hov a prosont for you!" Galatea called as they rose up.

"What is it?" Varia cried into the wind. She couldn't imagine what Galatea would have to give her. Galatea banked left and Varia slid sideways. "Aaaah!"

"Oi show you. Stop squeezing moi nock!"

Varia forced her hands to relax. It was exhilarating, but scarier than she could have imagined, riding on Galatea's back. The trees looked like potato plants, and her ears felt like they were filled with fluff. Galatea swerved back and forth, and Varia's stomach swerved with her. "Please don't do any loops," she begged through a mouthful of hair. Galatea's chuckle rumbled against Varia's clenched knees.

The dragon flew higher and higher, until the trees looked like shoots of weaving grass. It was cold this high up. Varia wished she had a blanket to sit on, to shield her from Galatea's cold scales, and mitts for her stiff fingers, and something to cover her ears. The emerald was beautiful in the sunlight though — almost as sparkly as Galatea's scales.

"Droizu pools," Galatea pointed. Varia squinted through the cold wind. Black, yellow-ringed buttons dotted the ground far, far below them. "And new droizu pools." Those were the grey ones without the yellow rings. There were also dark circles inside patches of green. Those were the pools Galatea hadn't transformed yet. Breathing the cold air dried Varia's throat. She looked hard for dark ribbons that were streams, but didn't see any. Maybe they were too narrow to be seen from so high up. Or maybe she couldn't see them because the wind in her face made her eyes blur with tears. She didn't dare take her hand off Galatea's back to wipe them.

"What's that?" Varia asked. Ahead of them lay a vast, sparkling circle.

"Loik. Moid boi da purokoot," Galatea growled. She banked right and down. Varia dug her heels into Galatea's side and leaned forward so she could hold on with her elbows too. Her stomach flipped and her ears popped. She squinted over Galatea's shoulder. If the purokoot was Draco, he must be enormous to make that huge, perfectly round lake. Or maybe the purokoot was a comet or a meteor.

The far side of the lake was rimmed with yellow, while the near side appeared to be covered by a dense, white fog. A ridge of grey around the lake trailed into the forest on the yellow side, giving the whole area the shape of a teardrop. As they came closer, the yellow resolved into sweet-smelling droizu. "A hundred dragons could eat at this lake," breathed Varia.

"Purokoot destroy drogons; purokoot keep drogons aloiv," said Galatea in a flat voice.

This was puzzling. It was clear how Draco or a comet could kill if it smashed into the Kettle. But how could either of them make the droizu and the bees grow big to feed a solitary dragon? Did Draco have the power to make things grow? The star child only made things smaller.

The white fog became clumps of bobbing, white balls. "Fluff plants!" Varia exclaimed.

"Droizu not grow in floff," Galatea muttered. It was true. Where the white met the yellow, the flowers drooped.

So the star child's fluff plants and the dragon's flowers were also at war. That was strange. It made sense that if Draco was the purokoot, he would want to keep the dragon alive, but then why was the star child against Galatea? Weren't Draco and the star child partners?

Galatea swooped toward the water. The surface rippled in the morning breeze and glittered in the sunshine. Floating bees dotted the water near the yellow shoreline.

They zoomed over the water . Galatea picked bees in her teeth and gathered bunches of them in her claws. She pulled sharply upwards at the end of the lake, next to a purple tree with twisted limbs. Varia's stomach clenched. What was she going to eat, she wondered as they flew back over the forest. And drink?

After a while, the yellow rings in the trees disappeared. Varia realised that Galatea had just flown easily past the farthest point she had been able to reach on foot.

"Look at so much water," Galatea cried. "So mony bees we con grow! So mony bees for so mony drogons." She angled down to a new pool and dropped a cluster of bees into it.

Varia closed her eyes as Galatea flapped back up. "You don't have to swim in the pools? The bees transform them for you?"

"Yos." They swooped over another pool and Galatea dropped in another handful.

Varia tried to look for the lander while Galatea seeded two more pools. What would a lander look like from up here anyway? A glint in the trees? There would be houses and fields too, by now — if there was anything. It was hard to focus her eyes with all the rising and falling. She didn't remember feeling airsick on the lander. Maybe it was a good thing her stomach was empty.

At last Galatea touched down beside one of her established pools. Varia rolled stiffly off her back. She peeled off her sweater and clung to the solid, unmoving ground. Ignoring the smell of the dead plants, she stretched her cramped limbs.

Galatea flopped down beside her, her wings draped loosely over the ground. "Oi do what moi moder toll me. Now Oi floi far." Varia nodded without opening her eyes. "Oi sleep here lost noight," Galatea continued.

"I know," mumbled Varia, remembering her disastrous visit to the cave with Dad.

"Moi moder also toll me moik Waria a prosont."

"Mmm," said Varia, her eyes still closed. She still couldn't imagine what Galatea could give her. She hoped it wasn't the skeleton from the pool.

Galatea was very talkative after her long flight. "Waria come bock orly in da morning."

Varia opened her eyes and sat up. "I had to." She described Dad's visit, his reaction to the empty pool, and what happened afterwards. "So we can't stay in the cave," she concluded. "They'll come looking for us." With weapons, and the star child, she added silently. She didn't feel up to making Galatea angry by saying it out loud.

Galatea's eyes flickered. "We floi soon. But forst Oi give you da prosont." She walked to the pool and pulled something out of the water. "Now close da oiys. No look."

Varia covered her eyes with her hands. She heard Galatea shuffling towards her.

"You hov moi moder's rong!" The accusation came so suddenly that Varia jumped. She opened her eyes to Galatea's huge snout in front of her face. Galatea quickly hid something under her wing.

Varia held out her hand so Galatea would back up a little. "I found it in the spring by the cave. It must have fallen off your mother's wing when you carried her out."

"Oi not corry her out."

"But she wasn't in the pool . . . " Varia suddenly realised what Galatea had said. "No, Galatea. It's my mother's ring."

"Moi moder woring da rong in da pool."

"Only because I brought it to the cave by mistake when I hatched you."

Galatea's eyes took on a yellow glint. "Moi moder loft da rong for me. Oi foind da rong when I hotch. I goiv da rong bock to moi moder."

That wasn't right at all. Varia remembered clearly how the tiny Galatea had dropped the ring when Varia gave her a piece of carrot, then knocked it into the water when she fell in. She hadn't even known her mother was in the pool yet. She still thought Varia was her mother. But Galatea's eyes were narrow and orange, and her breaths came hot and fast. Varia thought quickly.

"I took the ring to keep it safe. If I'd left it at the cave, my Dad would have found it when he came looking for me, and taken it away." Maybe she should have left it there for them to find when they came looking for her now. She put her hand beside Galatea's. "Besides, it won't fit your finger." Not even on the small, withered one she had burned in the pool the star child had tampered with.

"Yos." Galatea looked at their hands side by side. "Da rong too small. Waria will wore da small rong." She flicked her tail. "Now stond and close oiys. Oi hov da prosont."

Varia got to her feet and closed her eyes. The tip of Galatea's snout slid under her shirt and over her stomach. Varia jumped away. "What are you doing?" She glared at Galatea.

Galatea pulled back. "Oi toik off da short." A sharp claw scraped up Varia's side.

"Ouch!" Now she'd get another shiny spot — or maybe they only came from bites. She grabbed Galatea's wrist in her two hands. The yellow-brown claws hovered in front of her. One had a red tip. "I'll take it off."

Galatea sat back on her haunches, watching. Varia undid the ties behind her neck. "Why do I need to take off my shirt?"

"For da prosont."

"Can't it go over my shirt?"

Galatea considered the question. "Not go over da short."

"It won't fit?"

"Won't fot."

So it was something to wear next to her skin. "Do you have to stand there and watch me?" she asked. It sounded silly as soon as she said it. Galatea was a dragon, and a girl dragon at that. It wasn't like Sidran was watching her. Why should Galatea think anything of seeing her undressed? Galatea never wore clothes and Varia looked at her all the time. "Never mind. Stay there." Still, she felt daring. She'd had lots of baths in the same room as her parents when she was younger, but not since her body had grown up, and never in front of her friends.

She pulled the shirt over her head. The hot sun warmed the silver patch on her shoulder, and a prying breeze explored her bare skin. Galatea's gazed at her through deep purple eyes.

"Close oiys."

Varia's eyes trembled but she forced them shut. Galatea's musty smell came closer. Something scratchy slid over Varia's head onto her shoulders.

"That prickles."

Galatea's claw rested for a moment on Varia's silver patch. She made a raspy noise in her throat. Then she took Varia's hand and pushed it through a hole in the prickly thing.

"It feels like it's grabbing my back."

"Now da oder orm." Galatea slid her other hand through what must be the other armhole.

Cold prickles cascaded to Varia's waist. Galatea gripped her tightly under the arms and pressed her hands down Varia's body. Varia squealed.

Galatea let go. "Open oiys."

Varia looked down. "Dragon scales," she breathed. The glittering vest curved snugly around her body from the high neck to the scalloped waistline. It was hot to the touch but cool against her skin, and it moved with her, tickling, as she stretched and twisted. Shards of Galatea's eggshell glittered along the bottom edge. "How did you make this?" she asked.

Galatea was beaming. "Oi toik da scoils off da pools and Oi . . . moik it." She threaded her fingers together. "Oi work a long toim."

"The scales link together." Varia examined the vest. Each scale hooked onto two above and two below. Galatea must have made the holes with her claws. "This is so beautiful! And that's why there were no scales on the cave pool yesterday. Or eggshell." She moved her shoulders to watch the vest sparkle. The ring sparkled in front of it. "If Dad could see this, he'd believe me for sure."

Varia ran her hands over her stomach. "Could we show him? Could we fly into the settlement and show everyone?" It made perfect sense — and she could get some food and water. "If we fly in, the star child won't be able to stop us, and if I'm riding on your back and wearing this beautiful vest, they'll know you're not dangerous. Maybe Dad will even agree to come with us while we search. You can carry two of us, can't you?"

Galatea shuffled back to the pool and rummaged under the water. "Yos." She pulled something out of the water and held it up. It was another piece of her eggshell. "Da lost one."

Varia dug in her pocket. "Second last. I took a piece when you hatched." Galatea looked surprised, but not angry. "I kept it safe," she added, just in case. She took the piece from Galatea. "Here, I'll show you something. Lower your head." Galatea did, and Varia held the inside curves of the two shell pieces in front of Galatea's eyes. "What do you see?"

Galatea peered through the eggshells. "Oi see Waria."

"Don't I look different? Look at the sparkly vest."

Galatea looked again. "You look loik Waria."

Varia put the pieces up to her own eyes. "Everything looks different when I look through them. All sparkles and rainbows."

Galatea's voice was husky. "Now you see loik a drogon."

Varia arranged the two pieces side by side on her palm. She'd seen pictures of people wearing pieces of glass in front of their eyes, held on by stiff frames that rested on their noses and hooked over their ears. "If you make holes in them here and here, and if I pull some grass out of my shirt . . . " Galatea set to work boring holes in the shell fragments with her claw while Varia undid the bottom edge of the grass shirt and freed three strands. "There," she said a few minutes later, tying a knot behind her head. "Dragon eyes."

The dragon eyes probably weren't as comfortable as the eyeglasses in the pictures. The eggshell lenses rubbed against her eyelashes, and a piece of grass stuck stubbornly across one eye. The effect was spectacular anyway.

Flowers glowed against a background of dull green leaves. The shimmering pool looked luxuriously soft. Galatea became as brilliant as a many-coloured sun. Rainbows flashed from her body like lightning and surrounded her with colour. Varia covered her eyes with her hands. Sidran and Adriel would love this. She might leave it with them until they returned, if Galatea didn't mind.

Galatea cackled softly. "How is da prockles?" she asked.

Varia twisted and stretched. The prickles were gone. "It's almost like wearing nothing at all," she said. Her stomach rumbled. Nothing outside, nothing inside.

"Good," said Galatea. She turned brusquely to the flowers. "Waria come eat. Den we go." She skewered a bee and held it out.

Varia gulped. "I don't eat bees." But hunger clawed at her, and her throat was parched. She was far too hungry — and thirsty — to wait until they returned to the settlement. Far too weak to fly again with nothing inside her. She looked around.

Droizu, withered leaves, oily pool water, and Galatea's bees. "What am I going to eat?"

Galatea pushed the bee into her hand. "Eat bee."

Varia watched its black legs wiggle against her palm. "I'm so hungry I almost could."

Chapter 20

THE BEES HAD ALWAYS LOOKED ALIEN and creepy to Varia, with their bulging eyes, whiskered legs, furry body segments, and drooping honey sacs. "But I've never really looked at them closely before," she thought now, studying the one in her hand through her eggshell spectacles. Its soft, round body made her think of those wonderful strawberry turnovers they used to eat on the spaceship. The sticky nectar glistened like syrup, and its thin legs looked like slivered almonds. She could almost taste the turnover, tender and sweet and gooey. Her mouth watered.

She bit off the bee's abdomen. It was crunchy and gooey, sweet and flowery. She licked off the soft filling that was dripping down her hand, and bit off more. Mmm. The legs were no problem. It was easy to flick them out of her teeth with her tongue. She snagged another one when she was done, then another. Soon she was snapping up bees as quickly as Galatea had ever done. She would take one with her when they went to get Dad, she decided. He would find it a welcome change from barley bread and pea soup!

Now that her stomach was full, she brimmed with energy. She could easily look at her brilliant companion, crouched in the glittering water, drinking. Varia watched her, full but still desperately thirsty.

Galatea lumbered over. She picked up Varia and plunked her in the pool. "Waria drink."

Varia laughed. What did that star child know anyway? She gulped out of cupped hands. The warm metallic liquid flowed into every nook of her body, as if it was coating her all over on the inside. The sun's rays that moments earlier had felt too hot, now felt pleasantly warm.

Varia stood up. She felt strong and capable. She had flown on the back of her own dragon, the one that she herself had found, hatched, and raised. She had made a plan and carried it out, through cold and imprisonment and hunger. All that remained was the final step. "Let's go get my dad and find the lander, Galatea."

Galatea burped. "Soon." She disappeared into the bushes.

Good idea, thought Varia, slipping behind a bush on the other side of the pool. With no outhouse, you made do. I need my clothes, she remembered when she returned to the clearing. She would just carry them with her and brave the high, cold air in her new vest, so everyone would see Galatea's lovely present when she flew in. Oh yes — and a bee as Galatea's present to the settlers, so they would see that Galatea was in every way the equal of the star child. She snagged two for good measure, and wrapped them in her shirt.

Galatea returned and Varia climbed up. It more felt natural this time, sitting high on Galatea's scaly back. Sidran would be awestruck when they arrived. Maybe there'd be time for Galatea to give him a short ride before they left on their quest. "Ready!"

Galatea leapt into the air. The wind buoyed them up. Goosebumps rose on Varia's bare arms, but inside the vest she was warm. Her stomach stayed steady this time, and she could see clearly through the dragon lenses. In a short time, they were over the cave clearing. The gravel strip with its series of glittering flower pools was clearly visible snaking through the trees. Varia followed it with her eyes. "Your cave valley connects with that big lake." It was just visible in the distance.

"Moi coiv join Purokoot Loik," Galatea agreed.

In a few more flaps, they were over the settlement. Varia's stomach clenched again, this time from nerves. What if her people didn't like Galatea? What if they were frightened and attacked her even though Varia was sitting on her back? What if Dad refused to come?

"Land in the clearing." Galatea touched down, and Varia hopped to the ground.

"That's odd," Varia said. "No one is outside, and the shutters are all closed." Was everyone hiding? "You stay here for now," she decided. "I'll find Dad." She put down her shirt and sweater and walked to the sleeping hut, looking around uneasily. How run-down and dingy everything looked. The buildings were no more than rusty lean-tos, and even the crops looked scrawny and tired.

Something smelled strange inside the sleeping hut. Familiar too, but she couldn't place it. Someone — a girl, judging by the way her long hair was braided — lay curled up on a mat, sobbing quietly. She looked up when Varia entered. Her wet face was pale and pudgy, and her features blended into her skin as if she were wearing a clay mask. Her body looked . . . juicy, and full of bones.

Varia forced herself to focus. "What's wrong here?" she demanded. "Where is everyone?" Who was she speaking to?

"Hiding." It was Mom's voice. Why did she look so strange? The girl with Mom's voice wiped her eyes and stood up. "What's that on your face?"

Oh, the dragon eyes. That was why Mom looked so funny. "A present from my dragon," said Varia. "I'll take it off." She worked on the knot behind her head. "Why do you sound so frightened? You don't have to hide from Galatea." Mom choked back a sob.

Varia pulled the dragon eyes down like a necklace. She froze. Mom looked just about the same. Not quite as pale, maybe, but just as flat. Except for her wide eyes. Was losing your face the next stage in shrinking? "Where's Dad?"

"In there. But you don't want to — "

Varia pushed past the curtain, and the smell got stronger. It brought memories of sweat and dirt and horrible sickness . . . and something else too. She hardly recognised the man that lay thrashing on the mat. He too was pale and pasty, and his breathing was ragged. His curly black hair and beard straggled across his featureless face — featureless except for a scattering of shiny spots. Only his wildly staring eyes looked familiar. Varia's breaths came fast. She looked at Mom and then back at Dad. He didn't drink star water. Why had he lost his face? And what were those spots?

Dad coughed a deep, racking cough. "Ants!" he cried hoarsely, slapping at his body. "Get them off!" He kicked off the blanket. A chill crackled through Varia's body. Dad's foot was black.

"Dry rot," said Mom, behind her. "The circulation in his foot is cut off. He'll lose it soon."

"Like Reyk and Thora," Varia gasped. "How did this happen?"

Mom eyes were like steel. "You tell me. You took him into the woods."

Varia's mind raced. She vaguely remembered hearing Dad cough early this morning, but she'd been in too much of a hurry to look at him. And why should she have? He coughed all the time. She looked helplessly at pale, tiny Mom. "We didn't eat anything or touch any strange plants or go anywhere I haven't been."

She looked back at Dad. Her eyes prickled. He looked so fragile. And so precious. His eyes were closed again, and he lay shivering under the fluff blanket Mom had made for her when she was sick. She reached down and pulled the blanket back over his foot. The ring flashed on her finger. She needed to give it back.

"It's because of your dragon."

Varia whirled around. "It can't be! She wasn't even there." She tugged at the ring. It stuck at her knuckle.

Tears rolled down Mom's clay cheeks. She turned and left the curtained room. Varia took another helpless look at Dad, then followed her.

"That shiny vest you're wearing. What is it made of?" Mom asked.

"Dragon scales. Galatea made it for me." She tugged again at the ring. It was stuck.

"It smells like Dad's breath smelled this morning when he woke up delirious." She paused. "And his spots look like the ones on your ear."

"How can you even smell it in this stuffy hut?" Varia flung open the door. Her hand trembled on the handle. Mom was right. The unfamiliar smell in the room was something metallic. She stared at the splintery door. "The dragon wasn't there. You said Reyk and Thora's disease was caused by a fungus. Galatea isn't a fungus. Maybe Dad got sick from eating our food. He hasn't been well for a long time." But what about that smell? Her mind raced in circles. "Dad never even saw Galatea," she repeated. She glanced into the clearing, and stiffened. "Stop!" She raced outside.

Galatea stood on her hind legs in the clearing, hissing, surrounded by a circle of white-faced little people pointing crooked spears at her. "Stop!" Varia shouted again. She pushed her way between two spears and stood in front of Galatea. The dragon's breaths were hot and sharp above her. She blinked her eyes hard. Why couldn't she recognise anyone in this smattering of featureless faces?

"Put the spears down," she commanded. "Galatea is my friend, and she's not dangerous. Unless you scare her." That red-haired one must be Samuel. Or Sidran. No, Sidran must be the other one, holding his spear point down by his foot. At least he still believed her. She smiled gratefully at him. His face changed, but she couldn't tell if it was a smile or not. A few spears went down.

"I found her egg," said Varia, "and I hatched her. She was tiny enough to fit in my hands." A few more spears went down. Out of the corner of her eye, she could see Galatea scratching her belly.

"What made your dad sick?" someone asked.

Varia looked around helplessly. It would be so nice to know who she was talking to. "I don't know," she stammered. "I've been with Galatea many times, and I'm not sick."

"Why did you bring it here?" someone asked.

"We came . . . to get Dad," Varia said. "We're going to look for the other londer."

"What's a londer?"

Varia gritted her teeth. "The lander. Galatea was going to take me and Dad up to look for it." The rest of the spears went down. "But now with Dad so sick, I don't know." She looked up at Galatea. Galatea looked back at her. "Maybe we should stay here and help Mom look after him." But what about that smell in Dad's sickroom?

"What's that?" Someone yelped, and the closer people jumped back.

Varia looked down. One of the fat bees was crawling out of her shirt. She grabbed it and held it up. "It's a giant bee. Galatea farms these, which is why she doesn't eat people — and why she isn't dangerous." Something splatted onto her shoulder. She looked up. Galatea was drooling.

"May I see the bee?" someone asked.

That was a voice Varia recognised. It was Gretel, standing next to Sidran. But her face was a clay mask too. Didn't they notice what was happening to them? Varia held out the bee. "You can eat them. They're good. They taste like — "

It wasn't Gretel's hand that took the bee. It was the star child's. Its face had changed too. Its whole body had. Its stars were swirling vortexes, angry black holes waiting to suck her in. She backed away.

The star child snatched the bee out of Varia's hand. "LEAVE! NOW!" Its voices clanged into her skull. The bee burst into flame and collapsed into a handful of black ash.

Galatea snarled. She snagged Varia's hair and pulled her back. "Floi!" Varia grabbed her shirt and flung herself up onto Galatea's back. Her sweater was still on the ground, but there was no time to get it. The other bee tumbled out. The star child squashed it with its foot.

Galatea opened her wings and leapt upward. The star child stood in front of the crowd, blazing like a bonfire. Varia couldn't even see the little people cowering behind it any more. She hunched down behind Galatea's head to shield herself from the heat.

The dragon's belly churned between her legs. Caraahm-nop! Varia hooked her knees on tight and braced herself. Galatea's body swelled beneath her. Then it deflated all at once. A wall of flame gusted out. Galatea's body jerked backwards, and Varia held on by her fingernails as Galatea twisted in the air and flapped away.

Below them, the settlers scattered. The star child bobbed toward the trailhead and into the trees.

"It ron awoy," sneered Galatea. She angled downwards and Varia squinted over her shoulder.

Far below them, darting among the trees, was an eerie, pulsating light. Galatea raised her hand to her mouth. She swallowed, and dove.

Chapter 21

LEAFY BRANCHES ROSE UP TO MEET them. Varia closed her eyes against the wind and concentrated on clinging to Galatea's ballooning sides. She shoved her head into Galatea's neck and held on with her teeth to keep from sliding off. Just in time, Galatea hurled out her fire and angled back up. Below them, flames sputtered in wet branches, then died in smoke.

Varia sat up and felt her heart hammering her stomach back down where it belonged. Galatea grunted and banked right. Varia leaned left. She was getting the hang of this riding. All her senses were on high alert. She'd never felt so alive. "I bet that scared it!" she cried.

A gust of wind came out of nowhere and knocked them sideways. Through her hair, she saw a dark grey cloud rising over Purokoot Lake. The trees beneath them leaned to one side. The star child's light pulsed between the leaves.

Galatea steadied her course, tossed another caraahm-nop into her mouth, and dove again. Varia laughed as the trees speared the air around them and the flames licked their feet. Galatea tried to level out again, but the wind knocked them around like a leaf.

Once more, the light pulsed in the distance. Varia squinted through the wind. "It's heading for the floff field!" She wished the dragon eyes were tied on her face instead of flapping around her neck.

Galatea bucked her way forward. Varia huddled close to her neck and hung on. Galatea swooped low over the trees and followed the fleeing light into the fluff field, where it bobbed in and out of sight among the white balls.

Why are we doing this? Varia wondered suddenly. They had already driven the star child away from the settlement. But then she remembered blank faces, a wrecked dragon pool, and the star child's blind hatred of both her and Galatea. Dad was no friend of the star child either. Maybe that was why he sick. Fear, then anger churned her stomach.

"Dere it is." Varia pointed at the edge of the lake, and Galatea swerved, swallowing a caraahm-nop as she turned. The star child's flaming vortices swirled faster as they gained on it. Varia's shirt blew out of her hand and wrapped itself around her foot. She ignored it and concentrated on Galatea's boiling belly.

Flames flashed. The fluff plants' dry heads flared up. The wind stirred the flames and in a second the whole white side of the lake was ablaze. Varia lifted her feet, and her grass shirt fell into the flames as Galatea flapped away.

No eerie, pulsating light rose through the smoke into the darkening sky. Varia's hand trembled on Galatea's scales. They'd done it. They'd destroyed the star child. Mom and Sidran would be really upset now. She set her mouth. We're going to find the lander. Then they'll be glad. All the same, she watched the flames over her shoulder. Just in case.

The wind buffeted them as they fled. Clouds rose like night behind them. Varia shivered. Rain was coming, and both her shirt and sweater were lost.

Galatea touched down beside one of her pools and began stuffing herself with bees before Varia even got off. Varia rolled off her back. It was warmer down here, and the trees gave some shelter from the wind. She rubbed her arms with her stiff fingers. The ring felt icy on her skin.

Varia cupped her hands and drank, then snagged a bee and went to sit under a tree. She bit off the head and chewed it while she thought. So much had happened. Was it only last night that Dad had escorted her to the cave and then locked her in the hut? Was it only this morning she'd escaped? And now Dad was . . . she bit her lip. What on the Pot could have made him so sick? What if Mom couldn't make him well? Would he still be there when she got back?

"Galatea." Varia raised her voice to be heard above the churning leaves. "What do you know about plonts that make you sick?"

"Oi not eat plonts," Galatea mumbled through her bees.

"I know you don't. But my fader is very sick. He came back from da cave and woke up with black feet, like Reyk and Thora. They died. I want to holp my dad so he won't."

Galatea kept her back turned. "Oi not know how moik Wereeuh's fader not doi." Varia walked around her and looked into her face.

"Your moder saw our londer come to this planet. Did she see Reyk and Thora at your cave? Did she see what dey did?" Funny how she was talking like Galatea. She stretched her lips with her tongue.

Galatea swallowed her bee. She closed her eyes and rocked back and forth. "Moi moder see dem. Dey not see moi moder." Galatea opened her eyes.

"Did dey eat anything?" Varia prompted. She rubbed her jaw. It felt funny. Stiff. She must have had her teeth clenched while they chased the star child.

"Dey eat food from socks."

From socks? From sacks. Backpacks, probably, since they hadn't rotted away yet. "Nothing else? They didn't eat any plonts?"

"Not eat plonts." Galatea scratched her belly and stuffed three more bees into her mouth. "Dey dronk water."

That was something. "From the spring?"

"From da pool."

"The pool!" Dad had only drunk from the spring. She took another bite of her bee. What could be wrong with that? She'd drunk from it this morning. That was how she'd found the ring. Why hadn't Dad seen it, she wondered. It must have been there, because the skeleton was already gone, and Galatea hadn't returned to the cave until the next morning.

But Galatea said she hadn't moved the skeleton. What happened to it, then? Did it suddenly dissolve, and the ring fall off the wing-bone? But then how did it get to the spring? Varia stopped in mid bite. What if the water had carried it out of the pool through a hidden channel?

It made sense. The spring had to come from somewhere, and the cave pool was underground. Of course the spring came from the pool. Varia's heart thudded. Galatea bathed in the pool. Her mother's body dissolved in it. Varia's heart thudded. Dad had drunk dragon water. So had Reyk and Thora. She shuddered.

So had she.

"GALATEA!" The dragon turned around. Varia held her voice steady. "Why can I drink drogon water widout getting sick?"

Galatea opened her mouth in a toothy grin. She bent over so her enormous blue eyes looked straight into Varia's. "Waria is drogon."

Varia jerked up her hands. They looked the same as always.

"Scoils." Galatea poked her upper arm. Varia stared. The scales from the vest had attached themselves to the silver spot on her shoulder, and grown halfway to her elbow. She ran her hand up her neck. The scales had spread upwards and joined the spot on her ear. "More scoils." Galatea clawed at Varia's pants.

"Stop dat!" Varia screamed. "Leave my ponts alone!"

Galatea pulled her claws out of the fabric. "Da toil not loik ponts."

"Tail! I don't have a tail." But there it was — a small, pointed bump at the base of her spine.

Galatea skipped her tail over the pool, knocking over a swath of droizu. "Dronk. Drogon water moik you drogon."

"Dat's why you kept sploshing me." There were scales inside her pants too. She could feel the ridges through the cloth.

Galatea bowed her head. "Oi is moop your fader dronk da water. He need splosh forst, den dronk to moik drogon."

Galatea was apologising because Dad hadn't turned into a dragon? What kind of monster was she? "We don't want to be drogons!" wailed Varia.

"You be hoppy soster drogon," replied Galatea. "You loi oggs. We moik mony drogons. Den purokoot no hort us."

Wasn't the purokoot long gone? Lay eggs? "You moid a mistake," whispered Varia. "We're both girls. To make eggs that hotch, you need a girl and a boy."

Galatea scratched herself again and sat back on her haunches. "You is gorl," Galatea said calmly. "Oi is boy."

Varia's eyes widened. "You said you were a girl."

"Oi say Oi is loik moi moder."

"But a moder is — "

"Moi moder is girl and boy." Galatea's tail slapped the water and her eyes turned orange. "Da prosont of da purokoot."

How could a comet — or a star dragon — do that? It made no sense. But it made perfect sense that she was both. Otherwise, how could so many solitary dragon mothers have hatched eggs? Galatea was like those Earth lizards she had read about. But then why did she need Varia to help lay eggs?

Varia's lungs suddenly wouldn't hold air. She was turning into a dragon. That explained the shiny spots, her fast growth, her appalling interest in Adriel's blood, why everyone looked so strange, why she couldn't talk properly. She was going to mate with Galatea — and lay eggs. Her stomach lurched. She was going to be sick.

"I won't do it. I'm taking off this vest and going home. I'm sorry I ever hotched you!" She pulled the dragon glasses over her head and flung them into the bushes, then yanked up the bottom of her vest. But it didn't have a bottom any more. The scales were stuck to her skin — they were her skin. The eggshell pieces too. Frantic, she scratched at the scales until they bled.

Galatea stood silently, watching until she gave up. "Roin come," she said.

Small drops left dark marks on the dusty ground and on Varia's bare forearms. A big one hit her in the eye and rolled down her cheek.

"We stoy here," said Galatea. "You eat mony bees and dronk mony water. You grow fost now. When wongs come, you lorn to floi." She curled up in the clearing. "Now sleep."

The rain fell harder. Varia's hair dripped into her eyes. It must be dripping down her back too, but she couldn't feel it. She couldn't feel anything falling on her . . . scales. She shuddered. That's why Galatea could sleep out here in the clearing. Varia backed into the trees.

Galatea lifted one wing, making a little cave underneath it. "Waria come sleep?"

"Stay away from me." Varia backed into a tree. She moved over so her tail — her tail! wasn't poking the bark.

Galatea got up. Varia watched her through the rain, ready to bolt if she approached.

"It's not fair," she accused. "I hatched *you*. You're supposed to be *my* dragon."

Galatea yawned. She shrugged the water off her wings. "Oi go. "Oi come bock when you is drogon." She sprang into the air and vanished in the wet darkness.

Varia sat down and made herself small against the tree. Once again she was spending the night alone in the dark, rainy woods. Except this time no one would come looking for her in the morning to take her home. And if somehow they did find the missing lander, Connie wouldn't know who she was.

The rain fell harder until Varia couldn't see the pool. She stared into the darkness, running her fingers over her scales and feeling her tail twitch against the tree.

Chapter 22

In her dream, Varia flaps over the endless trees, following the light that is Connie. Again and again she dives; each time, Connie disappears. The light leads her to the settlement. Of course, she thinks. Where else would Connie be? She glides to a stop in the clearing — but the light isn't Connie. It's Galatea, huge and blinding. Connie hides behind the tower bars, clutching her kitten. Every way Varia turns, Galatea blocks her way.

Varia woke with icy feet. Her bed was soaking wet. She reached out and touched something hard and rough. Tree bark. Then she remembered. Slowly, she sat up.

Bits of leaves stuck to her. She picked them off. The scales hadn't spread much overnight. They were sticky, though, with clear, shiny stuff that rubbed off on her fingernail. She wiped it on her pants.

The sky was the colour of Mom's clay face. Varia's eyes filled with tears. Would she ever see Mom's real face again? Or Dad's? Or anyone's? Rain drummed on the leaves, the grey ground, the glittering flowers. Why hadn't she seen what Galatea was doing? The splashing, the bites, "Waria is moi ogg-loiing soster." How could she have been so stupid? Even the star child knew — well, it knew enough to tell her Galatea was dangerous.

More to the point, was there anything she could do to stop her transformation? What if she completely avoided dragon water? She could drink out of streams — there had to be some somewhere. A horrible thought seized her. Now that she was, at least in part, a dragon, wouldn't she turn regular water into dragon water just by touching it? And she had an uncomfortable feeling that the bees, which lived on the flowers that lived in the water, might have the same effect on her as dragon water anyway. No wonder the star child had incinerated the ones she brought before the others could touch them.

Her stomach rumbled, a painfully hollow canyon. It hurt another way too. She loosened the string at her waist and took a deep breath. Hesitantly, she slid her hand inside and felt for the tail. It was as wide as her thumb where it jutted out from her back, then curved down like a vine with a flattened end. She yanked her hand out and re-tied the pants lower down to make room for the tail. She'd seen a picture of a human skeleton with its slender, curved backbone made of bumpy, linked pieces. Hers must have added some new pieces. And grown new skin. New scales, actually. Baby scales, like Galatea's had been. But she had no doubt they would harden soon.

So it was really happening. She was going to be a dragon, and if Galatea had her way, her mate. No. She couldn't think of her beloved Galatea that way. That Galatea was gone. This was another dragon, an unfamiliar, malevolent male dragon: Galateor.

She felt light-headed. She needed food. But if she ate . . . She loped to the water. Enough thinking. If she didn't eat, she wouldn't be thinking anything soon.

The bees weren't out yet. She snarled. If she had to be a dragon, she might as well act like one. She ripped apart a clump of petals, buried her face in it and devoured the bees inside. All thought faded away as she ate her way around the pool. She didn't notice the scales creeping down to her elbows, or up to her chin, or the rain streaming down her broadening shoulders and thickening thighs. She didn't notice her lengthening jaw, or the changing light as the red sun slid up behind the low clouds.

Slowly, the rage in her stomach subsided. She closed her eyes and felt the wind on her face, the warm water lapping at her ankles. I belong to this place, Varia thought. To these sustaining flowers, this grey sky, these lush trees, this dancing water. She'd never felt that way before. The little, white-faced settlers with their limp cabbage leaves, sputtering tower, and rusty lean-tos were misfits, homeless vagabonds dropped out of the sky onto a planet that didn't want them.

She released a flower stalk and wiped the sticky pollen off one side of her mouth, then the other. The ring glittered on her finger. And yet they're my misfits, she thought. My parents, my brother, my community. Until now. Until I took my father and made him sick. Until I became a dragon. Suddenly the water smelled foul. Varia stepped out and huddled on the grey ground, her scaly arms wrapped around her legs.

What would she do while she waited for the changes to happen? Count the scales creeping across her arms, down her legs, and up her face? Feel her fingers and toes curl up and her nails thicken into claws? Practice flicking her tail? Scratch her itches?

Scratching didn't help. It only clogged her nails with slime. The rain didn't wash it off either, just rolled right over it. She knelt in the water and scrubbed wherever she could reach. An oily film spread around her, just like Galatea — Galateor's.

She couldn't reach her back; she'd rub it against a tree later. She walked around the pool to the cleaner side and cupped her hands to drink.

"Varia! Stop!"

Varia whirled around. Sidran!

Sidran sank to the ground, panting. "Don't drink that!" She stared at him. Either he'd shrunk in the last two days or she'd grown a lot. Or both. He looked so alien with his stringy red hair dripping down his blanked-out face. The only part that looked alive was his bright blue eyes.

Varia let the water slip out of her hands. "How did you foind me?"

"I sneaked out before dawn, like you did yesterday. I followed the trail to the sticky tree, then turned off like you described." A sack was tied around his waist. He worked at the knot while he talked. "I found the clearing with the boulders. I didn't know where to go from there, so I just walked down the valley until I saw a place where the bushes were all broken, and I followed them." He opened the sack and pulled out a handful of dried vegetables. "Want some?"

They looked like things she'd seen inside Adriel's diaper. "No thonks. I . . . already ate." She could still taste the sweet droizu nectar. But she couldn't offer any to Sidran. Do I look different? she wondered. Sidran was too busy munching on his food sticks to notice. She sat down facing him. Her tail jerked. She shifted so she wasn't sitting on it.

"It was a long walk," Sidran said through his food. "I've been drinking rain." He swallowed, then tilted his head back and opened the slit that was his mouth. He looked around. "So? Where's the dragon?" His eyes darted across Varia's scales.

She squirmed. "Gone."

"She abandoned you?" He kept staring.

"She — he'll be bock."

"Galatea's a he?"

Varia nodded and looked away. "Goloteor now. There's a lot I didn't know about drogons." She blinked her eyes hard. Sidran was so real and so close. And so, so far. She wanted to pick him up and hug him — something she'd never, ever wanted before. But she didn't know if it was safe even to touch him. Maybe dragon-hood was contagious. Or worse.

Sidran fiddled with his rope. "Your mom hasn't stopped crying since you left."

Varia twisted the ring on her finger. It was all she had left of Mom. It was all Mom had left of her mom too, come to think of it.

Sidran leaned toward her. "So. Was it the dragon that made your dad sick?"

Tears spilled out of Varia's eyes. She motioned to the pool. "Drogon water." She stretched her lips to make them work better, and spoke carefully. "Dragons swim in it. It comes out of the spring besoid the cave. If you drink it, you get sick, unless you've gotten wet with it a few toims forst." She couldn't speak properly even when she tried.

Sidran didn't answer right away. "Then you're immune and it doesn't hurt you?" he asked finally.

Varia's cheeks felt hot under the rain. "Then you torn into a drogon."

Sidran's eyes grew round. "Hopping marsh reeds," he murmured, getting to his feet and coming closer. "Do you mind?" he asked as he ran his finger down her shoulder.

Varia shrank back. "It might be contoigious."

Sidran pulled his finger away and wiped it on his shirt. "Are you going to grow wings and a tail too?"

"Yos," Varia snapped. "The wings come later. The toil . . . "
She stretched her lips again. "The tail has already storted."

Sidran gave a low whistle. "I guess now we know who's right."

Varia nodded. She picked a grey leaf and smeared it between her fingers.

Sidran paced. "They're working on bigger weapons, now that they know what the animal is. Especially now that your dad . . . " He looked away.

"I didn't mean to hort him," sobbed Varia. "I didn't know. I didn't!" She wiped her eyes on her prickly arm. She felt so, so... moop.

"I believe you," said Sidran. "That's why I came. Your mom doesn't know how to cure him. I thought maybe we could figure out how."

"I don't know," whispered Varia. "Goloteor didn't tell me, if he even knows."

"Then think!" prodded Sidran. "What's in dragon water that makes you sick?"

"Drogon scales," said Varia miserably. "And sloim." She pressed her toes into the grey mass beneath her.

"This place stinks," said Sidran. "That's another way I found the pools."

I used to think that too, thought Varia. Now I like it. "Everything dies in drogon water," she said, "except those toiny yollow flowers. They grow, and the bees that feed on them grow. Then the drogon eats the bees."

"And?"

"It grows too."

"But the dragons and the bees don't die."

"No." They sat in silence. Sidran's fingers tapped his knobby knees like twigs in the wind.

"Nothing else grows in dragon water?" Sidran blurted suddenly. "Nothing that doesn't change? Because if something did, it would have to be immune."

"The floff plonts," said Varia, sitting up straight. "Galateor said the only place the yellow flowers won't grow is where the floff plonts are." Her voice dropped to a whisper. "But they all borned up." She couldn't bring herself to add "with the star child." Or to explain how the fire started.

"We saw the smoke." Sidran pulled her to her feet. "We have to look, Varia. Maybe the fire didn't get them all. Or maybe the roots will help. They're the part that touches the water, right? You know," he added, "if some part of a fluff plant can cure your dad, maybe it can also change you back. It was dragon water for both of you, right?"

"Do you think it moight work?" She tugged at the string of her pants. It was tight again.

"We won't know until we try." Sidran looked at the sky. The red sun was just visible through the thick clouds. "This way," he said, and plunged back into the undergrowth.

They struck out silently, keeping near the trees when they passed through clearings in case Galateor was watching from the air. He wouldn't hurt her, but she wasn't sure any more about Sidran. At least they didn't have to worry about dangerous plants, or running into the star child. Varia shuddered. If only they didn't run into what was left of it when they got there. She wasn't sure what a burned-up constellation would look like.

Sidran paused several times to drink rain water that had pooled in leaves. Varia would have liked to drink from the pools, but then she might change drastically in front of him. Her tail was uncomfortable enough as it was.

They plodded on until suddenly the lake appeared in front of them, dark and glassy except for the reflections of the yellow droizu around the edges. The trees cast long shadows over the black stubble on the shore. From where Varia stood, there was no sign of a burned-up star child. But she didn't want to be the one to find it. Besides, her tail throbbed. She waited until Sidran stepped into the field before snapping off a twig and stabbing a hole in the back of her pants. She eased the tail through and felt it slap against her leg. "Dat's beder," she sighed. "Sort of." She followed Sidran out, careful to keep her backside turned away from him.

Sidran gazed around the field. "You didn't have to do this," he said. Varia swallowed. How soon would he find out what else they had done? She didn't feel brave enough to make herself tell him, and then watch him leave her here, alone, for good.

Sidran kicked at a broken stalk. "Let's dig some roots."

Varia tugged at one of the blackened stalks. It broke off in her hand. Sidran walked back to the forest and found two sturdy sticks. Together, they loosened the dirt around one of the stalks. Her stick went in further than his; after a while he stepped back and let her finish. When the dirt was soft enough, she wormed her hands in, then pulled out a clump of lumpy tubers covered with hairy, grey strings.

Sidran helped her knock off the dirt. He opened his sack, pulled out the remaining dry vegetables, and stuck them in his pants pocket. "Put them in here," he said. Varia dropped the tubers into the sack and Sidran tied it back around his waist. He stood up and wiped his forehead with the back of his hand, leaving a muddy smear. "I hope these work."

"So do I."

"I better go then." Sidran hesitated. His eyes darted over her face, then her scales, then away.

"The sooner Dad gets dem, da botter," Varia said. It was true, but if only Sidran didn't have to leave just yet. He nodded without looking up, and started across the field. But I won't know if the tubers work, she realised with a pang. "Woit!" she called, running after him. "I'll walk wid you."

They walked to the edge of the field and into the shadows of the trees. Varia recoiled. The star child was behind the first tree. Not an arm's length away, and not burned, but burning.

"Specto!" cried Sidran. "We've dug up some roots for Varia's dad. We think they'll make him better because . . . "

Varia didn't hear the rest of what Sidran said. The star child's glowing eyes spiralled wildly, sucking her into its head. She tore her eyes away and stumbled backwards, tripped over a piece of stubble, and fell onto the dirt, wincing as her tail folded underneath her. "I-I-I thought you were borned up," she stammered.

The star creature made a sizzling sound.

Sidran gave her his don't-be-stupid look. "How can you burn up a star?"

Varia tried to say something — she wasn't sure what — but it came out as a croak. The star child tossed a grass shirt onto the ground in front of her. One corner was singed.

"Why did you ron, then, if you weren't afraid of us?" Varia demanded, shading her eyes.

"Steer you away. Come here." Even without the light, its words whooshed dizzily into her head. Her hair fluttered off her face in a gust of hot air. Sidran backed into the trees.

Galateor would not be pleased.

"We dug up some tubers," Sidran said again. "We're hoping they'll cure Varia's dad."

"They will." This time the words were aimed at Sidran, and Varia just caught something like an echo. She felt a moment of relief — then more words, boring into her brain. "But what about you?" Varia buried her head in her knees. It didn't help.

The words continued to spin. "You . . . you . . . you . . . " Her scales felt uncomfortably hot. She rolled onto her knees and crawled to a cooler patch of dirt.

"Varia! You have a tail!" Sidran bounced out of the trees and crouched beside her.

"You . . . you . . . you . . . " The words slowed.

"I-I'll get my own tubers," Varia stammered, turning to block Sidran's view.

He walked around her. "May I touch it?"

"No!" Varia slapped his hand away.

A new wave of heat engulfed her. "Tubers not enough for you," said the star child. The voices brought a whirling image of Galateor carrying her in his claws and dropping her into a pool. Over and over and over.

Varia snarled. But the star child was right. Galateor would find her if she undid his plan, and turn her right back into his soster again. And he wouldn't be as gentle about it as Galatea had been. So what could she do?

"Star water." This time the words cascaded into her head like a rushing stream. She saw herself standing in a churning waterfall. One by one her scales loosened and floated away, leaving her white and naked in the misty air. She looked in horror at Sidran, but he was still ogling her tail. Maybe it was distracting him enough that he didn't see the star child's image. The image shifted. Now her naked self was becoming younger . . . and smaller . . .

"Stop!" she shouted. The image vanished.

"I don't want to be a drogon," Varia said. She scrambled to her feet. "But I don't want to shronk either. I jost want to be me again." Why was that so hard for the things on this planet to understand?

"You don't belong. You are . . . " It seemed to be searching. An image of a dragon's foot trying to jam itself into a grass boot thumped into her mind.

"A misfit." Varia supplied the word.

The image changed into one of a wrinkled, white-haired Dad, trying to eat something she barely recognised as a carrot. "Can't . . . can't . . . can't . . . " the words echoed. Varia's heart sank. That was also true. If Galatea hadn't started turning her into a dragon, their fungus-altered food would have weakened her too.

The image faded. The star child stood and pulsated. Sidran looked back and forth between them.

So she couldn't just be herself — whatever that meant now. It had been foolish of them, naïve humans, to think that they could move to a completely alien place and not be changed themselves. To imagine that carrot seeds and readers were enough to carry them into a new life. She ran her fingers up and down the scales on her arms. Star water, dragon water, or dirty tubers. Star child, dragon mother, or short-lived fugitive. It wasn't much of a choice.

She imagined herself small and pasty, spending her days weaving, digging, and gulping scalding star water every morning so she could choke down fungus at meals. She saw huge, armoured Galateor searching for her, enraged that his plan had been thwarted. She saw him carrying off her small, soft, weak body in his knife-sharp claws. She saw him, red-toothed, bending over screaming Adriel.

She trembled in spite of the star child's heat. If only she could open her eyes and watch this nightmare vanish in morning's new light. She took a deep breath and clenched her fists to give herself courage. It was odd how naturally her fingers curved into that position. Her throat swelled with emotion. When her voice finally came, it was thick and choked. "I'm going to become a drogon, so I can keep Goloteor away from you."

Sidran gasped. Varia watched him through a curtain of tears. Sidran wiped his arm over his face, smearing more dirt on it. He clutched his sack of tubers and turned away.

"Woit!" Varia grabbed his shoulder. He jumped. "Could you meet me at the cave — once a year, say . . . " she thought quickly. "On the day of the first frost, jost to tell me how everyone is doing? At sonset?"

Sidran nodded without looking at her. He squeezed her hand, then plunged into the bush. The star child followed. Varia watched the light until it disappeared in the forest.

She licked the dirt off her emerald ring. Good-bye Mom, Dad, Adriel. Good-bye Connie.

The sun had set, and it was raining again. She started to put on her shirt, but there wasn't much point. The parts it covered were protected by scales anyway. She draped it over her head like a scarf, and groped her way to the droizu shore of the lake, where she wove reedy stems together to make a shelter. Maybe she and Galateor would find another cave to live in. Or maybe they would just live outside, next to a far-off group of pools. The rain rolled off her shelter, enclosing her in a cave of tears. Varia curled up on her small patch of ground, using the balled-up shirt as a pillow. Her tail flopped into a rivulet of water, so she picked it up and laid it gently along her thigh. The blackness and the rain sealed out everything else, until she imagined herself a tiny seed buried alone in the centre of an enormous universe. A seed that would grow and change in soggy darkness, like fluff plants grew from dirty tubers in dragon water.

By morning, the rain had stopped. So had Varia's tears. She crawled out from her nest and yawned and stretched. The lake lapped at her feet, and the flowers glistened against the dark ground. Varia walked into the woods. She took off her pants, folded them neatly, and stashed them under a bush with the shirt. Galateor was right. She didn't need them any more.

She rubbed her itchy scales. They were slimy again, and she was caked with dirt. A bath would feel good. She took a deep breath, and waded into the lake.

Chapter 23

By the time Galateor found Varia, her transformation was complete. She could snap her tail and wave it in figure eights while snatching bees with both clawed hands. She could spread her wings and glide from the low branches of a bearded tree. Her scales were tough and dazzling. She was three-quarters his size, and used to skewering bees with her claws and following her long snout through the droizu. Strands of her black hair lay tangled among weeds, or wrapped around flower stalks at the edges of pools. Only the ring on her finger showed that she hadn't always been a dragon.

After that night in the tiny cave of tears, Varia hadn't wept. Dragons couldn't. Besides, she felt strong, and saw in the water that she was beautiful, and the bees were satisfying.

"You are porfect soster," Galateor croaked when he saw her. His eyes were deep blue pools. Then he saw her finger. "Whad is dat?"

Varia looked at her hand. The finger with the ring was smaller than the others, both shorter and narrower, as if her mother's gold band had tried unsuccessfully to prevent her from changing. It didn't hurt when she moved it, but she could feel its weakness compared to her other, dragon-sized fingers. She shrugged. "Now we both hov a small fonger."

Galateor growled, and his eyes turned orange.

"Teach me to floi," Varia said quickly.

Galateor's eyes turned blue again. "Forst you do what moi moder toll me. Oi hov anoder prosont." He pulled a long, curved stick from behind his back and thrust it at her. "Eat."

Varia recognized it at once. "Your moder's bone?"

"Moi moder floi," said Galateor. "You eat her bone; you floi too."

Varia's eyes widened. "You oit your own moder's bones?" Dragons were more ruthless than she'd thought.

"She not need dem." Galateor said shortly. He thrust the bone into Varia's claws.

We eat bees, not bones, Varia's mind protested. But the bone's scent made saliva drip from the corner of her mouth. I don't eat bones, she thought. But it wasn't her mother's. She nibbled one knobby end. It crunched, and tasted, like her memory of hard candy back on Earth.

Galateor watched her devour the rest. "Moi moder toll me fross bones is more yock."

"Not possoble," Varia mumbled through the last shard. The only fresh bones around were off limits. But if only! She pictured rabbits, deer, and squirrels running through the trees. "Toll me what your moder told you," she said.

Galateor lay on his back in the sunshine and closed his eyes. Sparkles danced across his belly. "Dere were mony oder onimals. Some in holes, some in trees, some floi loik us." He scratched his stomach. "Dey eat plonts, and we eat dem. No one eat us."

"Oi should hope not," said Varia with a shudder. She lay on her side beside Galateor and made circles and wavy lines in his stomach slime with her claws. "Did you moik droizu and eat bees?"

Galatea jerked to a sitting position. His eyes flashed. "Before pu-rokoot, no droizu. We not eat bees. We use onimals for food and for garoop."

"Whad is garoop?"

Galateor lay back down. "Garoop is moiking oggs."

Varia's heart fluttered. The thought of mating, and eggs, still worried her. Still, she better know. "Whoi did you need onimals for . . . garoop?"

Galateor looked at her, puzzled. "We use drogon water to moik onimals into drogons for garoop. Loik Oi moik you."

"But dere was no droizu. Whore dod you get drogon water?"

"Drogon water not need droizu. We always hov drogon pools." He rolled onto his haunches. "When we foind Waria's sosters, Waria moik drogons too."

Varia gasped. "We have each oder for . . . garoop," she said. "We don't need to moik more drogons."

Galateor looked down at her with yellow eyes. "Sometoims drogons foight."

Varia sat up. "Oi won't foight you." Why would she? Besides the fact that Galateor was bigger, stronger, and faster, there was no reason to. Unless she had to protect someone — but that wouldn't happen. That was why she was here, to make sure it didn't. And she better keep her word. "Teach me to floi," she said. So we can go far, far away, she added silently.

Galateor taught her to fly by lifting her high into the sky and dropping her. Varia would rather have started by jumping off a tall tree, but by the time she thought to suggest it, it was too late. "You eat da bone, you floi," he told her as he let go.

The bone must have worked, because riding air currents on her wide wings turned out to be easy. Flapping, even against the wind, was not too hard either. Steering was. Sometimes a flicker of her wing finger spun her right around, but other times her wing buckled and she plummeted like a stone. Fortunately, Galateor was a fast diver and a good catcher. It took most of the morning before she could bank to both sides, climb and descend when she wanted to, and catch an air current to lift her high above the clouds. Midday found them flying side by side, wingtips almost touching as they curved and dipped and rose again.

"Dis is trilling," Varia croaked. "Oi could floi all doi!"

"Oi know you loik to be drogon," replied Galateor. "Look." He pointed down. The forest, and the yellow-ringed pools in it, stretched out to all horizons. "Oi moik mony pools. We moik mony more. Bees for a hondred boiby drogons."

Varia stiffened and lost the air current. Galateor expected her to lay a hundred eggs? How could she ever keep a hundred dragons away from the settlement? Galateor dove underneath her and nudged her back into the warm river of wind.

"Sommer is eating toim,," he soothed when they were gliding again. "We not garoop ontil da droizu drop da yollow potals."

Presumably the droizu wouldn't drop their petals until the trees dropped their leaves. That sounded like a long time away. How far could they get by then, if they had to stop and make pools all along the way? She watched Galatea pull ahead. How many pools would a hundred dragons need anyway? If each one needed, say, twenty . . .

Galateor did a flip in the air and came up behind her. He nipped her thigh with his teeth. "You not fot enough for garoop," he said. "You eat more bees." His eyes twinkled.

Varia lowered one wing and butted him in the side with her head. He grabbed her tail and let her tow him. She zigzagged to fling him away.

"Oh! Oi is scored!" Galateor cried. He spread his wings and whizzed ahead of her.

"You botter be!" she called back, flapping as hard as she could to catch him.

They chased each other across the sky. Finally, they tumbled together into a sunny pool, where they spent the afternoon eating and scrubbing the slime off each other's backs.

Galateor meant what he said about her getting fatter. He hovered over her morning and evening to make sure she ate enough bees. It wasn't a problem. After living in the hungry settlement, Varia didn't have to be told to eat when food was available.

He also appeared to have meant a hundred baby dragons. Every day they searched out more pools to splash in — always travelling away from the settlement. They didn't get too far each day with all their stops, and of course had to return every night to the older pools for supper. But it was progress.

What a luxurious life, Varia thought one afternoon, lounging in tepid water surrounded by tiny yellow flowers soon to become food. She watched her rainbow-tinted slime, along with a few loose scales, drift to the edges of the pool and bunch up around the flowers as if they knew right where to go. She yawned. It just meant more bees. The settlement seemed very long ago. Why would she ever choose to pick grass and carry wood when she could live the lazy life of a dragon?

Maybe she should go back and transform her people. Once it was done, they'd be happy. They didn't know it was possible to live without working every hour of the day. Dad was probably working again, if the tubers worked. She closed her eyes and floated on her back. She'd ask Sidran when she saw him. Maybe he'd like to be a dragon.

If they found the other lander, she could also transform Connie. So far there'd been no sign of it — no smoke, no cut trees. Once they landed beside a strange tower of mud, vaguely house-shaped but without doors or windows. Banging on it produced a hollow echo, but dragon claws weren't sharp enough to tear it open. Galateor's mother might have known what it was, but it was too late to ask her. Next time they saw one, they flew on past.

Varia just hoped they didn't find a crashed lander with the bodies of the settlers inside. Galateor might want to eat Connie's bones. So might she. She shuddered. On the other hand, dead settlers wouldn't need them any more. She would save some for the settlers who did become dragons, so they could fly too. How sad to be a dragon that couldn't fly. But how much sadder to be a settler that didn't become a dragon, and became bones instead.

The next morning, they set off into low hanging clouds. The first unusual thing Varia noticed was the smell: like water, only heavier. Galateor noticed it too. She could tell by the way his nostrils flared. The trees thinned, then suddenly disappeared. In their place was a broad band of porridge-coloured dirt. Beyond that was only grey, undulating water stretching out as far as the grey clouds.

They landed on the pale, soft ground. When they tried to walk, their claws sank deep into it and they could only shuffle. "It's sond, besoid da ocean," said Varia suddenly. She remembered seeing the ocean from the spaceship, endless blue wrinkles fading into clouds as they pulled away from their home planet. From high up, it had looked small. Here, it looked immense. She and Galateor were like pebbles beside it.

Galateor lapped the water, then spat. "Not good."

"Oceans are solty," Varia remembered. "Nothing woll grow in it." Except the slippery-looking brown rope-things that littered the edge of the sand. The beach. "Dod your moder know about da ocean?" she asked.

"Oi not osk," Galateor replied. He backed away from the water. "Da water not good. We go bock."

Varia nodded. The water wasn't good. It kept them this close to the settlement. "We should floi da oder woy," she said. Maybe they could go further in that direction.

"Yos. We go to da oder soid of Pu-rokoot Loik."

It took several days of making pools in the other direction before they reached the ocean again. And several more in the third. They flew without making pools, just to see how far they could get. Every time, it was no more than one long day's flight from the lake, and one hungry day's flight back.

Sidran would call this a "star-shaped" search pattern, Varia thought as they turned their back on another beach to fly "home" to Droizu Lake. Now she knew why it rained so much: they were on an island. But the other lander wasn't — at least not on this one. Wherever it was, it would take more than dragon wings to find it. She and Galateor were chained to their droizu pools the same way the settlers were chained to their fields. Connie was as lost as ever.

Her own people, on the other hand, were about to be overrun by a hundred bone-eating, dragon-making predators — if Galateor's dream came true. She watched him pummel the air with his powerful wings, and matched him stroke for stroke with hers. There was no reason he wouldn't get everything he wanted. When the flowers lost their petals, he said. That couldn't be long now.

She needed to tell Sidran, so his people could plan their defences — or their surrender. The damp sea breeze blew shivers across her wings.

Chapter 24

As the nights got cooler, the dragons got hungrier. They spent less time flying and more time gorging on bees.

"We need anoder coiv," Galateor mumbled one chilly morning. "Outside too cold, and da old coiv not soif."

Varia nodded, shivering. Her scales clinked against Galateor's, seeking what little heat his body held. It was afternoon before she felt warm these days. She thought of the sweater she'd left at the settlement. It wouldn't even cover one arm, now. And there was no fluff in the field, even if she could figure out how to make a dragon-sized blanket with her stiff fingers. And they clearly couldn't live in the old cave so close to the humans.

"We not foind anoder coiv," Varia pointed out. Galateor's wing rustled against her shoulder. It felt like ice. She shuffled away.

"We moight moik a hole," Galateor suggested. "Hole is warmer don outsoid."

"Oi don't want to sleep in da dort," said Varia. "Whad about da mod towers? Dey is hord loik a rock."

"But dey hov no hole to cloimb in."

Varia could smell warmth in Galateor's armpit. She wormed closer again. "Moybe we can moik a tonnel into da bottom."

After the sun rose high enough to warm their wings and draw out enough bees for breakfast, they flew to the nearest mud tower. It was shaped like a gigantic mushroom. Varia knocked on the side. It sounded hollow like the first tower, but again, there was no visible way in. Galateor scraped aside some plants with his foot. "We moik da hole here." He gouged a trough in the ground with his toe claws. Tiny, white insects scurried out of the ground and away.

"White ants," Varia murmured. In the pictures she'd seen, ants were black or red.

Galateor scooped out dirt while Varia huddled in the sunshine. When the hole got too deep to reach the bottom, he climbed in. Dirt sifted onto his scales and caked on his claws as he tossed out clumps. White ants crawled up his body like water running the wrong way.

Varia watched, bemused. She had once imagined a dragon digging in the fields with a spade-shaped tail. She stabbed her tail into the ground. Ouch. No good; the dirt was too hard. But what about the pile Galateor was making beside his hole? She backed her tail into the loose dirt, and heaved.

"Rrrmppph!" Galateor stood up, shaking soil off his head.

Varia looked over her shoulder. Narrow yellow eyes stared at her over a blackened snout. She roared with laughter. Galateor clawed at the black dirt around the hole. He pulled himself halfway out, then slid back in, pulling dirt with him. Loud cackles rose from Varia's belly. She sagged against a tree.

Splat! Dirt spattered onto her stomach. She tried to stand up, but it was too funny. Galateor heaved himself out of the hose and glared. But his snout wobbled. She whipped her tail around and flung dirt at his chest. He dragged her to the hole by her foot, stuffed her in, then used his tail to pile dirt on her head.

Varia sputtered. Her chin was pressed against her chest. Her tail was jammed between her shoulder and the edge of the hole, and her wings were folded awkwardly half in and half out. Things were crawling on them. She looked up. "Oi am stock."

Galateor looked back at her. "You is." A white ant zigzagged up his snout. Varia watched his eyes cross as he followed it. His blue tongue flashed out the side of his mouth.

Varia giggled. Galateor snorted.

She wiggled her feet and hands. "Holp me!"

Galateor grabbed her arms and heaved. She flew out of the hole. Galateor toppled backwards, and she flopped on top of him. Dirt ground between their scales. Ants tickled her neck.

Varia started to roll off, but Galateor held her. His hot breath gusted over her teeth. His eyes were intensely purple. "You is Golotyor's soster," he said in a husky voice, scraping his teeth along her neck. She felt his claws in her back, and his heart pounding against her chest. He was trembling, or she was, or both. "Soon is garoop," he growled into her ear hole.

Varia was intensely aware of his close, muddy body. When the flowers dropped their petals. Any time now. A hot, shivery feeling flowed through her, and the egg place in her belly tingled. Suddenly, a picture of Sidran dropped into her mind, as plain as if he stood in front of her. She blinked. What was he there for? She wasn't going to garoop with him. "My torn to dog the tonnel," she croaked, pushing away.

While Varia dug, Galateor packed the dirt into a hard circle around the hole and collected twiggy branches to pile across the top to keep out the rain and snow.

The inside of the mound wasn't completely hollow, Varia discovered when her head broke through the floor and collided with a thin platform of hardened mud. It was completely dark inside, but she could smell that the bottom was lined with a strange, musky fungus and that the mound was teeming with ants. Slowly she stood up, pushing her head through layer after thin layer of mud. Mud crumbs showered her. Invisible ants swarmed into her eyes and nostrils. Gasping for breath, she shoved herself backwards into the tunnel and outside.

Galateor helped her lick off the ants. They were drier than bees, and it was impossible to catch them all. "We wont sleep wid so mony onts crawling on us," Varia complained.

Galateor solved that problem. "Caraahm-nop." He crawled in head-first.

"Woit! Da mound moight broik!" But it didn't even shudder. Galateor emerged coughing. Varia went in afterwards and scraped out the mud, fungus ashes, and charred ant-bodies. At first she had to work quickly, holding her breath, and scramble out for air. But the mound must have had vents, because surprisingly quickly the air cleared. They stashed a small pile of caraahm-nop inside in case the ants returned. Then they had a bath.

It was warmer sleeping in the mound than outside in the wind and rain. It was also darker, so they slept later. By the time they woke and found a pool, the bees were out. One rainy night they forgot to drag branches over the hole, and by morning the tunnel was slick with mud. After they slithered out, Varia wove the branches into a mat that would be easy to slide over the hole.

Winter crept closer. The leaves turned violet and orange and started to blow off the trees, but the droizu petals stayed firmly attached. The dragons dipped into the cold pools only long enough to scrub off their itchy slime. Fortunately, it didn't grow very fast in the cold. If they weren't sleeping in the mound, Varia thought, it might not grow at all.

As the warmth faded, the dragons' hunger grew. Varia and Galateor barely spoke; they spent every daylight minute searching for and stuffing themselves with bees. Often it was all Varia could do to let the queen bee return to her hive so they would have food in the spring.

One sunny day a biting wind blew in the smell of imminent frost. Varia dragged her sluggish body through the tossing droizu. Her fingers were clumsy, and her wings wouldn't unfold. The bees huddled in their hives, and when she ate one, its insides pulled apart in long strings. The water was glassy, too cold to wash the dusty clumps of nectar off her scales. By mid-afternoon, she and Galateor were worn right out. It took all their strength to drag themselves back to the mound.

Galateor flopped down asleep beside the tunnel hole as soon as he got inside. Varia clambered stiffly over him to her side of the bare floor. The walls blocked the wind, but the only heat in the mound came from Galateor. She wormed her way between his arms and legs and curled up with his breath flowing over her shoulder. Something nagged at her mind. Something unfinished. But she couldn't remember what it was.

Her dreams were as stiff as she was. Bees waddle past, but her cold fingers can't pick them up. They watch her as they walk, pity and concern etched on their strangely familiar faces. Suddenly she knows. The bees are Sidran. She is supposed to meet him at the cave the day of the first frost.

She opened her eyes to the darkness. It was time to go.

Galateor's stiff limbs held her like a cage, but his breath warmed her cold muscles just enough. Inch by inch, she slid free. Galateor never stirred, even when she stepped on him in the darkness on her way out the hole.

It was palest dawn when she emerged, and the air cut her lungs like a knife. A cloud rose from her nostrils with every breath. Through the puffs, she saw white twigs, white leaves, fat white shelf fungi jutting out of a silvery tree — everything was frosty white. She turned in the direction of the cave and slowly, creakily, began to walk.

By the time she reached the cave, the sun was well up — although it gave precious little heat. Sluggish bees littered the edges of the pool beneath stiff, glittering flowers. They crackled between her teeth, and she had to chew the hard middles. The cold followed them into Varia's stomach. But they were food. It took a long time to blunt her hunger. Afterwards, she stumbled into the cave and slept.

This time her dreams were filled with icy ghosts. *Ethereal Galateas groan and stagger across the floor, slide into the pool, and rise back out. Eggs flicker into existence like frosty rainbows, then vanish.* When Varia woke up, she felt like she hadn't slept at all.

The afternoon wasn't as cold as the morning. The stripe of sunlight falling on her through the ceiling crack actually felt warm. She heaved herself to her feet and lumbered to the door of the cave.

Sidran stood outside, covered in dry grass and white fluff. His angular limbs were clearly made of bones. Stop it, Varia warned herself.

Sidran jumped when she stepped out into the clearing. "V-Varia?"

"Yos," she said, suddenly conscious of her croaking voice and towering bulk. The sun's warmth spread across her scales.

"Your . . . your dad is better," said Sidran, backing up. His eyes explored her massive body.

"Good." Now that they were here, she didn't know what to say.

"Your mom sends her love. So does mine. I . . . we . . . everyone misses you."

Varia nodded. She hadn't thought about missing the humans for a long time now. She wasn't sure she did — Sidran looked so unlike her memory of him. She had to warn him, she remembered. And then get back to the mound before Galateor woke up.

"Do you like being a dragon?" Sidran asked, his eyes suddenly fixed on hers.

"Oi loik to floi."

"Any eggs yet?"

"No!" If she were human, she would have blushed. Instead, she ruffled her wings. It was funny how talking with him made her feel human again. Poor humans. Maybe it was better not to tell them what was in store.

"Would you . . . " Sidran began, and stopped. "Would you take me for a ride?"

Varia hesitated. She didn't want Galateor to see her. "A short one," she said. It was hard to talk to this small human as an equal. He was more like . . . a pet.

She knelt down and Sidran climbed lightly up her side and onto her shoulders. He hardly weighed anything. "Hong on toight," she warned, and felt his hands grip her neck. She leapt into the air.

"This is incredible!" Sidran exclaimed as the trees fell away. The low sun glared into Varia's eyes, so she banked away from it. Sidran's hands gripped harder. She levelled out into a smooth glide. Uh oh. The settlement was straight in front of them. How had she reached it so quickly?

She curved her wings to slow down, and made a steep curve away. Sidran flopped onto her neck and wrapped his arms around it. "Stop squoozing . . . " she said. Then she gasped.

Galateor was flapping hard toward her, his path jerky and erratic. His blue tongue flopped out the side of his mouth. His eyes were black as night.

"Why is you gone?" he croaked. "You is soster!" He wobbled around beside her. Sidran lay on Varia's back like a statue.

"Oi coim to foind bees," said Varia. The cave was in sight. "Oi am coming roight bock." She angled down and landed beside the pool.

Galateor sank to the ground beside her. "Today is . . . " He wheezed and waved a hand toward the pool. Varia's heart flipped. The droizu petals made a yellow carpet around the water. Galateor grabbed a bee from underneath one and swallowed it whole.

"Garoop." Varia whispered.

Sidran slid to the ground on the side away from Galateor and stared at him with wide eyes. Galateor had his snout in the pool and was making loud slurping noises. Varia jerked her head toward the trees. Sidran edged away. A stone clattered under his foot.

Suddenly Galateor was trembling in front of them, his eyes fixed on Sidran. His snout dripped water. His teeth dripped saliva.

Sidran's pale face went even paler. "No, Galateor," said Varia. But she could smell Sidran too.

"Fross bones is more yock," said Galateor, advancing.

Varia's own drool splatted against her shoulder as she plucked Sidran off the ground with one hand and knocked Galateor off balance with her hip. His jaws snapped on empty air. His roar chased her as she ploughed toward the settlement.

Sidran whimpered as Galateor's teeth snapped behind Varia's tail.

The settlers stood outside around an open fire. "Dragon!" someone yelled, and they disappeared in an instant behind slammed doors.

Varia swooped into the settlement and dropped Sidran near the largest building. The kitchen. Galateor plummeted to the ground between him and the door. Sidran screamed. Varia lunged between them. Galateor's bite grazed her shoulder, and she fell hard onto her side. Out the corner of her eye, she saw Galateor grab Sidran and leap away. She flung herself into the air.

She overtook them above the field. Shrieking, she dropped onto Galateor's back and forced him down. Galateor clutched Sidran close to his chest. Cold water enveloped them as they splashed into the creek.

Varia struggled to hold Galateor down, while he fought to roll her off his back. Through the tangle of teeth, claws, and tails, Varia saw Sidran stumble out of the water. She planted her foot on Galateor's head and pushed it hard into the creek stones, yanking her wing from under his shoulder at the same time. "You con forgot about garoop," she snarled as she took off over the trees, hoping Galateor was angry enough to follow her instead of Sidran.

He was. A steady stream of garbled words followed her as she fled. Her heart felt like stone. She had fought off one dragon, but she could not have defended Sidran against two.

Galateor wrestled her to the ground as the last ray of sunlight glinted across their sweaty backs. There on the brittle leaves, they garooped.

Chapter 25

VARIA HUDDLED INSIDE THE DARK MOUND, refusing to talk, refusing to eat. The icy egg seed grew inside her, promise of the end for her people. She kept to her side of the mound and snarled at Galateor if he touched her. A few ants straggled into the mound and settled in the crevices of her scales. She ignored them.

Dreams followed her in and out of sleep. *She is the girl Varia, running in terror from gleaming fangs and claws. She is the dragon, chasing faceless humans who turn to bones as they run. She is trapped inside a frozen egg, wanting out but unable to break the shell.*

The cold thickened outside the mound and inside Varia's body, pulling her deeper into sleep. The dreams faded. Galateor curled up beside her, and she didn't notice.

Varia woke to a warming mound with her stomach screaming for food. Galateor's scent was weak; he must have left. Gradually another scent intruded on her consciousness. She followed it to the crook of her leg. The thing was the size of a bee, and it wiggled when she nosed it. There were more of them tucked in the folds of her body. She tasted one. It was sweet like a bee, but crunchier. It hardly dented her hunger, but swallowing something made her feel more alert. She licked up a few more. Finally, curiosity overcame her lethargy, and she carried one awkwardly out through the tunnel on the tip of her tongue.

The light was too bright after so long in darkness. She closed her eyes and felt the thing crawl to the curled tip of her tongue. She fanned her wings and stretched, letting the sunlight caress her stiff body. Her toe-claws sank into the soggy ground, and her tail found a cold puddle. Branches creaked in the warm breeze. Her belly swayed. The thing on her tongue crawled backwards.

She opened her eyes and squinted at it. It was a bee-sized, slimy, white ant. Varia dropped it onto the round bulge that hung between her thighs. It slid slowly down, leaving a trail in her own slime. She ate it. Funny it had grown so big.

Varia sat back in the sunshine to think. Ants. Bees. Droizu. Dragons. All were abnormally big, and all were covered with slime. Was there a connection? She saw Luella, a long-ago Luella who still had a face, holding up a sweet potato so big she could hardly lift it. "Look how big this thing is!" And tired-looking Samuel. "It has a fungus. Plants grow bigger with a fungal partner."

Was this slime a "fungal partner" that made things grow big? A fungus that washed into water and made little flowers grow big and sticky with fungus too? Then the sticky flower stuff got onto the bees and made them slimy and big. That was why Galateor could make new droizu by dropping dead bees into pools. They took the fungus with them on their coats.

The sunlight shifted, and she moved with it to warm her groggy brain. What else had Samuel told her? Think! Fungi sometimes grew on two different things, alternate hosts like the barley rust that also grew on the silver berry plants. What if animals and droizu were alternate hosts for her fungus?

She closed her eyes to work out her idea. Dragon or bee slime infected yellow flowers, making them grow big and produce sticky nectar. The nectar infected dragons and bees right back, making them slimy. It worked on ants too. The huge white ants had slept in the flower nectar she hadn't washed off her body. When the fungus touched other plants, or humans who weren't used to it, it killed them. Like Reyk and Thora, who had drunk from the flower pool with Galatea's mother watching . . .

Varia felt sick with a sudden realization. Galateor hadn't told her the full story. Reyk and Thora would never have drunk that smelly water in the pool unless the dragon mother had forced them to. She had wanted to turn them into dragons, not knowing that humans were different from Kettle animals, that drinking dragon water would kill them. But Galatea did know. Her mother had told her what happened. And Galatea had made Varia drink anyway, hoping — *not knowing*, that it wouldn't kill her.

Varia kicked the ridge of dirt that surrounded the tunnel. So that was how much her dear little dragon loved her: not at all. She still didn't know why a dragon that was both male and female needed a mate anyway. She kicked again. Galateor could have laid his own egg, like his mother, and his mother, and so on back to the purokoot. Was it only loneliness that made him want a mate? Or was there something else he wasn't saying?

Varia smashed more of the dirt ridge into the hole. Let Galateor dig it out. She'd show him. She'd plant a fluff plant in every pool to kill off that evil fungus. He would be furious, and it would serve him right. But then what would they eat? Tiny bees, tiny ants...and tiny people. She stopped kicking. Human or dragon, her life butted up against a stupid fungus!

SHARON PLUMB

Varia splashed through the puddles to a patch of lacy snow. Her stomach was screaming murder. She needed food. She needed warmth to melt the lump of ice inside her, and get it out.

A strange sound cut the air — something between a whistle and a squeak. It came again. Varia cocked her head, then waddled in the direction of the sound. It took enormous effort to push aside branches with her wasted muscles, and drag her heavy belly over fallen logs. Not too far away, she found Galateor, also thin and gaunt, standing motionless and staring into a tree.

Two small animals sat on a branch. Their bodies were covered in brown, soft-looking fronds, except for their round eyes, four stick legs, and sharp, pointed snouts. The sounds were coming out of their mouths.

"Bords," Varia croaked. Four-legged birds. Her unused voice was raspy, and the birds immediately opened their wings and fluttered into the sky. The dragons stared after them.

"Bords," Galateor mumbled.

Birds! A miracle of birds! sang one part of Varia's mind. But she would have to think about it later. "Your ogg is hongry," she rasped.

Galateor turned and stared at her as if he'd forgotten who she was. Then he shuddered and blinked. "Hongry," he repeated. "Come foind bees."

Varia followed him through the trees. The snow was soft and wet, and it spattered onto their legs as they walked. It was easier walking with Galateor breaking the branches ahead of her. Soon they came to a clearing. The flower reeds were pale stalks in the still water. Varia lumbered forward and pushed them aside. A single bee floated at the edge of the water. She reached for it.

"Stop!" Galateor grabbed her arm and threw her aside.

She smacked onto the wet ground. "Moine!" she snarled. Galateor's voice trembled. "It born you. Look." He pointed with his withered finger.

Varia heaved herself to her feet and looked into the pool. In the middle of the water floated a soggy hive. "Jost loik lost toim," she croaked. A ruffle of grey on the side of a tree trunk showed where it came from.

"Da star choild come bock." Now Galateor snarled. "It wont to destroy us."

"It wants to protect da bords," said Varia. "From da fongus."

Galateor looked at her. "Whad is da fongus?"

"Dis sloim." She drew a stripe across her belly with her claw. "It grows in da dragon water. It moiks da flowers big, and dey moik da bees big."

Galateor snorted. "Moi moder not say dat."

"Your moder dod not know."

"How do you know?"

Varia moved into the sun and sat down. "Oi was sticky from da droizu and da big onts slopt on me. Dey grew big loik da bees."

Galateor stepped toward her. "Show me."

Varia shrugged. "Oi oit dem."

Galateor's tail waved in a slow circle and his eyes oscillated between blue and yellow. "When da flowers grow, we pock dem and rob da fungus on da bords. Da bords grow big. We eat dem."

Varia's eyes widened. "How will we cotch dem?"

"We will cotch dem." Galateor snapped off a tree branch. "Now we foind more bees."

The next pool was the same, and the next. Once Varia caught a glimpse of the birds flying. Galateor chased them, crashing through the trees with both arms, while Varia stumbled over tree roots trying to keep up. Galateor was scrabbling under bushes when she finally reached the next clearing. Again the hive floated in the pool. Galateor emerged with a caraahm-nop in his hand. His eyes looked glazed.

"Oi moik da star choild stop wrocking our pools."

Varia stamped her foot. "Caraahm does not hort da star choild."

Galateor snarled. He ripped off the stems and leaves, but kept the bulb in his hand. "When da flowers grow, we rob dem on da people, and eat dem."

"We don't eat moi people." Varia narrowed her eyes.

"Dey is not your people. Oi is your people. Da ogg is your people."

Varia glared at him. "Da ogg is hongry for bees."

Galateor looked at the lump hanging between her thighs. "Den feed it."

"You moik da ogg. You foind da bees." Rage swelled inside her. "You don't lov me. You only want me to loi your ogg so you won't hov to."

Galateor stepped back. "Moi moder — "

Varia stamped her foot. Icy water splashed onto her lump. "Your moder! Your moder poisoned two people wid pool water, and den you splossed me wid it!"

Galateor's tail slapped the ground. "Oi not hort you. Oi moik you soster."

Varia hissed at him. "You moid me for garoop. Oi did not want to garoop and you garooped onywoy."

"It was da toim for garoop. Da noxt doy too loit." Galateor's voice quaked. His eyes were dark.

Varia turned her back and huffed. Galateor was stubborn and totally self-centred. And the arguing had worn her out. "Oi am hongry," she said, sinking onto her haunches.

"Oi is hongry too," Galateor growled.

"Go to da Loik," Varia said without turning around. "Da Loik is too big for da star choild to wrock."

"Oi go foind food for da ogg," Galateor said.

Branches snapped. Varia felt a breeze and heard wings thumping the air. She considered following Galateor. To do that, she'd have to open her wings and then stand up and then jump, and she wasn't sure she had the energy, especially with her belly full of ice. She could just wait here until Galateor returned with his hands full of bees. But he could only carry so few. And she was itchy. He couldn't fix that. She creaked open her wings and used them to push herself to her feet. Willing strength into her legs, she jumped into the air.

It felt good to fly, once she was high enough to catch an air current and glide. After the initial effort, it was much easier than walking, even with the heavy lump swaying beneath her. The lump made turning trickier, but as long as she remembered it was there, she could manage. The lake shone in the distance. It was ringed with dry stalks, since the new plants weren't up yet. But there would be bees in the water, and buried in the bank. She gave her wings a flap.

Galateor wasn't there yet; she couldn't see anything sparkling on the lakeshore. She looked around the sky. There he was — flying toward the cave. Varia tightened her legs around the lump and banked hard. When she reached the settlement, Galateor was already on the ground beside the kitchen. There were no people in sight. She circled, watching. Galateor was bent over a row of small puddles.

Galateor thrust his hand into one of the puddles. A scale-bending shriek tore the air. Varia nearly stalled. Galateor half ran, half flew across the snow-dotted field and plunged his hand into the creek. Varia circled lower. What was he running from?

A few tiny creatures emerged from the kitchen, tiny spears in hand. Their warm scent rose to her nostrils. Her stomach clenched. Those twiggy animals couldn't really be her people. They must be related to the birds. Two of them ran toward a log contraption beside a pile of rocks. A very tiny one without a spear ran behind the outhouse. The others huddled in a cluster of spear points. "Star water burns it!" one of them cried. Their words sounded tinny.

Anger surged through Varia. Once more they were up against the star child, cousin to the purokoot. She growled and swooped toward Galateor.

Galateor turned away from the creek. He flapped low across the field, growling, his neck extended and his teeth bared. Varia swung around and flew beside him. The creatures pulled back their spears. A rock flew into the air. Galateor dodged it, but Varia was heavy, and it struck her on the belly. She faltered in the air.

Galateor roared. He swerved to the outhouse and snatched the tiny creature in one hand. The other hand, the one he had burned in the puddle with, he held curled close against his chest.

Varia recovered her balance and flew toward the safety of the forest. Galateor flapped after her. He waved his catch jubilantly in front of her. "For da ogg."

The scent of fresh animal assaulted her. Warmth. Food. And blood. She could see it, dripping down the creature's twig leg. "For da ogg," she repeated. Saliva rolled off her teeth. It's one of your people, a tiny part of her brain squeaked. Galateor's words drowned it out. "Da ogg is your people."

The tiny creature was flailing its limbs just like the bees did. Good. She knew what to do with those. The creature was noisier than the bees, but not for long. Her stomach growled. She opened her mouth.

"Varia! Drop Adriel in here!" a high, tinny voice shouted. Varia gagged. The speaker had orange fluff on its head. Sidran. More creatures ran beside him, holding a net. Others carried buckets of water. But she and Galateor were nearly over the trees.

Galateor snarled above her. "Food for da ogg. Eat."

"Adriel!" another voice cried.

Varia snapped her mouth shut. What was she doing? "Oidriel," she croaked to drown out her stomach.

"Oi eat," growled Galateor. He pulled the human toward his mouth.

Without thinking, Varia stiffened her neck and butted Galateor hard into the signal tower. It rocked with the impact.

"Wha?" Galateor caught his balance, but dropped the screaming Adriel.

Varia caught Adriel's twig leg in her hand. His delicious scent filled her nostrils — but she also smelled something else: laughter and love. Breathing deeply as Galateor streaked toward her, she swung around the tower and tossed Adriel inside. One of the humans jumped in and caught him. The others followed.

Galateor shoved his head into the tower, but he could not fit between the bars. His roar rolled across the clearing. He's going to push over the tower, Varia realized. I have to make him follow me.

She tilted her wing fingers into a sharp curve. She could just reach his tail. She bit hard and yanked to the side. Galateor floundered in the air. Varia turned and fled. She flapped as hard as she could over the trees, but her belly was heavy and her muscles were feeble with exhaustion. Roaring filled her ears. Flames engulfed her, and everything went red.

Chapter 26

THE FIRST THING VARIA FELT WHEN she woke up was something damp on her shoulder. Then there was a rustling sound, and another damp touch at her snout. She forced one eye open, and saw a mass of grey fur and two shiny, black eyes. Varia's eyelid fell shut. There was more rustling, and when she managed to open her eye again, the creature was gone. I'm dreaming, she thought as she drifted back into unconsciousness.

The next thing she heard was crashing in the bushes. "Here she is!" called a tinkly voice, and footsteps surrounded her.

"There's a branch through her wing." A stabbing pain jolted her awake, as her wing was jerked upward and folded by her side. "The bone is broken," the voice said. Her scales felt tight and stiff, and every touch, every movement threatened to crack them apart. She groaned.

"Lift her and we'll slide the hammock underneath." Hands pushed painfully at her scales, tugged, and heaved her up. Then she was lowered onto something that curled tightly around her sides. She felt herself being lifted and carried slowly through the trees. More crashing noises. Now and then branches tore at her scales, but more often they didn't. She had no idea how long she was carried, or where. The rocking motion put her to sleep. Finally the noises and the movement stopped, and it was dark. She felt warm, soothing water being poured over her. Then nothing.

Water was trickling over her when she woke up. She opened her eyes — it was easier this time — and saw a small, pale creature with a fluffy orange patch on its head standing beside her, pouring water out of a bowl. Sidran again. She tried to move her arm, and winced at the pain that shot through her shoulder. More water flowed over her wing.

"That was great, the way you saved Adriel. And me," said Sidran. She grunted. "We have to stop him, you know," he continued. "He'll be back. He wants to steal our bones."

Varia's stomach growled. Yes. Fresh ones.

"He'll be back for you, too, I bet."

Galateor. She nodded, and her neck creaked. "Ogg," she managed to croak. Her throat felt like it was full of dry leaves.

Sidran dipped its bowl in the pool and poured the water slowly into her mouth. "I thought so. Soon?"

She swallowed and nodded again. The egg was a lump of permafrost in her belly. Even Galateor's flames hadn't warmed it. If it didn't come out soon, her whole body would freeze from the inside out.

"We have a plan," Sidran said. "And we need your help."

Varia stared at him through heavy eyes. A plan? For what again? She closed her eyes. The egg jerked inside her body. Water washed over her and the creature continued to talk. The words bounced across her numb mind until she fell asleep.

When she woke again, she was alone. The bowl lay upside down beside her. She pushed herself up on her arms, grimacing at the pain, and managed to bring her legs around into a crouch. Her scales still felt tight, but not quite as raw as before. She was in the cave. She hobbled to the pool on stiff feet and took a long drink. The slit of light was painful on her burned skin. She moved back into the shadows.

Galateor's flames had come from behind. Her tail, feet, legs, underbelly, and back were scorched black, the scales curled up and brittle. The edges of her wings hung like jagged rags. The one that dragged on the floor had a gaping hole in the middle. And she was achingly hungry.

The doorway darkened, and two pale humans came in, Sidran and one with brown hair. They were carrying a roundish, hole-riddled bone. Drool splashed onto her foot. Sidran's eyes darted between the bone and her head, as if measuring the two against each other. The other dragon had been smaller. "We dug this up but we don't need it," he said. She devoured it while they watched. It was only one, but it eased the pain in her stomach a little.

"We've come to set your wing," said the brown-haired human when Varia had finished. The voice was familiar. It was her mother, of course. Varia closed her eyes. She wasn't up to another scolding. But her mother didn't scold. She set some long sticks, rolls of cloth, and a bowl containing something smelly on the floor beside Varia. "It will hurt," she said, but this will numb the pain." She scooped up some thick, creamy stuff with her fingers, and rubbed it over Varia's wing. Varia winced. "Help me, Sidran," she said. It went faster then. Within seconds Varia's wing began to feel thick, and when her mother touched it again, Varia felt nothing.

Sidran pushed and her mother pulled at the broken bone, and in spite of the anaesthetic cream, Varia howled when it snapped back into place. "That's it — now we just have to splint it," said her mother. She and Sidran folded the wing, laid peeled branches along the front and back of the bone, and wrapped it with long pieces of cloth. "We'll check it in a few days." She squeezed Varia's huge hand between her small ones. It was the hand with the ring. "Get well," she said, and left.

"Your mother is a good healer," Sidran said, "especially with those plants Specto showed us." Sidran dipped the bowl in the pool and poured water over Varia's back.

"Drogon water," Varia croaked.

"That's okay," said Sidran. "It won't hurt me."

Varia rolled over so the water would run across her belly. The cold stone felt good against her back.

"Your father is doing great," Sidran continued. "He's the one that jumped into the tower and caught Adriel, in case you didn't recognize him now that he's small." He stopped pouring and looked at Varia's face, as if this piece of news should interest her. She stared at the ceiling. Of course he would be on the star child's side now. Sidran continued. "That was quick thinking, by the way. I was afraid Galateor would lift the tower right up and attack everyone, but you distracted him."

Varia stared at the ceiling. She wouldn't be able to stop him if he tried now.

"Don't worry about him coming back. We're keeping a good supply of star water handy. There's some outside the cave."

Star water. That stuff that burned Galateor. She stiffened.

"If he comes back, I'll throw it at him."

"No star water," Varia croaked.

Sidran stopped pouring dragon water and looked at her. "I think we should find out if it's the same for you. It would be useful to know — in case we want to chase away Galateor without hurting you. I'll just try one drop."

Varia didn't want any more pain. One burning was enough for her. But he was right. It would be good to know now if she had to avoid it. She nodded miserably and closed her eyes.

Sidran went outside and returned holding up his finger. He carefully placed one drop onto her clawed toe. The water sizzled where it touched her. She shrieked and kicked. Sidran ran outside. When the pain dulled, Varia lifted her foot and pulled it to the side so she could see it around her belly. One of the scales had dissolved, leaving behind a smooth, pinkish-brown surface. It was the same colour as Sidran.

Sidran came back in. "I guess it burns you too," he said, reaching for the bowl again.

Varia nodded and let her foot fall back to the floor. That's what she expected. Star water burned her every time she touched it. But this time the burning had an effect she would have to think about. If she could stand the pain, she could get her human body back. That's what Specto had told her in the meadow, and the spot on her toe showed that he was right. But now the settlers had their own supply of star water, and they could change her back without her having to face the star child. If she could stand the pain. And if they could defend themselves from Galateor without her. And if she was willing to work for the star child.

Sidran dribbled dragon water over her foot. "Too bad." He poured some on her belly, and the egg jerked. "Your egg wants to come out soon," he said. "You'll have to think of some way to keep it from hatching. It will be harder to defend ourselves against two dragons. Well, three, but you aren't trying to eat us."

Varia closed her eyes. He didn't know how close she had come to doing just that. The icy egg made her belly so numb it didn't even feel the dragon water. What would happen to the egg if she became human again now, she wondered. Would it disappear, or would it continue to grow inside her? And how would she get it out?

"It's actually a good thing you're a dragon," Sidran said. "Our plan will work better that way." He continued pouring water over her. She fell asleep as he talked.

Varia the human girl stands on a ridge above a valley, holding her new baby dragon. Baby Sidran and Baby Adriel arch their wings and flick their tails and flutter around her head. "See down there," she murmurs. "Inside those mounds are fresh bones, sweet and sticky. Bring me some, so I can fly." Suddenly she realizes she has no wings. The dragons turn on her. "Bones, fross bones," they squeak, and tear at her skin with their needle-pointed baby teeth.

Varia woke, gasping. She lay, weak and hungry, on the cold floor as more and more of her body disappeared into the egg's cold circle. Sidran came every day with a handful of dirty bones and some bees. It wasn't enough, but it kept her from drooling over his smell. Usually. The cold spread from her belly to her thighs and her back. From time to time she saw the lump jerk roughly from side to side, so she knew it was still alive.

Galateor didn't come looking for her, until one afternoon he suddenly appeared at the door of the cave with a bouquet of young droizu blossoms in one hand. "Oi foind you!" His other hand was shrunken and grey.

Galateor glanced around. "Da coiv look small." He leaned against the far wall. and dangled the droizu blossoms against the floor. "Oi floi far. Oi look at da pools. Mony pools is wrecked, bot Oi moik more." A bee crawled out of a blossom. He slurped it up.

Varia pushed herself up so she was sitting next to the pool. It was uncomfortable. The egg pushed her legs apart and put pressure on her burned rump scales. She eased her feet into the bubbles, then leaned forward, scooped water into her mouth, and dribbled it over her shoulder and back.

"What is on your wong?" asked Galateor.

"A splont. Da wong was broken. Da splont is helping it heal."
Galateor looked slightly annoyed. He paced across the cave,
still dragging the droizu. Another bee crawled out, and this
time Varia snagged it. "Oi see mony new onimals," he said.
"Bords. Small onimals onder da booses and da trees."
Varia looked at the light outside the cave entrance. So she
hadn't been dreaming.

Galateor picked a bee out of a droizu blossom with his
withered fingers. It fell to the ground, and he kicked it toward
Varia. "Oi troi to rob da fongus on dem," he said, "but dey is
too fost."

Good, Varia thought, swallowing the bee whole. But was it
good? Bees didn't satisfy her the way they had before — before
the egg, and her injuries. The few tiny bones that Sidran brought
settled far more firmly into her stomach. She needed more than
bees — and she wasn't eating the humans. It would be good to
have choices. She pulled her feet out of the pool and wobbled
around so she could drop her tail in. The egg bobbed against
the floor.

Galateor arched his neck. "Da ogg want out."

Varia nodded. She certainly wanted it out. She hadn't felt
warm since last summer.

"Moi moder go in da water." Galateor said.

Varia stiffened. His mother had died in the water. Had she
drowned laying her egg? Was that why Galateor wanted her to
lay his? She waddled away from the pool. "Oi won't be oible to
cloimb out."

"Oi holp you." Galateor grabbed her tail and dragged her
toward the pool. Her burned rump scraped across the rock,
and she fell in. Galateor splashed in beside her. He was so
big he could stand on the pool bottom, but she couldn't quite
reach. She grabbed the edge. "Oi holp," Galateor said again.

Varia breathed out slowly. His mother hadn't had a helper. And Galateor had said he wanted her to lay a hundred eggs. He didn't expect her to die.

The bubbling dragon-water was soothing. Varia floated on her back and felt it slosh around her brittle scales. The egg felt much lighter when she floated. Galateor pushed on her belly, making a small wave. Varia bumped against the wall.

"Oi born you," said Galateor, rubbing the egg lump.

"Yos."

"You not eat da food. Oi born my hond and you not eat da food. Ond you boit me!" Galateor pushed her under the water.

Varia sputtered and clawed her way back up as water gushed into her mouth. "Oi won't eat Oidriel."

Galateor stood up straight. His eyes narrowed. "You eat Oidriel."

"Oi — " Varia's reply was cut off by a violent lurch from the egg. Her lump felt different. Further down. Icy water flooded her legs. Instinctively, she pulled up her knees.

Galateor stared at her with yellow-green eyes. "Or da boiby eat Oidriel."

The egg gave a final, violent lurch, and slushy water whooshed over Varia's feet, followed by an icy lump. Her legs relaxed and her belly deflated all at once. Her egg place felt prickly and numb, like her human feet had when she sat on them too long. She paddled herself upright. The water was covered with tiny ice floes.

Galateor dove and retrieved the egg. "Dat cold!" He rolled it onto the cave floor and climbed out, dripping water that froze on the egg. Varia clung to the pool's edge and looked at it. It was bluish-green, faceted, and tiny. Fifty of them could have fit inside her lump. The rest must have been full of water, protecting her body from the ice.

"Da boiby is a gorl," Galateor said.

"How do you know?"

"Boys are orange."

"Your ogg was mony colours," said Varia. Because the dragon inside it was both.

"Noxt toim Oi garoop two toims. Two drogons moik two oggs."

Varia's snout dropped open. "Bot — "

Galateor picked up the egg in his good hand. "Oi toik da ogg. You come loiter." He bounced it in his hand. It nearly fell, but he steadied it with his withered hand just in time. "Dat cold!"

"Woit!" Varia pulled herself up and rolled onto the rock ledge. It was easy now that the egg was out. So why had Galateor's mother drowned? She felt a fog lift from her mind, and a plan begin to form. She snatched up one of the droizu stalks. "Da humans will come to see da ogg. When dey come, Oi will rob da droizu fongus on dem. Dey will grow and moik fross bones. For da boiby."

Galateor hesitated, then rolled the egg onto the floor. Varia stopped it with her foot. He breathed on his fingers. "Oi moik more pools." He lumbered to the cave door, cradling his withered hand. The cave went dark as his bulk filled the opening. He turned to look at her with flat grey eyes, and stared for a long time. When he spoke, his words were so soft that Varia had to strain to hear. "If Waria not moik fross bones for da boiby, Oi and da boiby eat Waria." Then he left.

Varia felt colder than a hundred eggs. I could just smash it now, she thought, looking at the glittering jewel on the floor. It was so tiny. How could something that small grow so impossibly huge? She could crush it with one step — except that it was solid ice. And more important, it was hers. It had come out of her. She had suffered to bring it into the world. She couldn't destroy

SHARON PLUMB

it any more than she could have destroyed Galatea's egg, even
knowing the monster Galatea would become.

Smashing it wouldn't solve anything anyway. Galateor
wouldn't eat her — probably — without another mate. But he
could make other mates. All he had to do was catch one of the
new animals and feed it dragon water. She watched the egg
sparkle in the light from the ceiling crack. She couldn't destroy
it — but maybe she could keep it from hatching. She picked up
the egg and left the cave.

Chapter 27

THE SNOW MELTED; THE TREES BUDDED green and mauve; plants and mushrooms sprouted all over the forest floor. The air was full of smells. In the damp, rocky valley, the droizu grew tall and sparkling. Varia kept to the shadowed side of the valley to keep her scales from cracking again in the sunlight, and paused to soak them in each pool she came to.

By the time she reached Purokoot Lake, her fingers were frozen around the egg, just as they'd frozen around Galatea's egg on that so-long-ago day. If she'd given the egg to the star child then, she could have avoided this whole, horrible mess. But she hadn't — and she didn't particularly want to give it this one, either. Not until she knew what it wanted the egg for.

She studied the lakeshore. As before, yellow droizu grew on one side. The fluff side was covered with sharp, green shoots poking out of the black soil. Galateor wouldn't think to go there, especially if she didn't leave any footprints. Varia waded through the water and buried the egg in the bank. A small arrangement of five pebbles was all she dared leave as a marker. Then she swam across the lake to the flower side and ate until she was full. She fell asleep in the water at sunset with her head resting on the bank.

Days passed. In the water, her scales became glossy. Little by little her wing healed. The cloth holding the splint in place frayed till one day it fell off. Varia flew circles around the lake to rebuild her flying muscles, and on moonlit nights she flew over the cave and the settlement.

There was no sign of Galateor, although she knew he could come back at any time. Sidran's words echoed in her head. "It's actually a good thing you're a dragon. Our plan will work better that way." She scanned the clouds scudding across the sky. Yes, it would. One cloudy morning, she saw a dark smudge moving toward the cave. Her stomach clenched. The humans better be ready.

Varia spread her wings. She felt only the slightest twinge in her injured wing as she flapped to meet Galateor. He was spiralling silently down into the valley. His head was down, and he didn't see her approach.

The humans were there. One of them was crouched beside a tree at the edge of the clearing, fiddling with something. Galateor's roving shadow flitted across the muddy ground in front of it. Should she cry out a warning? But the human's head was moving, following the shadow's path. Galateor dove. Varia plunged after him, but before she had a chance to do anything, a huge net billowed out of the tree and engulfed the dragon. Varia pulled back up. Galateor writhed on the ground, getting more entangled the more he struggled. The human had somehow escaped, and a hoard of human children now emerged from behind rocks and trees and began hauling the net, with the dragon in it, toward the cave.

There was a new boulder beside the cave entrance; somehow the humans had moved it there. They must be hoping she would push it across the opening once Galateor was inside. Varia watched him slide through the mud, kicking and clawing inside the net. Varia's heart suddenly dropped into her egg place. This was the net she had made. The one she had sabotaged so her dragon would be able to escape.

Sidran spied her and yelled from the front of the net. "Varia! Over here!"

Galateor saw her at the same time. "Waria!" he grunted. "Holp me!" He opened his withered hand briefly and Varia saw a flash of red. Caraahm-nop. As soon as he got that to his mouth, the human's plans would be over even if the net held. Varia circled. They needed something else to hold him. But what did they have that would be strong enough?

Varia banked hard and flapped away, leaving both Sidran and Galateor gaping after her. Her wing muscles protested as she forged ahead. By the time she returned, with the signal tower dangling from both hands and feet, Galateor had found the weak knots in the net. One thrashing leg ripped free. The humans scattered. Some raced to pick up bowls from the edge of the clearing; others grabbed spears. A cluster of pulsating lights appeared on the cliff above the cave door. The star child. Varia's head reeled, but she forced herself to keep on course.

Two of the humans flung water at Galateor, then ran away. He screamed and kicked harder. The net tore, and he burst free. He put his hand to his snout, swallowed, and staggered toward the children clambering up the boulders around the cave.

The transmitter's whistle got louder and softer as the tower swayed back and forth in Varia's claws. She hovered for just a moment, then folded her wings and fell. The tower plunged over Galateor at the edge of the pool, neatly trapping him inside. He roared up at her, but she dodged the flames and held the tower steady. The humans watched.

Galateor threw himself at the rigid bars. Varia jumped on the solar panels to force the tower's legs into the muddy ground.

One of the panels snapped off. Galateor began to climb the rungs, snarling, his eyes a livid red. He must have seen that if he snapped off the other panel and the signalling device, the hole would be big enough for him to escape out the top.

Varia beat him to it. She snapped off the other panel, then the receiving dish, then the transmitter. It went abruptly silent. Galateor was only a tail length from the top. Varia tensed, willing strength into her body. With a sudden jerk of her wings, she yanked the tower out of the mud, aimed the top, and kicked it hard. It hit the ground with a splash. The caraahm-nop flew out of Galateor's hands. Before he had time to pick himself up, Varia shoved the top of the tower, with him inside it, into the mouth of the cave. She thumped to the ground and pulled in her wings, wincing at the return of the pain.

Above the cave, the star child plunged its hands into two bowls of water and handed them to two kneeling children, who trickled it over the edge of the cave door. The other children formed a line from the star child down the boulders to the pool. They passed bowls of water up to the star child, and the children on the top threw the empty bowls back. Galateor's snout pushed through the opening into the water. He howled and retreated. The children cheered.

Varia lumbered to the boulder and rolled it in a haphazard line into the open end of the tower. Sidran left his place in the water line and ran to her.

"You need to bend down the legs."

Varia looked at him blankly.

"He'll just push the boulder out again. You need to bend in the legs so he can't."

Now Varia understood. Of course Galateor would push the boulder out, as soon as the star water stopped dripping. She grabbed one of the tower's legs and pulled. The hardened steel didn't budge. Varia's eyes darted around the clearing. "Sidran," she said, pointing into the tower, "Oi need dose rod balls."

Sidran looked where she pointed. Galateor growled in the darkness behind the steady trickle of star water. Slowly, Sidran climbed into the cage. Galateor snarled. Sidran took one step, then another, staying close to the bars. The star water trickled faster. Galateor's arm pushed out of the cave, then pulled back. His bellow sounded like a sob. Sidran raced forward and dove into the mud, then flung himself out of the cage. His hands were full of muddy red balls.

Varia took one. "Stond bock," she said. She positioned herself in front of the tower bar, crushed the caraahm-nop between her teeth, and swallowed. Her stomach gurgled. Her insides expanded, pressed on her lungs so she couldn't breathe. The world turned red. Sidran backed away. Varia opened her mouth and roared. Flames licked her teeth and smoke scorched her nostrils. The tower bar glowed. She sagged to the ground.

Sidran jumped onto the tower and pounded the steaming bar with a rock. Varia heaved herself up, grabbed a larger rock, and helped him. The glow faded quickly into the same dull grey as the other bars. But the leg was bent.

"Now that one," said Sidran.

Varia took a quick gulp of water and did it again. By the third time, her tongue felt raw. But the top three legs of the tower held the rock firmly inside.

"What if he's strong enough to push both the rock and the tower out of the cave?" Sidran asked, holding out another caraahm-nop. Varia groaned. Her throat was raw too. But Sidran was right. Together, they dug out the dirt under the bottom three tower legs, bent them into the ground, and filled the dirt back in. Varia stomped it down for good measure. Then she buried her snout in the soothing pool and drank. She had done all she could.

The instant the star water stopped dripping, Galateor raced to the end of the tower and hurled himself at the boulder, his eyes oscillating between red and orange. He screamed with rage and rattled the bars. They settled further into the muddy ground with every shake.

The humans scampered off the cave roof with their bowls, cheering. Varia ran into the trees to escape the noise. It was true that Galateor had to be stopped or he would have eaten them all. He was a monster. But he had also been her child, her friend, her mate. She was grateful that she and her people were safe, but she couldn't rejoice. She huddled under a tree with her hands over her ear holes. It seemed like hours before Galateor stopped wailing.

It was getting dark, Varia noticed with surprise when she finally returned to the clearing. Raindrops dripped like tears from the glistening cage. Only Sidran and three others were still there. One had her mother's hair. Two others were studying the pieces of the smashed transmitter.

"Can't be fixed," said one. Maybe Hugo?

"They'll never find us now," said the one with curly, black hair. It sounded like Dad.

Varia turned away. If she hadn't hatched Galateor in the first place, they wouldn't have needed to trap him. Then the transmitter would still be working, and the other lander might yet be found. She felt a sob stick in her throat. If only dragons could cry. "Moop," she croaked. Moop for her people's dashed hopes, moop for betraying Galateor, and most of all, moop for her moolor self. She hung her head and trudged in the direction of the lake.

A small hand clamped onto her wrist. It was Sidran. "Aren't you coming home with us?"

Varia stopped walking. Go to the settlement? Like this?

"I'd like you to come," said Mom.

The one Varia thought was Hugo shrugged his shoulders. "You did the right thing. It's been three-and-a-half-Kettle years since we landed. If they were going to find us, they would have by now."

"We all make mistakes," said the one with the curly, black hair.

Varia looked down at her sweaty, slimy, leaf-covered body. "Not loik this."

Mom took Dad's arm. "You know where we are," she said to Varia. The three of them headed up the hill. Sidran stayed beside her, watching them fade into the twilight.

"We could still find the lander, you know," he said after they disappeared. "I could ride on you and we could look for it, like you wanted to do in the first place."

"We are on an oiland," said Varia. "Bot da oder londer isn't." He had to know.

"Well . . . " Sidran hesitated. "Couldn't we fly off the island? To the other side of the water?"

Could they? The ocean had looked so vast. "If we foind dem," she asked, "what will dey tonk of a drogon and a lottle boy?"

"Oh yeah." Sidran dug a hole in the mud with his big toe. "Will you give me ride home then?" he asked after a while.

Varia sighed. Her wing was throbbing. "Oi cont," she said. Besides, she'd been a dragon long enough. She wiggled her toes and looked down at the one with the dirty, pink spot.

Sidran pulled his toe out of the dirt. "I guess I'll walk, then."

"We moid a good team," Varia said. Sidran nodded without looking at her and trudged up the hill. He disappeared into the shadows before he reached the top.

Varia turned and walked down the valley.

Chapter 28

ONCE MORE VARIA STOOD AT THE edge of the lake. The smell of damp droizu filled the air. There were bees to fill her belly, even in the darkness, and warm water to soothe her sore muscles. But that wasn't what she wanted. She took a deep breath, and blew it slowly out. Fly away, fear. Fly away, dragon-girl.

She splashed into the water and swam toward the fluff plant shore. The tubers had worked for Dad. She climbed into the field, felt for the bottom of a fluff plant stalk, and yanked.

The tuber tasted mouldy. She spat out the dirt. Did fluff plants have a fungal partner too? Probably that was how they killed the droizu. Fluff fungus defeats purokoot fungus. She grimaced. Then she sat in the rain while her stomach churned. It was different from the caraahm-nop's churning. Instead of blowing her up, the tubers were melting her. Her limbs felt soggy; her head sloshed. She flopped onto the muddy ground and let the waters flow.

Dreams pulled her down and washed her back up, only to pull her down again. *Always there is water. Ice melting. Rivers tumbling. Oceans ebbing away from the shore. Dark and light and dark again.*

She woke to rain sliding over her face and birdsong trilling above her head. Her eyelids were heavy, and her stomach felt overfull. She opened her mouth and vomited. She must have thrown up in her sleep too — and more. The ground around her smelled like the outhouse in the settlement. She crawled away from the smell and tried to focus on her rubbery limbs.

Was she still clothed in scaly armour, or newly soft and naked? Did her fingers bend and flex, or were they still bound in tight curves? Had she crawled away on her knees or her feet? Was the rain dripping off a snout or a nose? If she tried hard, she could imagine a human body lying in the dirt.

But why was her tail twitching in the mud? And why did her wing hurt? She opened her eyes. The morning light glistened on a damp, silver-grey snout. Her muscular fingers still sprouted long, curved claws — the ringed finger was smaller than the others, but still large enough to trap the ring on her hand. But something had changed: she could tell by the size of the fluff shoots by her face. She was small. A small dragon with silver-grey scales. "Aaaaaah," she wailed, and her voice sounded small too.

She pushed herself up on wobbly arms. A shower of scales tinkled around her into the mud. Of course she wouldn't need so many scales for a small body, even if they were shrunken. Large, water-filled footprints showed her path from the lake. She stepped into one, dripping more crusty scale-shards. Both her feet fit easily, and there was plenty of room for another like her.

A small bee fluttered past, and she snapped it up without thinking. The bee tasted different from the big ones — it wasn't sweet. More like bread than cake, in Earth terms. That's how she felt too: like a plain dragon. The fluff tubers had done their job and gotten rid of the purokoot's fungus. But they hadn't undone the effect of the dragon water. She was an ordinary Kettle dragon, like the ones that lived here before the purokoot.

Varia wobbled toward the lake. Her scales flapped loosely around her, as if there were still too many for her new size. Fungus shimmer covered the water. This was no place for her any more, nor for her egg. She found the pebble marker in the ridge, and dug out the egg. It was still too cold for the fungus to grow on it. If the fluff were ripe, she could have used some of it to cushion her fingers against the cold. But it wasn't, so she picked up the egg and headed down the valley.

Scales tinkled behind her. She rubbed herself against a tree to dislodge more of them. How light and free this small body was! She felt as if running would lift her right up into the air. If she wasn't carrying the egg and her wing didn't hurt, she would have tried it. She slowed near the end of the valley. Galateor wasn't outside in his cage. She clutched the egg close and tiptoed past the tower and toward the hill.

"Waria!" His voice lassoed her. She turned around.

Galateor rushed out of the cave. His shiny scales were mottled with shrivelled, grey ones where the star water had struck. He looked punctured, like a puffball someone had poked over and over with a stick. He blinked through the bars. "You is so small!"

Varia nodded. "Oi got rod of da purokoot fongus."

Galateor measured her with his eyes. "How you do dat? Star water?"

"No." I could fit through those bars now, Varia realized suddenly.

"How den?"

She backed away. "Oi wont toll you."

"You toll!" Galateor smacked his tail against the other side of the tower.

"If you oscoip, you will eat us."

"If you not show me, Oi will doi."

Varia felt her face grow hot. Once again she wished for the release of tears. No matter what she did, everything got more tangled up. "Oi'll brong you food," she said. He could get his own food, for that matter. One side of the tower was in the pool. He could just reach out and grab bees.

Galateor was breathing fast. "Food not enof. Widout drogon soster, Oi doi."

Varia backed away. "You won't doi."

Galateor gripped the bars tightly. "Oi not eat you. Oi not eat da people. If we is small, da bees is enof."

Varia bumped into a rock at the bottom of the hill, almost dropping the egg. She would have, if the rain hadn't frozen and glued it to her fingers.

Galateor pushed his face through the bars. "Gov me da ogg."

Varia fled up the hill.

"WARIA!"

Galateor's cry chased her through the woods. Her heart felt mangled. She had to get far away before she lost her will to resist him.

The old hive was gone from the middle of the first pool. Small yellow flowers grew around the edges, and small bees hovered over them. This was the first dragon pool the star child had changed back. She leaned over the water. If it was still star water, how long would it take to change her back? How much would it hurt? She held her breath and dunked one toe. It felt . . . wet. The star water must have worn off. She waded through the water, drinking great gulps as she walked. Silver-grey scales floated away from her. When she emerged, her scales felt tighter. The queasy feeling was gone from her stomach, but in its place was a growing hunger. She would have to eat soon.

The trail to the settlement was well-trampled, as were the plants around the sticky tree. The mushrooms whose glow had led her here were gone. Looking up through the rain, she saw her black hair and Dad's boot still stuck in the branches. If she waited here long enough, the star child would come.

"Please, star child, will you make me human again?" she imagined herself asking.

"Yes, of course, if you give me your egg." The exchange sounded ridiculous.

It would want her egg, though. It wanted Galatea's. A whimper rose in her throat. What did the star child want to do with it? Its stars were so hot. What if it made the egg hatch?

The scent of a stale bone led her onto a fallen tree. She followed it down the trunk to a dark hollow where its great roots had been torn from the ground, and clawed aside the mass of rotting vegetation that covered it. Inside, it was dark and cool and empty. The scent of humans was also there; they must have removed the bones. Good. Then they wouldn't need to look here again. She tapped the egg against the log until the ice holding it to her fingers cracked. Then she rolled the egg into the hollow and replaced the vegetation.

She and Galateor hadn't thought to dig for bones, but she could do it herself now. Smells tickled her nostrils: wet leaves, damp wood, old bones, many shades of fungus. She didn't remember noticing so many scents when she was big. Maybe her own fungus smell had masked them — or maybe now she was just closer to the ground. More smells met her as she neared the settlement: smoke, freshly-dug dirt, bodies. Voices wafted through the air. Varia left the trail and slid behind some bushes where she could see into the clearing. It was easier to move quietly in a small body. She could feel her greyness blending into the rain-soaked shadows.

Humans moved in the field and walked between buildings. They didn't look so tiny any more. Patches of torn dirt near the trailhead showed where the tower had stood. Two humans, one with red hair, knelt on the ground beside the kitchen, where Galateor had burned his hand in a puddle. She stiffened. Star water. What were they doing with it? The star child must come to heat it up once in a while, so it didn't wear out like the water in the pool she'd just come from.

She watched, but couldn't tell what they were doing. Luella's whistle tooted the lunch signal, and the humans straggled into the kitchen. Varia's stomach rumbled. She followed her nose to one of the places with a bone smell, but it was empty. The next one was too. She would have to search further away from the settlement. Why were the humans taking the bones anyway? Were they eating them now too?

The humans emerged again and went back to their work. Suddenly, the two at the puddles stood up. Two small, brown animals sat at their feet. Varia crept forward to see better. They were furry, like the ones she had seen in the woods. The two people walked slowly toward the woods, the little animals scampering beside them on their six fat legs. Varia crouched behind a bush as they approached the trees.

The humans' faces weren't flat anymore! She could see cheek bones and brow ridges and lips, although they still looked too much alike — and still smelled delicious. The red-haired one had to be Sidran, by the way he bounced. Since they were with animals, the other was probably Gretel.

The animals were round-bodied and long-eared, with tails that floated behind them as they walked. Varia slid her own tail quietly under the bush. Gretel pulled down a leafy twig and one of the animals nibbled it. The other one sniffed around and nibbled a different one. Sidran knelt and stroked its back.

"We have to let them go," said Gretel.

"I know." Sidran stroked the animal one last time, and stood up. He clapped his hands, and the animals scampered into the trees.

Varia couldn't see them, but she could smell exactly where they were. It was amazing — like seeing with her nose. She closed her eyes and "watched" them come closer.

"That's two more done," said Sidran.

"The lizards will be ready tomorrow," said Gretel, stretching. They walked away.

Varia pounced. The animal squealed, and delicious flavours swam in her mouth.

White heat seared her face. The star child flared up in front of her. Varia jerked away, intent on her meal. Bushes crashed beside her and a hard kick landed on her leg.

"Spit it out, Varia!" Sidran scowled up at her from his new, chest-high size.

She turned again. "You bring death like the purokoot," a chorus of voices accused. An image exploded in her mind. She saw Varia the dragon, a half-eaten animal dangling from her jaws, crouched on top of a great, fiery snowball that hurtled through the air and smashed into the ground. Rocks, water, smoke, fire, and hot wind flattened the forest, and bones clattered around her.

Okay, she thought. I get it. She made her jaw go slack. Sidran caught the bleeding animal, and raced away with it. Varia licked the blood off her teeth. Her empty stomach whimpered.

"Not time yet." Another image dropped into her mind. This one showed the forest from above. Pinpricks of colour dotted the trees like raindrops until the forest was speckled with them.

Screeches and snuffles, barks and whistles filled the air. In a clearing, silver-grey dragons crawled out of eggs. "Dragon time," the voices whooshed, and the image disappeared.

The star child's light wasn't pounding in her head, she noticed suddenly. Its heat wasn't curling her scales either. Maybe it wasn't . . . angry any more. "Oi wont to be human agoin," she croaked. "Oi am sorry Oi didn't gov you da ogg. Oi didn't know . . . Oi didn't mean to moik so moch trobble."

Colours spiralled through her mind. In the middle was her egg — or was it two eggs? — flickering between blue-green and purple as the vortex spun. "You give me your egg now?"

Varia huddled in the leaves. Could she trust the star child now? The star child waited. Varia tensed for the onslaught of heat, but she only felt soft warmth. "For drogon toim?" she whispered.

"At dragon time."

"Oi will gov you moi ogg at drogon toim." The vortex broke into chunks of colour, like sunlight playing in leaves, but when Varia opened her eyes, rain was still falling out of heavy, low clouds. "Come," chorused the voices, and Varia followed the flickering lights back down the trail.

They stopped at the nearby pool. In the distance, Galateor banged on his cage. The star child stepped into the water. Light rippled across the water's surface, and steam rose. The little things floating on it — leaves, twigs, seeds, dust, dead insects, and discarded silver-grey scales — shrivelled and puffed into nothing. The flower heads drooped.

"Come." The voices sounded high and sweet, like trilling birds.

"Will it hort a lot?" she asked. The star child didn't answer.

Two humans ran up beside her. "Sidran told us. We've come to help." It was Mom's voice. She looked Varia up and down. "He said you were half-changed already."

The other one was Gretel. She tossed pants and a shirt on the ground. "Sidran wanted to come too, but we said no."

The star child stood in the water, waiting. Mom and Gretel waded into the steaming water up to their knees and held out their arms. Varia closed her eyes and jumped. She heard them squeal as she landed on her belly in the middle of the pool.

The water was hot — as hot as the fireball that had burned her hands so many lifetimes ago. It bit her scales and shrivelled them. She felt them lift away and pop like bubbles on the surface. She felt her insides sizzle, and her bones soften into clay. Cool hands supported her shoulders and her forehead, lifting her up to breathe, turning her, and lowering her back down.

The water bubbled, floating away her unneeded bits. Her tail melted; her wings liquefied; her wing-bones boiled away. Pieces of her snout broke off. Her joints pulled apart. Her teeth rose in long white threads. Water swirled around her like a living shell. Two blurred faces hovered above the frothy dome; two pale legs wavered on each side. It's like I'm inside an egg, Varia thought.

The churning increased. Gusts of hot, murky water buffeted her clay body, moulding her bones, weaving muscles, and knitting them together. Mom and Gretel continued lifting, turning, and submerging her. Somehow she breathed at the right times. Tiny bubbles flowed toward her and stuck on, making skin. Ripples around her head turned to hair. Her limbs stopped waving like water reeds and bent at the joints. She felt herself growing solid.

The water stilled and cooled. Varia grabbed onto the arms that supported her and stood up. Mom and Gretel were pink, wrinkled, laughing, and crying. Varia hugged Mom, then

Gretel, then both. They felt exactly right. They were all a similar size.

Varia pulled the ring off her finger and slid it onto Mom's. Mom smiled. "You better get dressed."

They splashed onto the shore. It was dark, but the rain had stopped, and here and there a star peeked between the clouds. Galateor was quiet. Did he know what had happened here? No, he couldn't. Varia pulled on her pants and buttoned up her shirt. They felt wonderfully scratchy. A pebble jabbed into her soft foot.

She turned back to the pool. "Thank you," she began. But the star child was gone.

Chapter 29

VARIA TUCKED A STRAY LOCK OF hair behind her ear and pounded her shovel into the hollow beside a fallen tree. Bulrushes, the dirt was hard! Having small arms didn't help either, and her back was itchy where she couldn't reach to scratch it. Oh — she was pounding a buried tree root. She moved the shovel over and tried again. This time it went in easily, and she unearthed a small skeleton. Some of the bones crumbled as she pulled them out, but the skull, three of the front legs, and some of the spine and ribs were still intact. She wrapped them in a cloth and added them to her bag.

This was only the third skeleton she'd found in a full morning of searching. She hoped Gretel wouldn't want all of them. She had promised to take Galateor some food, and she hadn't been to see him since she'd become human again. He would be hungry with only one hive to feed from.

She swung the sack over her back and stripped a handful of nuts off a pointy-leafed bush. Sidran said they were good to eat. Tomorrow she'd bring a basket and gather the rest. She'd bring a knife too, to cut off the shelf fungus on that nearby tree. Nara was drying that kind to make dye for the next batch of fluff wool. When she reached the field, Samuel was slopping water over some seedlings.

"I'm breeding the ones with the biggest roots," he explained. "They keep well over winter, and Luella's been using them in stews."

Varia walked carefully around the other rows of plants, none of which she recognized. The Earth crops weren't edible at all any more. The root vegetables were too mushy to pull. The peas were hard little cubes that refused to soften even after a full day in the kettle. The grain was so red and musty that Luella refused to grind it.

Gretel and Sidran were bent over one of the star-water pools beside the kitchen. It felt so good to recognize their profiles from as far away as the field. They looked just like she remembered — except their backs were broader. Everyone's were. Maybe they'd developed big muscles from working so hard in the fields. Or maybe she'd just forgotten how humans were supposed to look.

"What are they this time?" she asked when she reached the puddles.

"Some kind of lizard," answered Sidran, staring intently.

Varia looked into the steaming water. Two half-finished animals floated on their backs above a layer of compost. Gretel lifted and turned one of them, then the other. The creatures' filmy skins stretched almost invisibly over their pink muscles. Was this how she had looked?

"How do you know you put the bones together properly?" Varia asked. Each had a frilled, triangular head, a long body, six short legs with long toes, and a long tail.

"We start with informed guesses." answered Gretel. "Then we just keep trying until they fit."

"If we don't have all the right bones, we carve pieces out of extras," Sidran added.

They watched the creatures wave their limbs in the warm water while the colour in their new skins deepened to shades of orange. One was redder than the other. The lizards lifted their heads and paddled around the pool.

"Male and female," said Gretel.

Varia's heart swelled with wonder. She opened her sack. "Here are the bones I found today."

Gretel spread out the cloths and started laying out the new bones. Luella's whistle sounded and she stood up. "Leave them here. We'll figure out what they are after lunch."

Adriel was sitting in Varia's chair from the lander. "Vawia!" he called, pounding his spoon on the table. She sat down on her tree stump beside him and looked into her bowl.

It was a good thing she was starving when Luella first slapped a bowl in front of her. Today's stew consisted of slippery blue mushrooms, wilted dragon-wing leaves, slices of flabby, yellow, brain-jelly fungus, and circles of a starchy, white root — probably the kind Samuel was trying to grow. The blue-green flatbread was made from ground seed pods.

Sidran elbowed her. "Come on, Varia. You used to eat bugs!" He shovelled a yellow glob into his mouth with a torn-off piece of bread.

"I want bugs too," complained Adriel, pushing his bowl away.

Mom raised her eyebrows and looked pointedly at Varia. Adriel's chin quivered. Luella frowned. Varia tore off a piece of bread and put a tiny slice of blue mushroom on it. She closed her eyes and pushed it into her mouth. It was slippery and spread a musky flavour over the roof of her mouth. But it wasn't as terrible as it looked. "Much better than bugs," she said. Adriel opened his mouth and let Mom slide in a piece of mushroom. Varia nibbled on a leaf. She didn't want to eat bees any more, but this new food would take some getting used to. Dessert was very good: plump silver berries in a sweet sauce. The small bees made a delicious honey.

After dishes, she and Sidran went back outside. "You can have that pile of bones," he said, pointing. "They're lizard leftovers."

Varia put them in a sack and set off for the cave. She would gather bees from the valley pools for Galateor as well. Specto had left them untouched, so there were lots of bees. Birds chirped in the trees, and rustling sounds accompanied her through the bushes. She wondered if Specto was watching to make sure his new animals stayed away from the valley — and Purokoot Lake. They wouldn't like the smell of the water, but they might fall in, or brush against the droizu fungus.

She stopped briefly by the fallen tree and checked her egg. Still frozen. Specto hadn't yet asked her where it was. She picked and ate a handful of blue berries while she walked. There was a puffball beside one of the trees. If it wasn't overripe, she would pick it for supper on the way home.

Galateor was clutching the bars of his cage and staring down the valley when she reached him. Even gaunt with hunger, he was huge. Could she really have been nearly that big? She skirted the tower and stuffed bees into her sack from the other side of the pool. One bee would be enough for a human meal, if anyone would want to eat them, with those creepy, wiggling legs. She pictured Luella slapping boiled, mushroom-covered bees into bowls, and grimaced. Nectar stuck to her hands, but she drank star water now, and didn't have to worry about fungus.

Galateor growled behind his bars. His eyes were sickly green. He doesn't know who I am, she realized suddenly. All he sees is a tiny, flat-faced creature made of bones he can't have. She hesitated. How quickly could he grab her? "Stay where you are," she said. She walked to the cave end of the tower. If she threw the bees into the cave, they wouldn't be able to crawl away before he got them.

Something flickered at the edge of her vision. Instinctively, she jumped back. Galateor roared, and red flames licked the bars where she'd been standing.

Varia stumbled backwards. She turned the sack upside down. Lizard bones clattered at her feet. Dazed bees wandered away. Galatea snarled. Varia kicked the pile of bones away and stormed up the hill.

"You have to go back," Sidran insisted a few days later, pushing more bones into her hands. "Otherwise he'll die."

Varia trudged back to the cave. This time Galateor wasn't outside. Varia gathered up the bones she'd scattered last time and dumped them into the cage with Sidran's new ones. Then she hid behind a boulder at the top of the hill. After a while, Galateor stumbled outside and devoured the bones. He looked so pitiful slinking through his cage, so unlike the majestic dragon that had soared over the clouds. She would hate to be caged. She wished she hadn't seen him like this. She wished she hadn't had to cage him. She wished he had been satisfied eating bees. She wished so many things. But she would keep feeding him.

Spring passed into summer, and summer into fall. How thankful she was not to be a dragon tonight, Varia thought as small yellow petals blew around her feet beside the forest pool. She shivered. Galateor must also be remembering that night one year ago, for he was making a terrible racket down below, howling and hurling himself at the bars.

"Where is Waria?" he shouted when he saw her on the hill.

"I'm Varia."

He staggered as if he'd been struck. "Den brong da oder drogon," he pleaded as she walked down the hill.

"She is still in her egg," said Varia, stopping at the edge of the gravel. She was not going near his claws.

Galateor's body crumpled. "Oi is moolor." He trudged into the cave, and Varia left his food inside the bars.

Varia didn't see him again that fall. One day he left the food untouched, and she knew he had gone to sleep.

Winter came. The settlers did their usual chores, only now they dried mushrooms, leaves, roots, and berries instead of sweet potatoes, peas, onions, and cabbage. Sidran read about animal anatomy, and Varia read about animal care, when she wasn't reading stories to Adriel. She avoided the dragon stories. Nara learned how to knit cable patterns into sweaters. Samuel made detailed notes about the plants he was breeding, and Mom wrote descriptions of her new medicines.

Dad entertained them with magic tricks and taught them new games, which they played in the light from luminescent mushrooms. Varia's favourite was a pebble game called "Fox and Geese," in which a gang of beleaguered geese tries to corner a wily fox. It reminded Varia of the night they trapped Galateor, and she shuddered at how often the geese failed. Of course, they didn't have a dragon on their side. Or a star child.

Gretel continued to rejuvenate skeletons in the washtub. They kept the new animals in pens inside the sleeping hut. Some curled up and fell asleep in a cool corner as soon as they emerged from the water, while others needed feeding, cleaning, and company.

Varia's favourites were the long-legged, hoofed ones with pointed ears and large eyes like small Earth gazelles. They liked to eat grass, which was fortunate because the grass harvest had been good last year, but they had to be watched carefully so they didn't nibble the spare blankets and sacks. It was nearly spring when Varia, stroking their sleek backs while they ate from her hand, noticed the bumps on their shoulders.

"Wing buds," confirmed Gretel. "There were extra sockets in the shoulder blades when we put them together, but the bones we put there didn't grow. I guess they weren't big enough for wings yet."

"Now we know why they only have four legs, when all the others have six," said Varia.

"Do you think we'll be able to ride them?" Sidran asked one relatively warm winter afternoon. He and Varia had taken the gazelles into the clearing and were watching them chase each other, and Adriel, in circles in the snow.

"Maybe Adriel will." Varia considered. "I don't think they'll get very big."

"At least we'll be able to watch them."

Varia shook her head sadly. "Once they learn to fly, they won't stay here." Her throat tightened. Adriel skipped past, flapping his arms and roaring like a dragon. "Adriel woke up crying this morning," she said. "When I asked him what was wrong, he said he dreamed he could fly, and when he woke up, it wasn't true."

"I have that dream too," said Sidran. "I'll never forget the time you took me for a ride, Varia." He reached over his shoulder and scratched his back.

Varia didn't answer. She tried not to think about that evening. She tried not to think about flying, either. It hurt too much to know that she'd never do it again. It also hurt to remember that she'd given up her chance to find Connie and the others. Unless they found another way to cross the water, they'd never find them now.

Sidran elbowed her in the side. "I said, if you do want to become a dragon again, I'll be happy to throw you in the lake."

Varia lunged at him, but he was off with the gazelles. Laughing, she joined the chase.

When the snow melted, they opened the pens and let the animals slip into the woods. Varia filled a sack with leftover bones, and picked her way around the puddles to the cave. Galateor was awake and watching the hillside, gripping the bars with both hands. The bones from last fall were gone.

"Oi am hongry!" he screeched when he saw her. She stared down at him. His tail dragged, his scales hung loosely over his thin arms and legs, and his wings drooped behind his back. Poor Galateor. She tossed the bones into the cage one at a time.

Galateor lumbered awkwardly toward them. Then Varia saw the lump, hanging heavily between his thighs. "You have an egg," she gasped.

"Dat's roight." He glared at her. "Oi is Galatea agoin." He — she crunched fiercely at the bone.

"Would you like . . . a warm blanket?"

Galatea's grey eyes smouldered. She turned her back.

"What will happen when it hatches?" Sidran worried when she told him. "The baby dragon won't stay in the cave."

It was true. And Galatea wouldn't wait for the star child's "dragon time" before hatching it. The baby would carry the fungus back to all the forest pools, and there were lots of animals now for a dragon to turn into mates. Would there be enough animals to feed it, or would it go after the humans too? Would other animals get infected by the fungus and grow big like the termites and bees? Would Galatea tell the baby what had happened, and would it want revenge? What if the new dragon baby freed Galatea? The settlers tried hard to think of a plan. Varia worried, but she also remembered how hungry she had been in Galatea's place, and took her all the bones they could spare.

Galatea stayed in her cave. Varia climbed the boulders to watch her through the crack, shivering and devouring the bones, which were never enough. Her belly grew so large that it dragged on the ground. Varia's lump had never been that big, or that stiff. She remembered it wobbling when she walked. When Galatea wandered into the light, Varia saw a dark stain on her belly scales. Every day it grew larger and darker, and Galatea clutched it and moaned.

One afternoon, Varia saw Galatea doubled over at the edge of the pool. "Go in the water," she urged, peering through the crack. "You'll be able to climb out once you lay the egg."

Galatea stared dully up at her with grey, sunken eyes. Her belly was black and rigid. It lurched to the side, and Galatea staggered against the wall. "You not know," she gasped. "Oi is not real gorl. Da ogg connot come out." The lump lurched again, and a crack appeared on Galatea's belly. Her face distorted with pain. "Da prosont of da purokoot."

Her lips pulled back over her teeth as the crack in her belly gaped open, the flesh around it splintering into shards like cracked ice. Varia watched in horror. That was why Galatea's lump was so stiff. Her body was literally frozen from the inside out. She watched helplessly as Galatea clawed at her solidified flesh, until finally the egg rolled out onto the cave floor.

Galatea stumbled toward the pool while the torn remnants of her belly flapped stiffly around her ankles. She toppled in, and sank. The ripples on the water faded away. The cave was empty except for the egg, which glistened like a frozen, multi-faceted jewel.

Chapter 30

"I NEED YOUR EGG."

It took a minute for Varia to hear the voice. She turned around, wiping her eyes on her arm. Specto was standing behind her on the rock, but she could barely feel his heat. He looked different — pale, insubstantial. Small. If the sun had been out she might not have seen his stars at all.

"I need your egg." Only a faint flicker appeared in her mind. She froze. He had only one voice.

"I'll get it." Varia half-slid down the boulder. Specto was inside the cage when she returned with the frozen egg. She climbed in and followed him into the cave. His stars were easier to see in the dim light. She gave him the egg and watched him walk to the edge of the pool. Galatea's egg was golden orange. A boy. Specto knelt and rolled both eggs into the bubbling water.

Varia stayed by the door. She didn't want to see what was in the pool. As it was, the odours of sweaty dragon and rotting flesh stung her eyes. "How did the purokoot do this to her?" she asked. Her voice broke. "How could it create a fungus and make a dragon half male and half female?"

Specto walked to her and held out his hands. Varia took them and knelt down so she could see into his face. This close, she could still feel his heat. He stared into her eyes. There were no words, only pictures.

Varia, holding the star child's hands, flies toward a misty white comet with a feathery, two-pronged tail. They dive into the puffy snow around its head. The star child squeezes her hands, and the snow becomes hexagonal columns of ice crystals interspersed with minerals: glassy peridot, green olivine, white diamonds. And other substances she doesn't recognize. He squeezes again, and the minerals enlarge into whirling clusters of flickering energy. She is seeing molecules, she realizes, constellations of atoms, like sub-microscopic stars. "For building life." The words slip into her brain.

The star child points his toes and falls, and Varia falls with him. They are back on the Kettle, hovering above the shore of Purokoot Lake. Desolation lies on all sides. Grey clouds hang over a forest of charred logs. Nothing moves. The star child looks down, and Varia sees a tiny, green shoot pushing through the rocky soil: the plant with the small yellow flowers.

They slide down the stem and follow the flower's branching roots to a thin, clinging thread: the flower's fungal partner. They burrow into the thread. Another squeeze, and the thread grows into clusters of flickering energy like the ones on the comet, but entwined into twisting, towering sculptures. Something whooshes above them. Varia looks up. It is the energy clusters from the comet! They attack the sculptures, pull off pieces, and fit themselves in. "But they're on the wrong sides," Varia protests. "They're backwards."

The star child squeezes her hands, and they swoosh out of the thread, now a thick, heavy rope, up the flower's roots, now obscured by the fungus, and out over the lake. The plants grow and leaf out. They are droizu.

Varia felt a shock of wind. She was back in the cave with Specto. She understood now, that alien molecules from the comet had altered the natural fungus that grew on the flowers' roots. She would have to look up molecule shapes on the reader, and see if she could figure it out more exactly. "Did the fungus make the dragon male and female too?" she asked. "Oh, no. I remember. Some animals just become like that when they have to." But it didn't work so well for these dragons.

Specto let go of Varia's hands and made a noise like a small explosion. Another gust of wind slammed into Varia. A cloud puffed out of his body and floated away. He was smaller yet. He gripped her shoulders. "No more misfits," he said, and shot out of the cave. Something prickled on her back.

Varia ran out of the cave and looked around the clearing. A faint light was flickering over the rocks in the valley. She caught up with him at the last droizu pool before the lake. "Wait!" He couldn't leave yet. They weren't ready. "When the dragons hatch, they'll spread the fungus!" she shouted.

Specto waved his arms, still running. Another cloud of gas exploded from him.

Varia braced herself against the shock wave. "Galatea's bones will tell the babies to eat us!"

Specto mouthed something at her over his shoulder. He stopped on the ridge overlooking the lake. Varia lurched to a stop. He was growing again. In a second he was back to his usual size, then as big as Galatea, then as tall as a tree. The rocks glowed red under his feet, and heat blasted out. His voices nearly bowled her over. "RUN!" She turned and fled.

Sidran met her at the cave, his face flushed. "What's happening? I heard thunder."

"Specto." Varia pointed, gasping for breath. The gravel was hot under their feet.

"Bulrushes!"

Sidran grabbed her hand and pulled her up the hillside. They crouched behind a boulder and looked down the valley. Steam billowed from each droizu pool, and above the trees a great, white cloud rose out of the lake. Steam curled out of the crack in the cave's ceiling.

"He star-watered the whole valley," Sidran murmured. "All these pools must be connected."

"He was fading away," said Varia. "And then he puffed up so big — like a . . . "

"Supernova."

Varia gulped. Yes.

"Then he's gone."

She nodded. "So is Galatea."

Sidran wanted to know everything. She told him as well as she could. Sidran put his arms around her, and she buried her face in his neck and wept. Sidran wept too.

When the steam from the pool thinned to wisps, they climbed down. The droizu flowers lay on the water like ropes around the soggy hive. Sidran followed Varia into the cave. The water bubbled gently, and the air smelled freshly washed.

At the bottom of the pool lay a small dragon's skeleton. In the dim light, they could just make out the two eggs lying between its arms, one blue and one orange. Varia reached into her pocket and pulled out a handful of small bones. She placed them in two piles on the floor. Then she and Sidran left the cave.

Hand in hand they walked home.

Epilogue

"ANOTHER SUPERNOVA!" EXCLAIMS VARIA, WATCHING IT blaze inside its expanding halo of dust. The wind slams into Draco, and comets whirl around his stars. He stands as still as he looked in the Earth sky, watching. Slowly, the supernova fades, until all that remains is a brilliant jumble of magenta, gold, and cyan. Stars blink on. Draco trembles, and the end of his tail swirls in a figure eight. The new stars wobble in their birth-nebula, and a child steps out of the cloud.

"Specto!" Varia jumps up and down where the tower used to be, waving both her arms. The night air feels cool on her wrists and ankles. She will have to lengthen her sleeves and pants again.

The star child turns to her, and one starry eye winks out for a moment. Draco bounds toward the cloud, his eager feet splashing sparks. Specto spreads his arms and legs and lets the last of the stellar wind blow him toward the dragon. They collide in a blurry whirl of light and roll across the sky, leaving behind a choppy, sparkling trail.

"Look out!" Varia cries. She cringes, waiting for the crash. But in the last instant, Specto leaps and Draco dives. Cygnus the Swan ruffles his starry wings imperiously and stretches his long neck after them. Specto somersaults three times and plops onto

Draco's back. Before Cygnus has time to hiss, they swoop under Pegasus and fly circles around the Big and Little Bears.

Varia smiled and dreamed she was flying with them. On the next mat, Adriel murmured something, and Dad mumbled a reply. Sidran muttered on the other side of the curtain. Varia rolled onto her stomach and snuggled into her pillow. Two small peaks jutted up in the back of her nightgown. The wing buds were starting to grow.

SHARON PLUMB lives in Regina, Saskatchewan, where she writes stories and creates websites. She has published one picture book, *Bill Bruin Shovels His Roof. Draco's Child* is her first novel.